LIFT AND SEPARATE

LIFT AND SEPARATE

A Novel

Marilyn Simon Rothstein

Text copyright © 2016 by Marilyn Simon Rothstein
All rights reserved.

Published by Lake Union Publishing, Seattle

www.apub.com

Amazon, the Amazon logo, and Lake Union Publishing are trademarks of Amazon.com, Inc., or its affiliates.

ISBN-13: 9781503940307
ISBN-10: 1503940306

Cover design by Janet Perr

Printed in the United States of America

For Alan M. Rothstein

Chapter 1

Three days after my husband left me, I stood in the master bathroom with my best friend, Dana. "I would throw out his toothbrush," I said, "but I don't know which is his and which is mine."

Dana had arrived at my house direct from Kennedy Airport, vaulting up the stairs to find me staring stun-gun still into the bathroom mirror while squeezing a family-size tube of Colgate into one of the double sinks. I hadn't brushed my teeth in three days.

"Buy a new toothbrush," she said. Dana was in advertising. She had a retail solution for everything.

I shut my eyes and shook my head.

Dana reached for her summer bag. "I'll buy one for you."

"Please don't go anywhere. I'm so relieved that you're here. I need you here."

"Okay, Marcy, okay."

I glanced at the tub. "Harvey and I never went in the hot tub together."

"Maybe that should have told you he was unhappy." Lightly, Dana knocked her shoulder against mine. A shoulder knock from Dana always made me feel like the most popular girl at the popular table.

But I didn't feel like knocking. What was there to knock about now?

"Actually, I thought of drowning myself in the tub, but no one was around to rescue me and I didn't want to die. I just wanted to stop breathing long enough to make Harvey come home."

"News flash, Marcy. You're not the first woman to be left by a man."

"So why do I feel like the first?" I wiped a tear across my cheek—one tear. Even my tears were alone now.

"You must stop taking this abandonment personally when it's nothing but the human condition." Dana lit a cigarette. She cranked open the window, exhaling into my stellar acre of backyard woods.

I loved that backyard. I focused on the spot where the cedar playground with three swings, a slide, a seesaw, and a fort with a canvas roof had once stood for eternity, it seemed. When my husband, Harvey, suggested that we call someone to dismantle it, our children were grown; our youngest, Ben, our only son, was a junior in college, on a semester abroad in Florence. I found it amazing and poignant and comforting that now, no matter how much miracle, magical seed our landscaper tossed down, a portion of that spot remained forever brown.

"You're so right, Dana. My problem with Harvey isn't personal. It's universal. Harvey didn't leave me. He left every woman in the world."

"Of course I'm right. I'm only fifty-six, and I've been married three times."

Apparently, my husband's departure was not enough aggravation for me. My best friend needed to remind me that I was older than she was. "Oh, yes," I said. "And don't forget—you're not only younger than me, you wear a smaller size."

"Give me a break. You always look great."

I pulled down and straightened my sweatshirt from high school, worn over baggy sweatpants, and took another shot at eliciting husband-leaving-size sympathy from Dana. "When I was in my twenties and I threw my lot in with Harvey, I didn't think I was starting a *new* life. I thought I was starting *life*."

"I'm telling you—you're going to be fine."

I started pacing between the granite counter and the steam shower. "I keep thinking how well Harvey will do without me. I'll be in a nursing home clutching a walker—lime-green tennis balls on the bottom— eating soft food for dinner at noon, and my daughters will be lunching with Harvey's new wife."

"That's ridiculous."

"Why? *She* never told them to turn off the television, to clean their rooms because the cleaning lady was coming, to find a boyfriend who speaks to adults in at least two-syllable words. And Harvey. Harvey will morph into Disneyland Dad—or, in his case, Saks Fifth Avenue Dad. I can't stand thinking about it."

"Get a grip. It's all going to work out."

"You just watch. Suddenly, Harvey will start a diet. He'll join a gym or hire a trainer. He'll eat egg-white omelets. He'll pour protein powder into spinach shakes."

"Harvey can scarf all the egg-white omelets he wants—you're in good shape."

"Not after this hell. I guarantee you that the way I've been stuffing myself through this debacle, I'm going to gain two hundred pounds— mostly in my inner thighs." I was aware that I had to stop thinking up these awful scenarios, but somehow projecting ahead was less painful than dwelling in real time.

"You can stop pacing right now, because you are certain to do better than Harvey. It's not even a contest. If it's necessary, and I'm not saying it will be, you'll lift yourself up and create a whole new life."

I didn't want a whole new life. I wanted my life—in Connecticut—with my husband, an endearing family man who would do anything for our three grown-up children, a man who was smart and hardworking, a man who had built a brassiere and lingerie empire. Okay, so Harvey's corporation, Bountiful Bosom, wasn't Victoria's Secret—and that vexed Harvey to no end.

Dana was wearing white linen cuffed trousers, a wide silver belt cinched tight, and a billowy red blouse. Her hair was soft, wavy, naturally blond, and long, down her back. In fact, her hair was longer than it was when we first met, which was in front of the dairy case in a supermarket, back when yogurt sold for sixty cents and the only acceptable brand was Dannon—with its famous "fruit on the bottom."

We were about the same height, about five foot six, but Dana would traverse a tightrope in her stilettos, so she always appeared taller. Anyone we met for the first time was surprised to hear that Dana was old enough to have a thirty-year-old son, Jeremy, who lived in Boston. In addition, she had two daughters, twins, who were seniors at the town high school. Dana was hunting for colleges as though she were going to buy one.

I wished Dana would quit smoking. And I wished she would say something that would actually make me feel better. I'd been married longer than I'd attended school, longer than I'd known Dana. I was married in a Priscilla of Boston empire gown and a white daisy crown, before the existence of Vera Wang bridal couture, microwave popcorn, corporate greed, virtual reality, destination weddings, cable news, global warming, stay-at-home dads, and frequent-flyer points.

I was married when the smartest phone was a Princess, and the World Wide Web was science fiction. In fact, I may have been born married; I had no inclination not to be married. And what I needed in my master bathroom right now was a head-nodding, hand-wringing, soggy-eyed friend with a wholesale supply of tissues.

I sat down on the cold tile. *Good thinking, Harvey. Thank you for the ultimate necessity item—a custom floor, a replica of the ceiling of the Sistine Chapel, installed by artisans, in a bathroom in Connecticut. Harvey Hammer—what a magician. He can make thousands of dollars disappear.*

Dana glanced at the wristwatch her current husband, Calvin, had given to her for their anniversary. I had no idea why anyone would care what time it was. I hadn't seen a clock in days.

I hoped Dana wasn't consulting her watch because she needed to leave my house at a particular time. If Dana left, I would be alone— with a liter of Diet Coke, a Sara Lee pound cake, and a party-size bag of Cape Cod potato chips—about to undo years of struggling to live healthy.

I rubbed my bleary eyes, panicking at the thought of her departure, petrified that she would say she had to go pick up the girls at gymnastics or the dog at the vet or that she had a meeting at her advertising office miles away, on Old Cow Lick Lane. A meeting at Dana's agency would be worst of all. I could always join her to get the girls or the dog— although I had no inclination to ever leave my house again.

"Let's sit in the hot tub," I suggested, trying to be more engaging and less morose.

The empty tub was grotto-style, roomy enough for four adults. Fully dressed, Dana and I stretched out next to each other with our legs crossed at the ankles.

Dana kicked off her shoes and rested her head on an inflatable pillow. "Okay," she said. "Let's go through it from the beginning."

Although I had told her every detail, through face-staining tears, on the telephone, I was not going to surrender this opportunity to tell her again. I needed to go on and on about Harvey, and I had no desire to share my burden with anyone beyond Dana. I had lived in a pinch of a New England town long enough to know that gossip regarding Harvey's departure would spread like influenza in a preschool. If Harvey changed his mind and returned, as I prayed he would, I didn't want this mishap on my permanent record.

"On Monday," I began, "which was doomsday—pouring rain, crackling thunder with lightning—I called Harvey at the office to ask when he'd be home. I've done that forever. I like to have supper ready when he arrives. But this time, Harvey said he wasn't coming home. He spoke slowly, softly, as though someone close to us had died.

"I said, 'What do you mean you're not coming home?' Then, without warning, he launched into this maniacal monologue. He said that for the first time in his life, he was uncertain of everything, especially our marriage. He said he needed to think. I begged him to come home so we could think together. He blew his damn nose into the phone.

"He said, 'Marcy, I'm leaving you.' Click. Clicks are so cruel."

"Did you call him back?"

"No," I said. "I haven't done anything yet."

"What?"

Dana's "what" had a stop-everything screech to it, and I was flooded with anxiety as I worried that I had made a colossal mistake. I could still call. My cell was on the vanity. But would calling Harvey make things worse? Maybe time did heal all. Or maybe time was a waste of time.

"You're tough," Dana said as she knocked into my shoulder.

"As what—a cotton ball? I didn't call him because when I raced upstairs to check his closet, I saw that all of his favorite suits were gone. The man packed enough clothing to open a menswear store."

I needed a tissue desperately, but no way would I climb out of the tub to get one. If I stepped out, Dana might follow me and tell me that she had to leave.

"Where did he say he would be?"

"I guess he's holed up at Bountiful." Easy enough—Harvey's office had a six-foot leather couch the color of butter, as well as a stocked wet bar, a refrigerator with an ice maker, and a microwave oven.

"Maybe," Dana said weakly.

"Maybe what?" I snapped.

"Maybe he's sleeping at the office."

So now where was her optimism? "Come on, Dana. He's Harvey."

Dana flicked ashes into a yellow-duck soap dish I'd bought years before, when I was happily married, or so I'd thought, and my house was vibrant with the sights and sounds of my children and their friends—Reeboks scattered on the floor, homework projects amassed on the kitchen table, hands reaching into the freezer for treats, our house phone always busy, the anything-but-sleep sleepover parties on our carpeted family room floor, the girls' field hockey team standing and cheering on my kitchen table, over-the-top holiday celebrations and birthday parties, always with a cake from Sweet Heaven Bakery. I missed the days when my life was chock-full and there were too many things to do, when I collapsed into bed dog-tired and slept through the night as though I had participated in a world-championship triathlon. But most of all, I missed my family depending upon me.

Dana was a big ash flicker. She tended to flick ash the most when she was trying to keep her mouth shut. I was certain she was no more than several flicks away from suggesting that my once-devoted husband, the attentive father of my three fabulous children, might be having an affair. I didn't want to hear it. I didn't want the repugnant thought released into the smoke-filled air. I reached for the Febreze and sprayed in circles, up to the ceiling and down to the floor, until Dana insisted that I stop.

From her experience, Dana assumed that every man with a gold band, except her third husband, Calvin, who didn't wear a wedding ring, was a cheater. She enjoyed going on and on about cheating being easier than ever. Even an oaf with hiked trousers, no job, and the under-arm scent of half-eaten food rotting in a trash can could score on the Internet. I could hear her speech coming. But I was surprised. Dana didn't voice a word about infidelity and the Internet. She said, "I'm sorry I was away when you called."

"Are you serious? I'm so proud of you. Speaking in London at an advertising conference—you're such a success. You have the career people dream of. You have the career I dreamed of."

"Yes, my friend, I am amazing," she said with her characteristic sarcasm. "But honestly, Marcy, there is nothing I do that you couldn't have done."

"Did I tell you that last spring Harvey and I went to the Jewish cemetery to choose our burial plots? We rode around looking at headstones. How morbid is that? We agreed on one large headstone for the both of us. Harvey would be buried on the left, and I would be on the right. You know what? I think Harvey wants to be *buried* with me. He just doesn't want to *live* with me."

"We don't know that yet. He's been gone only three nights. There are men who go out for a beer longer than that."

Only? Three nights was not an "only" in my house. An afternoon would be an "only."

"He's coming back," Dana said, swiping her hand through the air as if to say this was absolutely the truth. Then she knocked my shoulder to reaffirm.

"Quit knocking my shoulder."

"We always knock shoulders."

"Harvey has never done this before. We argue, but not that much, not like when the kids were growing up. Then we had things to disagree about. Our most recent dispute concerned this floor. Should I watch Harvey order a floor that costs more than a presidential election without saying a word?"

"Not if it's as ostentatious as this one. Who puts a replica of the Sistine Chapel on a bathroom floor? And what's with that parrot downstairs?"

"The parrot is Harvey's latest acquisition—some rare breed, of course. From Africa."

"So Harvey likes expensive things. My first husband considered a water bed on the floor the height of luxury—as long as he could roll over and reach his bong."

"Our last argument, before the Sistine bathroom, was about his weight. We went to Dr. Port, the endocrinologist. He suggested that Harvey drop thirty pounds, because he's prediabetic."

"What's 'prediabetic'?" Was Dana actually lighting another cigarette?

"Prediabetic is one M&M away from a major artery exploding in your chest," I said. "One Sunday, before noon, Harvey was about to barbecue a marinated steak the size of Kansas. I took the steak, on a platter, out of his hands, refusing to give it back to him. Harvey stomped out of the yard and drove off, probably to a fast-food window. I stopped haranguing him about his weight when I realized that if Harvey had to choose between me and a sheet cake, I'd be tossing the bakery box in the garbage on my way out of the house."

"So Harvey likes food. It's always something. What about your kids? Do the kids know?"

"Yes. Harvey phoned Elisabeth, and of course she rushed over here to be with me. Elisabeth called Ben, then Amanda in California. They both called me. They were so sympathetic, so good to me. Made me wish I had had more children. Not with Harvey. With another man."

My lower back was beginning to hurt. I'd had enough of the tub. I had no choice but to stand up and step out. Dana followed, fussing with her hair.

"Elisabeth came straight from her shift at the hospital. When I heard the side door slam, I ran to the staircase. I was praying, hoping, it was Harvey. I tripped on the belt of my robe and tumbled down a few steps."

I showed her the bruises on my side.

"Whoa, that's ugly," Dana said, shaking her head. "Did you put anything on it?"

"Ice," I said as I pulled up my sweatpants.

"You should take Tylenol," Dana advised, and she turned her attention to my makeup drawer. I watched as she touched up her mascara with my wand. She rifled through my compacts to find the bronze blush she favored. She passed a round brush to me.

I ran the brush through my hair. It was easier than telling Dana that I didn't care if I looked like the afflicted woman in a commercial for extra-strength head lice remover. "Do you want to know the worst part? The entire time that Elisabeth was here consoling me, Harvey's new parrot wouldn't shut up."

"The parrot speaks? What does he say?"

I imitated the irritating bird. "Harvey. Harvey. Harvey."

"That's it?"

"What would you like him to say?"

"Dana is beautiful. Dana is beautiful," she said with a squeaky squeal—part fowl, mostly pig.

"I'm calling an animal trainer today."

"I like this shade," Dana said, displaying an open lipstick.

"Keep it."

"I will."

Maybe she would keep the parrot too. Harvey had bought the bird one week before leaving home. Damn cruel—to the bird—if you ask me. Harvey had mentioned that a parrot could live for forty to sixty years.

"Any chance you would take the parrot to your house?" I asked Dana. "Just for a while?"

"No."

"The girls will like him."

"Great. Now you're using my children to get to me?"

"Dana is beautiful. Dana is beautiful," I said.

"What did Elisabeth have to say?"

"She said she was going to talk to Harvey."

"Good. What else?"

"She said, 'Mom, I feel so bad for you. If Dad was going to leave, why couldn't he at least take the parrot?'"

If Dad was going to leave, I thought, *why couldn't he at least take me?*

Dana carried the dome-top cage to her car. I followed with a healthy bag of supreme veggie-blend pellets, gluten-free, with omega-3.

I hugged her good-bye. I forced a smile.

"You can survive this," she said.

Chapter 2

That night I drew an *X* on the calendar featuring New England scenes that I kept on a wall in my kitchen. I had begun the *X* routine the day Harvey had left. I found placing an *X* over a day, with black marker, very depressing—the day is done but shot to hell, and by the way, your husband may never come home. But I did it anyway.

I kept my cell phone in my pocket during the day in case Harvey called. I slept with it next to my head. When it rang, I reacted like a drowning person within arm's length of a lifeboat. I wandered about my own house, a nomad. Our town, Atherton, was small, so if I went anywhere I would bump into someone I knew and feel obligated to smile.

I decided that I was on permanent strike, done doing work for Harvey, even though I had a title at Bountiful. I was his director of consumer affairs. From an office in our house, I handled the most disgruntled customers. After all, not one was more disgruntled than me. Harvey's staff at corporate headquarters dealt with happy customers and the minor complaints. Now, they could have the kvetchers from hell as well.

My real job, though, the one that made me feel like a person, had nothing to do with my husband. I was part-time program coordinator for Guild for Good, a nonprofit association of artists from throughout the region. Two successful painters and two illustrators had launched Guild for Good on Main Street, so the office was a zip to my house. We promoted the work of our members, raised funds for art programs in inner-city schools, and provided scholarships for college. When I'd attended NYU, during the Age of Aquarius, before going to business school for marketing, I had majored in art history. Small wonder that I enjoyed Guild for Good and the people I met through it.

The phone rang. I looked at the number, praying it was Harvey. But it was Dana. I could hear her daughters in the background, repeating their names to the parrot.

"Are you all right?" Dana asked. "Tell me he called."

"If he called, I would have called you. But thanks for checking in."

"By the way, we're heading up to Boston for a few days. We're going to meet Jeremy's new girlfriend. And the twins want to take a second tour of some colleges."

I was happy for Dana, but the thought of her brunching on Newbury Street with her family made me feel lonely. Wineglass in hand and potato chips in mouth, I went to the door and pressed my nose against the screen, watching as summer in Connecticut left me behind.

The High Hills Day Camp bus belched to a halt in front of my neighbor's house, the Yankee blue colonial on steroids. A nanny waited at the bus stop with a toddler in a stroller; two teenagers—their blond hair in lopsided pigtails—jogged by.

Then I saw Harvey.

He pulled up deliberately, stopping behind the bus, waiting for the children to step out, waiting for the stop sign to retract. I watched him swaying his bald head back and forth. The man was killing me, and he had the audacity to enjoy himself, listening to music. On the other hand, music might be a positive sign, a sign that he had come to the correct decision and was coming home to me.

I prayed that he would turn in to our driveway. I prayed that he was not just passing by. I loved my husband—more now than when we first started out. I realized, even if he didn't, that we had created a good life together, that our shared history was a passion, a love potion of its own. The compromises I'd made, I chose to make. And in thirty-three years, I never—not once—gazed at another man and thought, *There he is—the guy I should have walked down the aisle with.*

I closed my eyes and recalled other summer days, a long time ago, when my kids were the ones returning from day camp and Harvey appeared in his car to take us all to Friendly's for ice cream. We would crowd into a booth, laughing at each other, laughing with each other. Always, Harvey had a chocolate ice-cream soda, Elisabeth and Amanda shared a Fribble milk shake, and Ben ordered a Cone Head sundae—an upside-down cone on top of a scoop of ice cream decorated to look like a happy clown. My regular order was a small vanilla with a drop of butterscotch syrup, because I was always dieting, but now I would order a Jim Dandy, a kitchen sink of a sundae with three kinds of ice cream and three kinds of toppings, and I'd do it without a second thought.

When the bus moved, Harvey turned in to our driveway and Emmanuel Perez, our landscaper, pulled up and parked on the road. Harvey stepped out of his car, conversing with Perez, who sat in his truck, which held a tractor, tools, and several workers on the flatbed. I knew that Harvey got a kick out of practicing Spanish with Perez. I was a mess, and my husband was polishing past tense in the August heat.

"Calm down," I said aloud to myself. *He said he was leaving, but, thankfully, he's back. Is it to pick up something? Is it to explain? Is it for good? You can't handle any of this if you're crazed. Calm down. Think.*

I knew Harvey hadn't seen me at the door, so I dashed into the family room. I wasn't going to be waiting with my hand out for a shake like the welcoming committee outside a polling place. I was devastated and confounded by his departure, but I still had self-respect and no intention of playing the hysteria card.

I ran my fingers through my shoulder-length red hair. Had I known he was going to dawdle, I would have showered and changed in record time. Now it was too late for me to futz around, so I sat rock-still with a month-old town newspaper, the type seeming to shake in place. I was biding my time, gathering every iota of self-control to prevent myself from reaching out to Harvey when he first entered the house. I had battled impulses to call him, and I was not about to initiate the conversation now. I wanted Harvey to speak first. To say what he had come to say.

I heard the door open, his heavy footsteps in the hall, the jingling of his keys as he placed the loaded silver ring on the mahogany console. For thirty-three years on nights when he worked very late, I lay in our bed waiting for those sounds. Some women loved jazz; some, rock and roll. I liked the sounds of Harvey coming home.

"Marcy," he called out as though it were any other day, as though he had taken a trip to the town dump, which looked like a park—and returned with a smile on his face, ready to tell me who he'd bumped into or, at election time, who was campaigning there. Or, what treasures—bicycles to appliances—townspeople had donated to the giveaway shed.

"Marcy," he called again, because I was too choked up to answer.

"In here," I said several times, until my voice could be heard.

I was wearing khaki shorts, sandals, and a thin white T-shirt, with his bestselling sports bra underneath. He was in a suit, his natural casing. He lingered at the edge of the room—rubbing his hand over his head as though smoothing the hair he didn't have. His tired eyes were on my chest. "How's that sports bra? Did I mention that we now carry it in larger sizes?"

If Harvey and I were refugees fleeing the cruelest dictatorship—our children on our backs, suitcases stacked on our heads, a crust of bread in hand—Harvey would talk about bras. I'd never found it annoying. I understood what his business meant to him.

"Let's sit in the living room," he said in a formal voice. We sat in the living room only for state occasions or on holidays or when we had visitors we invited over once a year or less. If we didn't have visitors, why were we going to the living room?

In the living room, he turned on the Leaning Tower of Pisa lamp, bought in Rome during his first trip to Italy sponsored by Amore More Lingerie. He removed his navy suit jacket, loosened his tie, and rolled up his sleeves—a positive sign, I thought, until it occurred to me that that's what Harvey did when he had a daunting amount of work.

As I anticipated Harvey's words, I sat down and clasped my hands, attempting to evade any tremors.

"I have to make a confession," he began, standing at the entrance to the room as though he expected a four-alarm fire.

Good, I thought. *He's talking. Bad,* I thought, *because it's not going to be good.*

"The recession has gotten worse," he said.

The man was missing in action, breaking my heart, ruining my life, and he made a guest appearance to provide a consumer report. I felt my self-control unraveling.

"Only the most expensive lines are selling," he whined.

"That's your confession?"

"No, it isn't my confession. But the economy is important."

I tried to stay collected, but I was about to blow, the heat coursing through my face reminiscent of the worst hot flash I'd ever had, so I walked out of the living room, into the kitchen. I pulled myself together, settling on a Windsor chair, one of eight matching our long English pine table.

Harvey followed me, which was what I wanted. We were knee to knee, hand in hand, at the oval end of the table on the edge of two chairs.

"I could use a cup of coffee," he said.

I could use an explanation, I thought.

"We're out of coffee," I said, which wasn't true. We had more coffee than Brazil.

"I have so many problems."

"I'm your wife. Tell me your problems."

"Where to begin," he said with a heavy breath.

"I'm listening." I squeezed his hand to emphasize my willingness to listen. Then I sat back in my chair.

"There's a crisis at Bountiful Bosom."

Was Bountiful the problem? Was he stressed by his business? Why had I even spoken to Dana? She would bet on a monk committing adultery. Dana was driving me crazy, and this whole thing was probably about his business.

"I may need to shutter a store in Westchester—the one in White Plains." This was a huge deal. Harvey had never liquidated a store before.

So this was all about his business? I should have known. Bountiful Bosom was Harvey's life. When I first met him, he operated two shops in Manhattan. Since then, he'd cut ribbons in four states and begun an international wholesaling business from his headquarters. He couldn't pass a woman without informing me why her bra style and size was an unfortunate choice, and what would be best.

"It's the economy," I said, to support him. "What's that saying? 'It's the economy, stupid.'"

"Exactly. I'm a victim."

No wonder he appeared haggard, so trounced-upon that he didn't notice his bird was gone. Maybe I shouldn't have given the parrot to Dana. It was callous. I was wrong.

"Why didn't you tell me?"

"I couldn't tell you. After the ceramic arrived from Florence, I went ahead with the floor in the master bathroom so you wouldn't suspect that something was wrong. I didn't want you to worry."

"Are you serious?"

He nodded, but I knew finishing the floor wasn't about me. It was about Harvey. He was embarrassed by his new financial predicament. For a lifetime he had enjoyed success, and to him the smallest economic debacle was failure.

Maybe he had left because he'd had some kind of nervous breakdown. But that was okay. I could hunt down the name of a therapist who was experienced with type A men suffering from a major recession.

This rupture wasn't about me. This rupture was about bras.

"There's an excellent chance we can reorganize, pay our primary vendors with a percentage on the dollar, and ward off the IRS with installment schedules. But we'll have to retire quite a few old-timers," he said.

"Not One-Eyed Bobby." One-Eyed Bobby was eighty-some years old. He'd joined Bountiful Bosom before the invention of the wheel, holding many positions. Now Harvey paid One-Eyed Bobby to sit on a stubby stool in the warehouse, boning up on the *Daily Racing Form*, with reading glasses at the bottom of his nose and a paper cup of water from the cooler in his hand. Harvey bought him breakfast every day.

"Yes, One-Eyed Bobby. Sadly, the big layoff might also have to include Hungry Hannah. I'll miss Hannah at the Christmas party. We both appreciate good cold cuts." For a moment, his mind seemed to wander. I assumed he was imagining the platters of roast beef, pastrami, and corned beef under cellophane, about to be opened. "I'll need a dead serious sale."

I was so delighted that Harvey's departure was related to business I would have walked from store to store redlining each bra by hand, using my own blood instead of ink.

"I agree," I said. I hadn't been this agreeable since our first date.

"I'll talk to Feldman," he said.

Elisabeth and Amanda were December babies because Martin Feldman, CPA, MBA, CFP, had suggested to Harvey that we have children at the end of the year and take the deduction. I gave birth to Ben in January because the boy was a week late and apparently didn't care much about the tax consequences.

"Maybe you shouldn't listen to Feldman," I said, certain that this financial fiasco was Feldman's fault. *Why didn't Feldman walk out on his wife?*

"I already spoke to a few advertising agencies about the business. The consensus is, we have to change our name. Bountiful Bosom is prehistoric."

"Harvey, don't you recall that I suggested a name change? And it was a while ago—when the kids were little."

"I remember, but it's not easy for me. Bountiful Bosom is the name my great-grandmother gave the company, and she made bras back when most women were wearing corsets."

"You could shorten the name to Bountiful. How often do we just say Bountiful?"

"You're right. We call it Bountiful all the time."

"And maybe we need to make other changes."

"What changes?"

"We could sell the house," I said. "The kids are gone. We can downsize. Lots of people downsize."

He frowned. "Feldman is only concerned with the business. Besides, people who sell houses wind up in condominiums. I don't like condominiums. There are too many rules: Don't walk on the lawn. Don't look at the lawn. No barbecuing after eight p.m. No kids in the pool. Where are our grandchildren supposed to swim?"

Asking where his grandchildren were going to swim before he had grandchildren was so trademark Harvey that it was as good as a portrait of him. I had married him for sentences like that, and I didn't care

19

where I lived as long as I lived with him. I thought of that song—something about "you are my home." *He* was my home.

"Anyway, it's not a good time to sell. The housing market is on life support."

I opened the cupboard. "Oh, look," I said. "I do have some coffee."

I slipped the pod into the machine. I cut a hefty piece of the banana cake that I'd bought in case the kids came to visit. All three kids worshipped the cake with chocolate icing and sprinkles that Amelia at Sweet Heaven Bakery had told me was her aunt Sylvia's recipe. I placed a plateful of banana cake in front of Harvey.

Harvey looked around the table like something was missing, and I quickly passed him a fork and napkins.

"I wish you had told me about the problems at Bountiful. I'm devastated that you had to deal with this alone."

"I wasn't alone."

"Harvey?" I whispered, spooked, like I was afraid of the dark, in my well-lit kitchen.

"That's all. I wasn't alone," he said.

"What does that mean?"

"It means what I just said."

"Right, of course—you had Feldman," I said, wishing the discussion would wash up on another continent. I didn't want to know more. I was afraid to know more.

"Yes . . . No . . . Sort of," he said, perusing the cake, memorizing the sprinkles.

"Look at me. You're scaring me. What are you talking about?"

"I'm sorry."

I was overwhelmed by a swell of nausea. My hands began trembling at my sides. "Harvey, don't say you're sorry. Don't say there's anything to be sorry for. You're here now. Everything is fine."

"I am truly sorry."

Harvey was not a breather—he could barely breathe deeply with a stethoscope on his chest—but he was huffing from the bottom of his belly.

I could feel my eyes getting wider, the nausea caught in my throat. It was the worst kind of nausea, lodged and unable to come all the way up.

Harvey took another breath—through his nose, then his mouth.

"Stop breathing. You're making me nervous."

"I don't know how to say this," he said.

I grabbed the cake plate. "Look at me. Look at me and say it."

He stood up from the table. "I slept with someone."

I was motionless, a monument, staring straight forward, past his head. The room shook with silence. I raised my hand to slap him, and he stood there like he knew he deserved it, like he was willing to take it. But then I recognized that a blow might actually make him feel better, that he'd confessed to me to divest himself of guilt and he would be satisfied to toddle off with a whack. From the elbow, I backed up my right hand. My eyes froze and I didn't cry a single tear, but I could feel my hands burning. I dug my nails into my palms, clenched into two fists.

"You can hit me," he said. "I deserve it."

"Then hit yourself," I seethed. "I'm not giving you that satisfaction."

"Look, I admit that I made a mistake, but I was under a lot of pressure. After all, I've never been in this financial position before."

"I understand. You were forced to step out and have an affair. Bet business is better now. You're a genius, Harvey."

"I didn't step out."

"What does that mean?" I said, still gripping the plate as I backed up across the room and held steady against the sink.

"She's a fitting model. A new fitting model."

The plate shattered on the floor. "Don't tell me she's underage."

"She's twenty-two," he said sheepishly, guiltily.

My body boiled with rage, a level of anger I had never felt before. He was such a salesman; he starts off with his hard-luck it's-the-economy story and cranks up my sympathy, then he stabs me in the heart.

"I'm sorry," he said. "I am really sorry."

I stared at him.

He began coughing. "I need water. Can you give me water?"

"Get your own water." I was never going to hand him another thing again. He could be dehydrating in the Sahara and I would pour orange juice on the sand before I gave it to him.

Harvey held his throat with one hand as he rushed to the sink. He turned on the faucet and cupped his hands.

"Start explaining," I said.

"Can't you see that I am choking?"

"So choke," I said.

When he was done drinking, he splashed water on his face and throat, then wiped dry with a dish towel. He paced around the kitchen, as though searching for a reason to leave. "I can't believe you're blaming this on me," he said.

"Now it's my fault?"

"Once every thirty or so years isn't a bad record."

"Was it once? Or do you want me to *believe* it was once?"

"She was there. It's over. I didn't have to tell you."

"She was there? What is she—Everest?"

"I'm only human."

"No, I'm the only human in this room."

He cupped his head in his hands. "I knew you would start like this."

I slumped into a kitchen chair, tears streaming down my face. He handed me a napkin.

"I don't need your damn napkin. I don't need anything from you," I said as I cleared my eyes with the back of my hand.

He looked around furtively, like he had lost something, but I knew him well enough to know that he was just hunting for a way out.

"Marcy," he said with the tone of a man who has lost his child in the mall. "I don't hear the parrot. Where's the parrot?"

"Don't you dare change the subject."

"Where's the parrot?"

I whistled into the air and held up my hands, as if to say "I have no idea." With this act came some silly satisfaction, because I knew it would make Harvey explode. His face went red, and I imagined ragged pieces of Harvey, like stretched Silly Putty, on the wide-planked floor, the textured ceiling, and the etched molding around the windows, along with a generous splattering of Harvey on the pantry door.

He grabbed his keys from the console in the foyer. "Dana has the parrot, right? You gave him to Dana. I knew you didn't like my pet."

"Harvey. Harvey. Harvey," I said loudly, in fluent parrot.

Chapter 3

After Harvey took off, I couldn't move. Dusk to dawn, I sat erect, stunned in my kitchen on a Windsor chair—my body stiff but my mind on a trapeze all night.

Why did this happen now, when we were done raising our kids, when we were free of those responsibilities? I knew it was better for the kids that they were grown. But why did I think everything was fine when clearly it was not? Why was I living a life focused on Harvey and his business when apparently I was on the outer perimeter of his world?

If the affair was over, why did he mention it, and why did he leave the house we had bought? He'd said he wanted to live in it for eternity. Was he still seeing her? If so, what reason would he have to lie to me? What was the truth about my husband and his relationship with this girl? Each time I thought I had the answer to this mind-boggling jigsaw puzzle, I came up with another piece that didn't fit.

When at last I heard the shrill, continuous ring of the alarm clock upstairs next to my bed, I shook off a heap of disgust, held my breath, released my breath, and stretched both arms wide.

Harvey could dash off and retrieve every yack of a parrot in the world, but first he was going to talk to me. There was one thing I knew without question: I wanted my life back. And my life was Harvey.

I decided that if he had truly broken up with her—permanently, forever, until the end of time—I would struggle to look past his indecency. I would mend the marriage even though I knew I'd never completely file away what he had done.

I stepped into the shower. I washed my hair until my scalp hurt, rewashing as though I could scrub my problems away.

Wrapped in a towel, I hunted through my closet for something to wear to his office. I studied a short scoop-neck dress that I knew he liked a lot, a clinger that was perfection on me until Harvey had announced he was leaving me and I'd turned full-time to bottles of wine and tins of carbohydrates. But how much could I have gained? The whole Harvey mess had started less than a week before.

At the freestanding full-length mirror, I held the dress, still on a hanger, to my body. It was too obvious a choice. I wanted to look good, but I didn't want Harvey to know that I was trying to look good. I needed an outfit that was less revealing of my mission. *Keep it simple,* I thought. *Maybe dress down. Maybe wear jeans.* The trouble was that in my jeans, I would appear like I was straining to be young, somehow competing with a twenty-two-year-old—which I wasn't, because I couldn't.

I worked through my wardrobe until there were more outfits on my king bed than in my closet. I sat on the pile of clothes, some possibilities in my hand, and I cried. It was true. I was so appallingly pathetic that I didn't have any idea what to wear to get my husband back. When I was done despising myself, clean out of reasons I was a loser, I went to the bathroom, dried my hair, and concluded that what I needed was a new dress.

I felt horribly alone. I decided to go to Nordstrom, because the department store was renowned for its customer service. At Nordstrom, I would have company and polite, well-perfumed, friendly people to fuss over me. I pulled on a pair of cropped pants and a polo shirt and headed to the mall.

～❧

It was ten o'clock on Friday, and there were only a few customers in the store. I took the escalator, near the piano and armchairs, to the dress department on the second floor.

"Excuse me," I said as I approached a salesperson scented of Chanel No. 5, with the name Millicent on her chest. "I'm looking for something to wear that my husband will like a lot."

"It must be your anniversary," Millicent said with charm as she looked up from the rack of reduced-price items she was organizing by size. "I suppose you're going out on the town."

"He's out on the town already," I said.

"I see," Millicent said. She was easily in her early seventies, and her response seemed almost motherly.

I noticed her thick gold wedding band. "That's a beautiful wedding band," I said.

"I've been married forty-eight years. I have six grandchildren."

"What's your secret?" I said, wishing that Millicent had the answer to all of my problems and that she would now tell me everything I needed to know: how to work things out with Harvey, how to accept his treason and move on, how to share six grandchildren with the man sometime in the future.

"Cranberry juice," she said.

"I don't understand."

"With vodka in it," she said.

I laughed.

"I'd go black," she said, directing me to a lineup of one- and two-piece cocktail frocks. "Why don't you start here? Don't worry—I won't stand over you. Just let me know if you need help."

Millicent proceeded to the cash register, where she approached another salesperson, a man with a tight face and a rose in his lapel. I saw her point her head toward me. In no time, I would be renowned as the woman shopping for a dress to get her husband back.

I felt lonely again, so I approached the register. "I need some help," I said.

"Black is wrong in your situation," said the salesperson with the rose. He was wearing a pin-striped suit and a pink shirt. His hair was slicked back. He was folding tissue paper for gift wrapping. "You need color. Maybe green. No, I take it back. You need a cream, maybe an almond—simple yet sophisticated."

"It depends where she's meeting him, William," Millicent said.

"I'm going to his office, and I need something more casual than those cocktail dresses."

"But not a church dress," Millicent said.

"Something between church and purgatory," William said.

William told Millicent he wanted to help me, and he scurried to my aid. On his third try, he showed me a cream-colored sleeveless wrap dress. He displayed it on the hanger in front of me, then steered me to the dressing room. I knew it was the right dress, and I smiled for the first time in days when I tried it on. Fitted and demure, it was the ultimate go-to-your-husband's-office-to-repair-your-marriage dress. It should have had a label that said that.

William wrapped my street clothes so I could wear the dress out of the store. Then he called the women's shoe department, and a salesman brought a wobbly stack of shoe boxes. All of the shoes were cream, brown, or black stilettos worthy of Dana.

"These won't work," I said, imagining myself towering over Harvey.

"Height is power," William said. "Did you know that eighty percent of CEOs in America are six feet tall or taller?" If that was true, William had no chance of becoming CEO of Nordstrom.

"My husband is only an inch taller than me," I said, closing the lid on the box William was holding open for my inspection. Then suddenly I felt the need to defend Harvey. "He's short, but he is a CEO."

Next thing I knew, I'd be saying that Harvey was a dedicated father—and that his children, not a fool among them, loved him. That he was salutatorian in high school, and would have been number one if it hadn't been for a gym teacher who gave him a B minus. High school seemed too far back, so I said, "Also, my short husband graduated at the top of his business school class. He was the speaker at graduation. He spoke for ten minutes."

The shoe consultant snapped to it, stacking up his boxes. "No problem. We have some elegant dress flats and low heels."

"Would you like a bottle of water?" Millicent asked.

"Yes." I nodded.

As she brought the water, my heart warmed at the thought of someone doing something nice for me.

"You must be drained," she said.

"Sapped," William chimed in.

"He's having an affair," I said to my new friends.

They shook their heads, almost in unison.

"I hate that," William said with a shiver. "I'll call a consultant from our cosmetics department. You don't mind if I explain the situation?"

"Oh, no, it's hardly a secret here."

"Bobbi Brown okay?" William asked.

I nodded. I had never used Bobbi Brown cosmetics. But my old makeup line certainly hadn't helped in any way.

After the Bobbi Brown rep worked her magic with an array of products, I purchased waterproof mascara, left the mall, and headed for Harvey's office.

⌒

I referred to Harvey's corporate offices as "nouveau colonial," meaning that the building appeared prerevolutionary from afar but had been built in 1998—which was when Harvey moved Bountiful operations to Connecticut. The building was five stories, with colonial-style windows overlooking woods. It was unadorned, except for the cursive company logo—large and loopy and gold—above the door.

As I entered, I checked both ways for a fitting model. There was a young woman with an iPod, snapping her fingers while waiting for the elevator. Was she the one?

She was not. Her hair was greasy, and I knew Harvey would never go for that. Harvey was a cleanliness freak. Every day he showered morning and evening. And as long as I'd known him—predating the proliferation of Asian nail shops—he'd had a weekly manicure. I stepped into the elevator with the girl and a tall man.

Whoever Harvey's juvenile delinquent was, I had no desire to see her. If she was a knockout, I would be devastated, branding myself an Oldsmobile with smoke rising from under the hood, replaced by a late-model sports car. If she was certifiably abhorrent, it would be even worse.

The receptionist in the foyer was a new employee, wearing long silver earrings and a leotard top. Noticing me, she stashed her cell phone, scrunched her vacant eyes, and asked my name.

"I'm Harvey's wife. Marcy," I said, certain that she knew my husband was having an affair, and that she was either snickering to herself about it or feeling sorry for me.

She stood awkwardly. "Pleasure to meet you."

I started walking past her.

"I have to buzz him," she said.

"No, you don't. Because as I mentioned, I'm his wife."

I was no Navy SEAL, but I had the daring to walk in on him and the 32DD.

I was relieved to find Harvey in his leather office chair—alone—at the antique desk with its black lacquered top, which was the only family heirloom I had ever heard about. His silver reading glasses made him appear even more successful than he was. He was reviewing his year-to-year sales record for the date—which he always hand-recorded, as a matter of pride, in a series of ledgers—and looked up in surprise. I closed the door behind me. My eyes went to the picture of our three children at Ben's college graduation. Ben was in the middle; the girls were on either side. I had given him that picture.

As usual, lingerie was all over the office. In a hurry and in silence, Harvey cleared a slew of half-slips and body shapers from a leather chair, one of six at his conference table. I looked out the windows facing the woods. Harvey sat down across from me, opposite his door.

"You look very nice."

My eyebrows furrowed, and I dropped my chin.

"*Okay* then," he said, emphasizing the *O*.

I had no patience. I got right down to it. "Are you still seeing her?" I asked. If the answer was yes, the conversation was over. If the answer was no, I would accept it.

"Can I first say again that you look nice?"

I stared at him.

"No," he said assertively, as though under oath. "No. I am not."

"Tell me something. Are you lying?"

"I don't lie," he said.

"Are you sure? Because I think you were *living* a lie." My voice cracked.

I knew if I wanted him back, I needed to stop beating the drum. He'd said what I wanted to hear: he wasn't seeing her. How many times did I need him to say it?

"There you go with the accusations. I'm always the bad guy. You always turn everything on me," he said. "Is anything in this world ever your fault?"

"You have an affair, and I turn everything on you?" I was intent on his paperweight. It was a replica of Stonehenge—so heavy I could knock his head off with it. And I was considering it.

Harvey folded his glasses.

"You hypocrite," I said. "You instructed your own daughter not to see a married man."

"I didn't see a married man," he said.

Did he actually think I would laugh? Did he actually think there was anything about him that I found the least bit amusing?

"And how can you compare Elisabeth to me?" he marched on. "She's my daughter. It's my responsibility to watch out for her, to protect her from pain. As I recall, you smoked your head off in the '70s, and told her not to as much as stroll past a joint."

He eyeballed fabric samples, white and blush and nude, on the conference table.

"Do not look at microfiber—or anything else—when I am talking to you."

His office phone interceded. I slapped down my hand, covering the receiver. "Don't even think about taking a call."

He went to the door. He stuck his head out. "Switch on the voice mail and go home for the day."

"Thanks, Mr. Hammer," the new receptionist responded.

He turned toward me, and suddenly, in a pleasant tone, he said, "Tell me something. Would it help if you knew where I'm staying?"

My hand was still on the receiver. I glanced at the couch. It was buried under sapphire cartons of My Lovely Lady plunging bras. "I thought you were staying here, but I can see that once again I'm the fool."

"I'm at the inn," he said.

"What? You check out on me and check into a hotel?"

Five Swallows, the only inn in town, was a five-star accommodation. At charity auctions, Harvey and I had won weekends at Five Swallows. All the important social functions were held there. I knew the place up and down. And, as much as I wanted to believe Harvey was done philandering, that we could put everything back together, I was on a steam train to hysteria. He'd been luxuriating while I was sitting up at night in a kitchen chair.

It was as easy as it was painful to imagine Harvey at Five Swallows—humming "My Way" or some other self-centered song while carrying his freshly cleaned suits as he inserted his key card in the door to his grandiose set of rooms with flat-screen TVs larger than billboards on the Connecticut Turnpike. This scene taking place as I bawled in our stagnant house, each bedroom a shrine to a child who no longer lived there and was never going to live there again.

"I tipped my way to the Presidential Suite," he said proudly.

Harvey always thought that palming out a gratuity and then getting his way was an achievement worthy of recognition. *And the gold medal goes to Harvey Hammer—for tipping!"*

"Stop bragging about what a schmuck you are. And for once, give me credit, Harvey. You actually think I believe that you checked into the Presidential Suite at Five Swallows all by your lonesome?"

"I *did*."

"Really, Harvey."

"I'm there alone," he said without raising his voice.

"Stop selling. I buy the lie."

"It's not a lie."

"I think *you* should live in the house, and *I* should be at the inn."

"Ridiculous. You're the wife—you belong in the house."

"I belong in the house? I'm done with the house. I'm selling the house."

"Don't you dare," he said.

I stood from the table, swiping all the underwear off the couch onto the carpet, glaring at him from across the room.

"I swear," he said. "I swear I'm living alone. Solo, by myself, with nobody, nada."

"I see you've been at work on your Spanish. *Bastardo.*"

"I have a lot to think about. I need to decide what I want to do."

"What *you* want to do?" That's what I had wrought. A husband who thought—no, *believed*—he was holding all the cards.

"Well, I know exactly what *you* want to do," he said to me.

I was fifty-eight years old, had centered my life around him, and was heartbroken at the thought that there was anything I was supposed to do other than live my life the way I had been living it. "So," I said, "what do I want to do?"

"You certainly don't want to break up our marriage," Harvey said, as though he had discovered the wheel and was the only one who knew what to use it for.

"You know that because . . . ?"

"You'd never do that to the kids," he said. "We're family people."

"Damn you, Harvey the Home-Wrecker. You didn't think twice about pillaging our marriage, hurting me, hurting our kids. You tossed everything, a lifetime, down the drain. And I don't want to be buried anywhere near you—so stay out of my cemetery and get your own damn headstone."

"Marcy, how many times do I need to tell you I'm sorry?"

"A first time would be nice."

"The relationship is over."

My aorta toppled into my large intestine. "Relationship? It was a *relationship?*"

"I chose the wrong word. It was nothing. You're blowing this out of proportion."

"How long?"

"It doesn't matter."

"It doesn't matter to you. Tell me how long."

"A month."

"One month?" I didn't believe him.

"Okay, three months."

"This isn't a negotiation. How long?"

"Four months. Just four months."

"You were seeing her in May, June, July, and now August? You were with *her* while I planned *your* company celebration, under the damn whale at the damn museum?"

"She wasn't at the party," he said. "She wasn't even on my list."

"Well, that's a relief. I feel much better now."

"I'm sorry. It's over. You're blowing it out of proportion."

"Blow yourself, Harvey." I walked out the door, slamming it behind me.

In the Bountiful parking lot, as I searched my bag for my keys, my wallet fell out. Credit cards scattered, along with some singles and a few coins. I bent over to gather the mess. At last, I felt the gold Swiss cheese–shaped key chain with holes in it that Harvey had bought for me when he went to Zurich. I took the keys off and threw the Swiss cheese to the ground.

Hovering over the steering wheel in my sweltering car, the keys and plastic membership tags in my sweaty palm, I thought of all the miserable moments I had bawled inside my car whenever I'd had a problem with Harvey. But it turned out that those had been false alarms, petty tiffs compared to this. This time, I bawled in my car like I had been told about the sudden death of a friend.

My new dress felt as though it were melting. I blinked repeatedly to make room for more tears. I leaned over the steering wheel, and soon it was all wet.

It was a Friday in summer, and people were leaving work early. The vehicles around me started moving, backing up, pulling out. Slowly, I stopped sobbing, whisking my hand across my face. I blew my nose into a piece of composition paper on which I had scribbled my mother-in-law's address in Scottsdale so I could mail her a birthday present. "Buy my mother something," Harvey said each August. He did one thing for his mother a year, and I was the one who did it.

So he'd dropped his 32DD model. So he was living alone. He had no one, and he didn't want me. What was worse than that?

I was wretched, and I didn't have the newspaper outside my door in the morning; no one delivered fat pumpkin muffins stuffed with cream cheese or made my four-poster bed fluffed up fresh with one-thousand-thread-count cotton sheets. Fool that I was, I had trusted him with everything. He knew everything about me; I couldn't even think of something he *didn't* know about me. And suddenly he was my enemy. Harvey was the person to look out for—a merciless spy for another country, living as a fraud yet effortlessly returning unscathed to the motherland. My husband was the definition of human betrayal.

Chapter 4

At home, I dragged myself up the stairs and collapsed on Elisabeth's bed, flat on my back with my head on a pillow. The room was the same as it had been on the day she departed for college. The room and I had a lot in common—we were both dull, unused, stagnant, wasted, waiting as Elisabeth, now a doctor, made her own way in the world.

My eyes were closed, but I could still envision the room. On the twin bed there was a yellow gingham quilt with matching pillow shams. The ruffled curtains were gingham too, tied with bows. There was a hand-hooked oval rug on the oak floor. Elisabeth had begged me for the wallpaper, enormous yellow and blue polka dots. When we bought it, she loved it; mere months later, she hated it.

Elisabeth's ceiling was covered with pictures. Amid the sticky-back photos and memorabilia was a fading Red Cross poster. After Elisabeth had volunteered for the Red Cross, she decided to go into medicine. She rewrote her college application essay; "Changing Our World through Good Film" became "Changing Our World through Good Medicine." It would have been a far better essay if she had grown up destitute in a mobile home with no toilet and no father, or if she'd had to overcome a completely crazy mother. As for the latter, maybe she did.

I sank my head deep into one of Elisabeth's pillows. I wasn't sure what to do, but I knew it was time to do something. Maybe it was time to sell the house—a house that was now emptier than I was.

But if I moved, where would I move? I figured that there were only two choices. I could stay in Atherton and resettle in a cottage-type place, a dormered Cape with a rocking chair on the porch. Or I could go the other way—and move back to New York. What a deal that would be: I could buy an alcove studio in need of total renovation for the price of my house in Connecticut. The truth was that I had no idea whether moving to a new home would actually move me forward, but thinking about it made me feel like I might have options.

I called Elisabeth. "I'm thinking of selling the house. But to do so, I would have to close the History of Elisabeth Museum. Do you think you could dismantle your room? After all, you haven't touched a thing since you went off to college."

"Oh, Mom, I don't think you should make rash decisions. Besides, my apartment is spatially challenged. Where would I put everything?"

"Well, let's see. You could ask Brian's wife whether you can store your things in her basement." I started laughing, a bit too wildly. It made me nervous. "I'm sorry that I'm laughing, Elisabeth. But you have to admit that was funny."

"One day he's going to divorce her," she said.

"And you think that's all right? You think that's okay?"

"It's not anything. It's the way it is."

"But she probably put him through medical school," I said.

"You don't know that."

"She had his children."

"Child."

"How old is he?"

"Twelve or thirteen?"

"So you're planning to bring up his child?"

"I'm not planning anything."

"Do you have any idea how fragile a teenager can be? You don't need this. You're ruining your life and his before it begins."

"Why do you always need to project ahead, to imagine situations down the road? Live for today, Mom. Live for today."

"What have I got to live for?"

"What does that mean?"

I paused. I swallowed. I closed my eyes. I felt bloody with pain.

"Mom?"

"Your father has someone."

"What? No way. I don't believe it," Elisabeth said, her voice rising high.

Thank heaven Elisabeth was aghast. What would I have done if she hadn't been aghast?

"She's single, like you," I said.

"I don't believe it. Tell me. Tell me about Dad."

I bit my tongue. Hard. "I think Dad should tell you about Dad."

"Oh, Mom. I am so sorry."

"I know you are, honey," I said softly.

"The first summer I went to camp, there was this miserable girl on the bottom of my bunk," Elisabeth said. "It turned out that her parents were separating. They visited her on two different days. She cried after each one left, and all I could think about was *What would I do if my mom and dad split up?* But I didn't think it would happen when I was an adult. Maybe you can work it out. Maybe Dad will realize how fortunate he's been to have you."

"Maybe," I said.

"You need a plan, Mom. I want you to think of a plan."

"I have a plan," I said. "Right now, my plan is to kill him."

"That's not funny. Mom, you love him. We love him. I know he spends most of his time working, but he's there for us at every turn."

"I know. Believe me, I know." I reached over for the tissues on Elisabeth's night table. The girl had moved out eons ago, and I still kept tissues on her night table.

"There's something I want you to think about, Elisabeth. Unfortunately, you are about to see firsthand the tumult that can result from an affair. Your day at the beach, your picnic by the pines, is at someone else's expense. His wife is a good person. She doesn't deserve this."

"How do you know she's a good person? Maybe she's a bad person, a very bad person. Maybe she sells heroin to children."

"She doesn't sell heroin to children."

"And how do you know that?" she asked.

"Because she's married to a doctor," I said.

"You're ridiculous," she said.

"Okay, tell me what his wife will do when he leaves her. She's too old to hop from bar to bar. I guess she could look for a new man on a dating site, but she'd have to post a picture taken when Jimmy Carter was president."

"Mommm," she groaned.

"Incidentally, who's going to teach her how to get a picture onto the computer screen? Are you?"

"Nice rant, but you're talking about yourself. For all you know, Brian's wife is a lesbian who took a Rosie O'Donnell cruise with a partner and her adopted multiracial children."

"Is she?" I said.

"Is she what?"

"Is she a lesbian who took a Rosie cruise?"

"No," Elisabeth answered firmly in her I've-had-enough-of-you voice. "But maybe she has her own lover and she's relieved I'm with Brian."

"She doesn't have a lover. She has ten pounds she wants to lose."

"Mom, you have a gym membership."

"I am not talking about myself. I am talking about a woman who wasted her twenties and thirties and forties, and maybe even fifties, on a man who never appreciated her."

"Mom, I have a patient waiting, but you can call Amanda and bother her. I hear she's seeing *two* married men, a fire-eater and a born-again porn star."

I knew she wasn't cutting our conversation short for a patient. She was getting off the phone to call Harvey.

"I love you," I said.

"And I love you," she said. "Dad will come back to you, and it will all work out."

But what if it didn't work out?

What the hell then?

Chapter 5

I imagined them sideways.

I imagined him entering her from behind.

Insane images, since Harvey was a come-on-top man with little to no imagination. But who knew where she was leading him—for all I knew she was an Olympic gymnast.

She had the soft, poreless skin no one appreciates until they are too old to have it anymore, too aged to remember having it. When she smiled, her cheeks didn't drop to her chin. Her eyes hadn't yet lost their light. Her plump breasts perked up, practically said hello. Harvey was amazed by these breasts, the small waist, the skin smoother than cream, the skin that was cream. Every inch of this new body was a country he believed he had never been to before. He had forgotten I was once, a very long time ago, that very country.

There was a time that *I* was his fitting model.

∽

The evening after our first date, at a steak house, a messenger knocked at my door and handed me a box with a large bow on top. Gingerly, I opened it. A scented card fell from the tissue paper: *For Marcy. Because you deserve my best.*

Harvey had sent four Bountiful bras, two pairs of tap pants, and two string bikinis. The bras were different styles, but each was natural—skin-toned. The size was exactly right.

With my favorite dangling from one hand, I thumbed through the Yellow Pages, looking for the Bountiful Bosom corporate headquarters. A receptionist with a heavy New York accent connected me to Harvey.

"I received a delivery," I said. "Thank you."

"Can I come over?" he said confidently.

"I'll be wearing your lingerie in fifteen minutes," I said.

There was no question—when we were young, there was passion. But as we grew older, the sex aged as well, until one day it seemed older than we were.

After years of marriage, we had fallen into a pattern. We made love only on federal holidays—the type of holidays when public schools, banks, and the post office were closed. We'd come up with this plan because it seemed we weren't having enough sex. At least not according to the magazine surveys of married couples. I dug back in my mind, trying to remember the last time we'd had random sex. Then I remembered. It was the night Harvey had returned from another business trip to Italy for Amore More Lingerie.

When I'd heard him climb the stairs to our bedroom, I slipped off my sweats to reveal his latest product, the Precious Plunge bra and matching boy shorts in tropical yellow. But he had been in Italy observing young women parade about in underwear, so all he said to me was "Precious Plunge in Saint Martin Sun."

Then he said he was going down to the kitchen to make a drink. I pulled on a robe and followed, waiting as he poured Scotch neat. And then somehow we wound up in an hour-long discussion of his business trip and his corporate plans. I updated him on some of the recent complaints lodged by his consumers. There was a woman who was bellyaching that her Bountiful bra had caused cut marks on her chest. She blamed it on the underwire, but the bra she kept referring to had no underwire.

"I offered to send a gift certificate, but she began screaming at me that her brother-in-law was a lawyer and she was planning to sue."

"Is there anyone in the Northeast who is not related to an attorney?" He raised his glass. "To lawyers," he said.

Some might call this idle chatter, but for us this was foreplay. It was what we loved most about each other. It was what was most likely to lead to sex.

And so we were at peace just sitting there, in the kitchen of a long-emptied house, mundane as mundane could be. When Harvey finished his second drink, I moved to his lap, then we made our way upstairs. The rest was lovely and romantic, then he fell asleep.

But I couldn't sleep. So I put on my robe and went down to the family room, where I dozed on the couch to the sounds of CNN. At about three a.m., I awoke abruptly from a dream in which I was kissing Anderson Cooper on Veterans Day.

⤳

When Dana returned from Boston, it turned out I wasn't the only one with sex on my mind.

"Perhaps you need to have more sex with him," Dana said as we occupied a table at Starbucks. It was early afternoon in deepest suburbia, and most of the patrons were women.

"Dana, you say that as though we only have sex on federal holidays."

"You have sex with him that much?" She was stirring a straw in an iced latte with whipped cream. She had also bought two packages of madeleines. We loved the madeleines at Starbucks. Why didn't they put more than three in a package?

"Okay, Dana, that's enough."

She laughed. "You can't even discuss it."

"I can too discuss it."

"Can*not*," she said.

"Fine. I'll discuss it." I took a breath and leaned back in my chair. "I don't think this is about us having or not having sex."

"Denial. At the very least, he wanted to have new sex. Years and years go by, and then one day you want to fall into bed with someone who isn't totally predictable. You want something new."

"Well, she's new," I said. "Twenty-two years new."

"The two of you need to get away. I know—go on a cruise with him."

"I get sick on boats," I said.

"Then plan a two-week trip to someplace that's romantic."

"Like Harvey is going to take two weeks off from Bountiful."

"Okay, so stay home and do something he would never expect. I think you should suggest tantric sex."

"What the hell is that?" I asked.

"I read that John Kennedy Jr. loved tantric sex. Sting is into it too."

"Yes, and that makes sense, because Harvey has so much in common with Sting."

"You're knocking everything I'm suggesting."

"Okay, what is tantric sex?"

"You delay orgasm as long as possible, making the actual act sacred."

"If a man in his sixties gets hard, you don't delay the orgasm. You're lucky there's going to be an orgasm."

"Then how is he doing a twenty-two-year-old?"

That's right, Dana. Go for my heart. Get that knife in there.

44

"Maybe it's more exciting," I said weakly, certain I had lost all color in my face.

"He's taking Viagra," she said.

"No. He refused."

Often, I had wondered when and how our sex life had dwindled. Was it having kids? Was it Harvey traveling so much? Was it about me? But then I read an article that said men prone to diabetes were likely to have a low sex drive. I had asked Harvey to take something, had gone so far as to schedule an appointment with a urologist in town, an appointment Harvey canceled. I let it go. We weren't malcontents. We had a full life, or so I'd thought.

"Well, maybe he changed his mind. About the Viagra."

"That's enough. Not another word. Shut the hell up. You're making me even more miserable. I don't want to talk about this. I don't even want to think about it. Naive me. I thought there was more to a lifelong marriage than sex."

"I know we've never discussed this, but it's important: How many men did you sleep with before Harvey?"

"We've never discussed that?"

"Never."

"Two."

She rolled her eyes. "I've been married more times than that."

"So that's a reason to brag?" I said.

I wasn't one for yakking at length about my sex history, but girl talk with Dana was keeping Harvey off my mind. "There was the first guy, but he didn't really count, because he was random and unexpected. He crept out of my dorm room in the middle of the night and took my James Taylor album with him—so much for 'You've Got a Friend.'"

"Then Michael?"

"Yes."

Michael the Premed was my college boyfriend. He owned one pair of jeans ripped at the knee, played Frisbee on the quad, and ate whole overly ripe cucumbers while walking his pet hamster, King George, on a leash. He was mine from spring of freshman year until January of junior year, when he scored an A in organic chemistry. That day, when I brought a celebratory jug of sangria to his dorm room, I noticed a diaphragm in a pink case on his university-issued dresser. I confronted him, eyeball to eyeball, diaphragm in hand. And that was the last time I ever trusted a guy who walked a rodent with the name of a king.

"And this all matters right now because . . . ?" I asked Dana.

"Because we never talked about it before," she said.

"What about you?"

"Let's just say I'm in a statistical dead heat with a sex slave."

"Nuh-uh. The count," I said after I swallowed the last of my coffee.

"Twelve," she said, nodding her head up and down, looking delighted with herself.

I didn't know much about how many men most women had slept with, but twelve seemed like a lot.

"Give or take a dozen," Dana said, practically snorting cookie as she laughed.

"I wonder what the average is," I said.

"Four," Dana said, taking a small bite into another madeleine. "But of course I read that statistic in the bestselling book *Confessions of a Eunuch*."

I laughed. Dana was the best.

"So now that I've cheered you up, what about Harvey?"

Chapter 6

After meeting Dana, I went home. In the living room, I went to the bookshelf and pulled out a brown leather photo album. I opened it up to the first picture taken of me with Harvey, back in the late '70s. We were standing next to each other at my cousin Leona's engagement party. It was an event I had attended only because my mom had practically held a gun to my head.

Leona was my mother's sister's daughter. Even at the age of twenty-nine, she'd acted like the oldest person in the world.

"You never liked Leona," my mother had said on the phone, whispering to me as though Cousin Leona could hear.

"I like her. I have to study" was what I said. *I shall not be moved* was what I was thinking.

"She's having a brunch in two Sundays. What do you need in your apartment? Tell me what to bring and I'll give it to you at Leona's."

"I am *not* going."

"Do you need tampons? Sanitary napkins are better for you. No toxic shock. But if you want, I can bring tampons."

"Bring an economy-size bottle of extra-strength aspirin."

When I arrived at Cousin Leona's hot, crowded apartment, my mother threw up her hands in delight, then pressed me to her chest. My mother's face was wrinkled perfectly, as though an illustrator had placed each line there. Her hair was light gray around her face and darker gray in back. Her eyes were the deepest green, wide and bright. As for her straight nose, I was fortunate in the gene pool to win one just like it.

Leona buzzed about in a full-length crimson caftan, with braiding at the neckline. She was beaming to the point of exploding. She hugged me, then flashed her left hand and shoved her engagement ring in my face. Her precious diamond was so close I could have eaten it.

"Beautiful," I said dutifully, then smiled. What, after all, *was* there to say about your cousin's new elephantine engagement ring? *"Looks a little discolored to me?"*

When Leona dashed off to greet a friend from college, I noticed a guy who looked to be about thirty, with a well-groomed mustache and wavy hair almost the same color as mine. Men with reddish hair were rare in New York.

I watched from the doorway as he adjusted his gold wire-rimmed glasses, then returned to what he was doing, which was slicing a dried log of salami at the groaning dining room table.

"He's a friend of Leona's fiancé, Steve," Mom whispered to me. "His sport coat is very expensive. From Barneys," she said.

"He's not wearing a sport coat," I said. He was in a blue oxford shirt with a button-down collar. His sleeves were rolled up.

"He complained that he didn't understand why the air conditioning wasn't cranking, so I offered to hang his sport coat in Leona's hall closet."

"I'll bet you did. Did you get a look at his underwear label as well?" I teased.

Friend of Steve smeared his slice of salami with spicy brown mustard. He was older than the guys I'd dated before, and I wasn't a mustache person. However, it was the '70s—facial hair came and went. There was a sweet boyish ruddiness to his full cheeks, and warmth in his demeanor.

When I approached the buffet table, the object of my attention smiled at me. A slight tingle shot from my head to my knees.

"I spoke to your mother," he said. "She told me Leona was a colicky baby, the cheesecake is from Brooklyn, and I'd be fortunate to meet you."

"Did she mention my leprosy?"

He smiled and introduced himself. "Harvey Hammer."

"Marcy Kinderman."

He shook my hand. It was a solid, dependable shake.

"Are you on the bride's side or on the groom's side?" I asked.

"Actually, I hope the groom is on my side. He's my attorney."

I didn't know anyone in my generation who had ever needed a lawyer for any reason other than a misdemeanor for selling pot. "You know, Harvey, you wouldn't need an attorney if you stopped hopping the fence and selling drugs at the day care center."

He laughed. "I'm in business. Steve is my corporate attorney. I have never been arrested."

"What kind of business?" I asked.

"It's my family business. Fourth-generation," he said proudly.

"Your family has been in the United States a long time."

"Yes. We arrived on the boat preceding the *Mayflower*."

"What boat was that?"

"The *April Flower*," he said deadpan, then grinned when I laughed.

Harvey wasn't my usual type, which was collegiate sloth, but I liked him. I liked his smile, his sturdy handshake, and his sense of humor, and the way he built his sandwich after he wolfed down the slices of hard salami. The sandwich was on a bulky seeded roll, with chunky chicken salad even all around, sliced tomatoes in a pyramid, and pickle chip on top.

"What do you do, Marcy?"

"I'm in graduate school for marketing—almost finished—and I work part-time at an advertising agency. I supervise Mr. Coffee."

"That sounds like a big account."

I laughed. "Not the account. I just make sure there's coffee in the machine."

I also delivered mail, brought in lunch, organized mechanicals—sizable pieces of cardboard on which advertisements were pasted the old-fashioned way—one block of copy, one picture, at a time. I was an assistant to a traffic manager, haranguing art directors when layouts were due.

I loved my job. I was hyperentertained, fueled by the creative people around me. I planned to work full time at the agency when I received my graduate degree, and I could see staying in the advertising business forever.

"Would you like to sit down somewhere?" he asked.

I glanced around the living room, an *L* off the dining room.

"Quick," he said. "I see an opening on the couch."

We seated ourselves on the couch, paper plates on our laps, drinks on the coffee table in front of us.

"So, Marcy, tell me something about you."

I thought for a moment. I didn't want to give a run-of-the-mill answer. "I played the oboe in college."

"So I'm talking to a musician."

"No." I laughed. "You're talking to someone who played the oboe in college."

"Why did you choose the oboe?"

"My mother thought I'd meet a better class of people."

"Tell me something else."

"I'm pretty sure it's your turn. What's your business?"

"It's called Bountiful Bosom. Have you heard of it?"

"Yes," I answered. I had heard of Bountiful Bosom, but I had never been in one of the stores, because I bought my bras on sale at Alexander's.

Cousin Leona's sorority sister approached and asked us to remove our drinks from the coffee table. Harvey snatched our party cups as she plopped her dribbling son on a rubber changing pad and opened his soggy disposable diaper. Cousin Leona was not going to think it was funny, a pee-soaked nine-month-old on her furniture—during an engagement party or any other time.

Harvey grabbed my hand and pulled me out of my seat, across the room, and through Leona's apartment door as though we were fleeing an oncoming train.

"My hero," I said as we stood in the deserted corridor, opposite each other.

As he asked more questions, I was beginning to think maybe Harvey, not Steve, should be the lawyer. On the other hand, I was pleased he was so interested, and tried to keep it that way.

In the hall, I learned that Harvey was an only child, and that he had graduated from high school two years early and attended Syracuse University. Harvey's favorite movie was *Butch Cassidy and the Sundance Kid*. He read multiple business books at a time, left open here and there in his one-bedroom apartment. His ideal Sunday involved reading the *New York Times*. He started with front-page news. I started with the magazine.

The fluorescent ceiling fixture began blinking. Harvey and I snapped our fingers, bobbing in rhythm with the light. We were laughing, our legs lightly touching, when Cousin Leona poked her head out her door to summon any guests smoking in the hall. Stop the world—the engagement cake was about to be cut. She grinned knowingly when she saw us—and only us.

∾

My mother loves to tell this story, the story of how I met Harvey: all because I listened to her and went to the party, all because she spotted him first and told him exhaustively about me.

I flipped backward in the old photo album, wanting to see who I had been BH—Before Harvey.

I had taken several proud pictures of my studio apartment—the first place of my own—where the shower was next to the oven, and my knees touched the door when I crouched on the toilet. My portable Smith-Corona typewriter, carbon paper from the stationery store, newspapers, hair rollers, a knife, a fork, a loaf of Wonder Bread, and a cup of coffee from Sol and Jean's Luncheonette were on a metal desk. My stereo was on a shelf with albums. I slept on an orange-and-lime tweed couch, and my madras quilt, made in India, was a mess on the floor. I stored all of my clothing behind hanging brown beads. I stored marijuana in a zippered makeup bag I got free as a gift with purchase from Estée Lauder.

In the photos, I had waist-length strawberry-blond hair and was most often wearing a peasant shirt and my favorite jeans. These jeans were blotched, washed-out, wiggle-in tight, ragged with holes. My mom, who deplored any garment evidencing the least sign of wear, thought these jeans were a shame, not just for her but also for the entire borough of Queens.

What had happened to those jeans? I wished I still had them. But the jeans had disappeared when I went home for the Jewish holidays one year. I always pictured my ragged jeans in my mom's garbage can all those years ago, under the breakfast cantaloupe. But I had never called her out on it.

I closed the photo album. Carefully, I put it on the floor next to the couch. Then I dialed my mother, who answered on the first ring.

"Hello, Marcy."

"Hi, Mom."

"What are you doing?"

"I was looking through photo albums. I'm fifty-eight years old, but I have to know: Did you throw out my jeans all those years ago?"

"When I was a young girl, they were called dungarees."

"When you were a girl, they were sold out of Conestoga wagons."

"That's funny but unkind."

"I came home for the holidays one year, and those jeans weren't in my suitcase when I returned to Manhattan and unpacked. I loved those jeans. Those jeans had holes in all the right places."

Like my mother would appreciate the importance of strategic holes. Mom had contributed so much "gently used clothing" to the Salvation Army I was surprised she wasn't a general. She had an aversion to other people's towels, open bottles of soda, borrowed books, used cars, and any home or apartment lived in first by another human being. When I had informed her I had rented a walk-up studio apartment, she asked me how I planned to live in another person's dirt.

"Buy a new pair tomorrow. I'll treat," she said. "You don't have anything more important to think about than an old pair of jeans?"

I did have something more important to think about, of course—but I had not as yet told my mother about my husband's departure.

I knew that telling her would be excruciating, one of the most painful experiences in my life—worse than wearing saddle shoes and having frizzy red hair on the first day of junior high.

Telling her was the mother-daughter equivalent of slicing off my right arm to avoid the spread of gangrene as I struggled in the aftermath of an avalanche. I imagined blood dripping in the snow as a member of the ski patrol reported the news of my survival to the townies praying at the bottom of the mountain. *We found the skier.*

And it could be worse. She could have told her mother about her husband leaving."

Mom was as rabid as a Red Sox fan when it came to Harvey. She'd liked him from the moment the two had met at Cousin Leona's engagement party. Mom was the warm antithesis of Harvey's own disinterested mother, and Harvey had been saintly to her since day one. In fact, it was Harvey who had suggested out of the blue that Mom relocate to Connecticut. I said she would never leave Queens. He said she was almost eighty and too old to be alone. I said she wasn't alone—she had her synagogue and her friends. He asked me how long I thought her friends were going to live. I told him that Mom would never move to assisted living. He said we could buy a house, everything on one floor. Within months, Harvey had sold Mom's home and found the perfect renovated ranch in a neighboring town. No other man would have suggested it and handled it all for me. That act alone had qualified him for sainthood, and I'd worshipped him for it.

Soon after her move to Connecticut, Mom had a heart attack and had to stay at the hospital. Once during her recovery, Mom mentioned to Harvey her complaints about the hospital gown—no pocket for her heart monitor, scratchy on her skin, and too much southern exposure. She advised him of the opportunities he would find in the hospital gown business and then suggested new fabric, colors, and patterns. Harvey brought her a selection of comfortable nighties with slit backs and breast pockets, and based on Mom's recommendation, he created a division at Bountiful, a line of patientwear he peddled to hospitals, nursing homes, and hospices. Harvey considered Mom the founder of the line, and he sent her a check once a month.

But the main reason to stall telling Mom about the situation was that if Harvey and I reconciled, I wouldn't have to tell her at all. That would spare her the bad news and spare me the phone conversation I could already hear in my head. My mother would insist I do something to get him back, because, as a thousand country songs will tell you, no woman wants to live without her man. Mom would complete her monologue with the excusatory comment "What do you want? He's a man." After all, this was the woman who wrote to Hillary Clinton advising her to look the other way—for Chelsea.

I was thinking about all this while inserting a pod in my Keurig.

"How's Harvey?" she asked inexorably.

"He's fine."

"I have to hear what's going on in your house from Leona? Harvey moves out and you don't call to tell me?"

"I didn't want to upset you," I said, thinking I should be making a martini instead of coffee.

"What happened?" she said, as though she didn't already know all the details after talking to Cousin Leona, who naturally had heard it all in detail from her husband, Steve, who'd been Harvey's attorney since the invention of yellow legal paper, and who was the reason I had met Harvey in the first place. Come to think of it, Harvey was loyal to everyone but me.

"Apparently, Harvey has a twenty-two-year-old girlfriend."

"That's exactly what Leona said."

"If you heard it all from Cousin Leona, why are you asking me to tell you all over again? It's not much fun talking about it."

"I want to hear it from you," Mom said. "Tell me the whole thing."

"That's it. That's the whole thing. She's a fitting model."

"Not even a real model?"

Great—now I was supposed to feel bad that she was parading about in bras in his showroom instead of being airbrushed on the cover of *Vogue*.

"What else?" my mom said.

"He's living in a suite at Five Swallows."

"That's Harvey. Everything first-class."

"Mom, maybe I need to remind you that *I* am your daughter. Harvey is the son-in-law. Please don't be proud of where he's staying."

"I am coming over," she said firmly.

I dumped my coffee in the sink, opened the kitchen cabinet, and reached for a bottle of something stronger. I looked at the label. Grey Goose. I poured the vodka into a mug, added ice cubes.

"Mommm . . ." *Oh no*, I thought. *I'm becoming my daughter.*

"I can keep you company."

"Maybe tomorrow. Right now, I need to be alone."

"That's ridiculous. No one needs to be alone. When you have a private room in an old age home, your husband is dead, and your children don't visit, then you can be alone."

"Is that what you think is going to happen to you?"

"Who knows what will happen to me," she said. "Look at what just happened to you."

"Mom, it's going to be okay. Harvey just needed to think."

"The man is married over thirty years, has three children, and now he has to think—in a hotel room."

"Mommm . . ." She was killing me.

"You need me."

"I don't want to drive."

"I could ask a neighbor to take me," she said.

"Just call me. Check in."

"Okay, you don't want me to come, I won't come. I'm not like some mothers who don't know when to stop. But I'm calling Harvey and telling him that I treated him like a son from the day I met him, and I won't allow him to do this to me. And I'm not fiddling around. I'm going to get right to the point, like a regular Dr. Phil."

"Maybe I should go on *Dr. Phil*," I said.

"*Dr. Phil*? What? Do you want the whole world to know about this?"

To my surprise, Ben came through the door, the same noisy way he did when he was a kid. Ben was twenty-four and six foot two, with a body by Crunch, curly brown hair, black glasses, and a beauty mark above his lip, on the right side, since birth. He wore a Yankees baseball cap, T-shirt, and jeans. He was holding an empty duffel bag.

I used his sudden appearance as a way to say good-bye to my mother.

"Give Ben a kiss," she said, "and call if you change your mind. You don't have to come pick me up. I can find a way to get there. I'm very resourceful."

Chapter 7

"What are you doing here?" I asked Ben, wrapping my arms around my savior.

"Warm welcome," he said.

"I'm surprised—happy—to see you."

"Elisabeth said you wanted us to clear out our rooms. I figured that was your smoke signal for 'I need company.'"

"You know me like I'm your own mother," I said. "But now that you're here, I don't know if I actually want to do it. Maybe I would brood even more. We could just sit in the kitchen. We could do the room another time."

"Also, Elisabeth told me that you're thinking of selling the house. How are you planning to sell the house when you can't even stomach the thought of dumping my high school jerseys?"

He was right. "Would you be upset?"

"Don't you get it? Dad gave you a pass. Do whatever you want."

"I guess I can now," I said.

"You could before. But you didn't think about it."

"That's true."

He put his arms around me, and I could feel my heart almost burst. "Are you hungry?"

Ben opened our fridge, a cavernous Harvey purchase. "Buy a few groceries?" he said sarcastically.

"Don't I always?"

"That's why all the kids always wanted to come to our house."

"I always love a full fridge." But the fridge wasn't just full. It was brimming with enough food to feed a medium-size country. I reached over Ben and shut the door.

Ben checked the side freezer. "Mom, you have Chubby Hubby."

"It's your favorite," I said.

"It's my favorite, but I don't live here and you didn't know I was coming." Ben placed his foot on a kitchen chair and tied the open lace on his boot.

"But it reminds me of you when I buy it," I said, standing in front of the freezer door, a goalie because I didn't want him to open the door again and point out the rest of my stash, such as the frozen squash soufflé for Amanda—who lived across the country in California, where she was opening the newest Bloomingdale's store.

"I have thought about buying less food," I said, "but I'm not an express-line person. What would be more depressing than standing on a grocery line with a sign that said 'Express—Ten Items or Less'? That would be the death of me, my complete undoing. Can you just see it? Me holding a lonely Greek yogurt—vanilla, no fruit—and the impatient single girl in front of me with two ounces of Swiss cheese."

I picked up a dishcloth and wiped the counter. "Would you like to eat? I made a turkey, and it's almost done. A few more minutes."

Ben peered into the top oven. "You cooked a turkey that could feed every Pilgrim in Plymouth and you're the only one home."

I was embarrassed. "I make turkey soup and hot sandwiches with the leftovers."

He shook his head as though I had committed turkey genocide. "Whatever, Mom. I'm not hungry. I grabbed pizza on the way up. By the way, since Amanda might not be home for a while, I can come up another time to help you clear out her room."

"That's sweet of you, but how do we know what she wants to keep?"

"She said she took everything she wanted from the room years ago."

"She did? You're telling me she doesn't want a thing?"

"Why would Amanda need anything from home? She gets a discount at Bloomingdale's. Come talk in my room while I go through my stuff."

I looked at the time and turned off the oven, then I went up to Ben's room, without any turkey but with my Grey Goose. The walls were neutral—tan with white molding. The carpet was beige. There were wooden mini blinds on the windows, and a patchwork quilt made by Aunt Dottie, Leona's mom, on the twin bed.

Throughout high school, Ben strove to be as colorless as his room. He chose to blend in with the crowd, a popular white-bread crewneck group, with parents who summered in Nantucket and owned ski houses near mountains in Vermont.

One Saturday night after returning from a movie with the happy-go-lucky girl he'd been seeing on and off, he told Harvey and me, in the family room reading newspapers, that he was going to come out in college. Neither of us was astonished, or even surprised. It was a relief to both of us. We had wondered for a long time.

When we took Ben to college in Middletown, we watched the gay and lesbian groups chalk messages on the sidewalks at the top of the hill:

Say hi to a bi.

Give us a year and you'll be queer.

Have you told a parent you're gay today?

Ben was smiling.

Ben and Harvey moved the station wagon out of a load zone, and I waited on a creaking swing in front of a building with the school flag, the American flag, and the state flag waving on top. Peace washed over me as though I had taken a pill for it. *I* wanted chalk. I had something important to say on the sidewalk: *Have you told your son you're happy for him today?*

◦᳴

As I sipped my vodka, Ben opened the trunk at the foot of his bed. "What have we here?" he said as he dangled his basketball shirt from high school. He sniffed. "I guess I should have washed it before I tossed it in the trunk."

Watching Ben examine each item made me remember that there was nothing I enjoyed more than time spent with my children. I'd be happy sitting on his bed and watching as he emptied a trunk with no bottom. When Ben was in high school, I often peeked into his room while he studied on the beige carpet, writing in his binder, with a plastic bowl of microwave caramel popcorn and Gatorade at his disposal. I lingered until I thought he had seen me, and then I said hi, as though I had been passing by.

Ben inspected a tattered green folder and showed the pages inside to me. "Mom, remember this? It's the Oakley paper from freshman English. Ms. Oakley was the teacher with the lisp and the cane with the duck bill on top. Her slip was always longer than her dress, and her dresses were all floral. She had her hair blown big on the weekend, and by Friday it reminded me of a nest someone sat on."

I looked at the title of the typewritten paper: "The Great Gatsby." That paper was family legend. I laughed. As he had been all his life, Ben was my elixir.

Ben went on with the story of the paper, because he loved telling it. "I needed a three-page paper, and I had a horrible cold and I couldn't come up with anything. Even after I read the CliffsNotes. Before I went to sleep, I had only a paragraph. I was sick, a wreck. That night you wrote a paper. Left it on my desk."

"And you handed in the paper, and Ms. Oakley gave you a C on it."

"That's when we all started calling the paper 'The Not-So-Great Gatsby,'" Ben said as he flipped through the pages marked amply with red pen.

"Then Dad decided to call Ms. Oakley and tell her exactly what he thought of the grade I received. I remember that you horsed around, trying to grab the kitchen phone from Dad, and he was holding the receiver up in the air." Ben deposited the paper in his bag, on the carpet next to his trunk. "But Dad called anyway. He said, 'Ms. Oakley, Ben's paper is an A, not a C. My wife would never write a C paper.'"

"What a dork," I said, remembering how endearing Harvey could be.

"I guess we have to love him."

"I do love him," I said to Ben.

"I know you do."

"Do you want to know the truth about the turkey?"

"Sure, Mom," he said as he dropped his photo album into the duffel bag.

"The truth is that I cooked that turkey because I knew it would stop me from feeling alone. A woman who lives by herself would never roast a turkey. You need a family for a turkey."

He looked at me quizzically. "But, Mom, you have a family. We have a family. And I honestly believe that Dad will be back. He needs you."

Ben put his arms around me, and I sniffled and I cried, and we sat on the twin bed and I prayed he was right.

⌒ⲟ

Ben stayed at home for the entire weekend. We went to three movies and put enough butter in our popcorn to create an oil slick. We had dinner at a McDonald's with an indoor playground, because Ben said he wanted to relive the old days. Ben removed his boots and attempted the slide. A little boy told him he was too big, that he was going to get stuck and a superhero would have to come rescue him. Ben said he was right and put his boots back on.

I hadn't been in a McDonald's since the kids were, well, kids. I ordered a Happy Meal, hoping it would make me happy. I gave my toy to the boy who had been kind enough to warn Ben.

On Sunday evening, Elisabeth came to the house between rounds. We poured wine like bartenders at a wedding. We parted with a three-way hug.

Chapter 8

The camp buses were gone. The school buses were running. I turned the page on my calendar. The New England picture of the month was a red one-room schoolhouse with a bell tower in a field. I put an *X* on the day, September 1, the anniversary of my first date with Harvey.

Unable to stop myself, I got in my car and drove to Five Swallows. Maybe I would see Harvey. Maybe he would walk, serendipitously, out of the inn while I sat in the car. Maybe I would go in, to the desk, and ask for him.

Whatever happened, I wanted to know if he was with someone or alone.

I sat in my Volvo, in the circular stone drive in front of the inn. There was a special event for families and friends of Atherton Academy, one of the prep schools in town. There were handsome people chatting quietly, their children running about in blazers with the school insignia, along with golden retrievers and black Labs wearing bandannas. In the middle of a life crisis, there isn't anything worse than looking at well-groomed, well-heeled people with pedigreed dogs.

A doorman approached. He asked if he could valet park my car, and I said yes, but I couldn't seem to let go of the wheel. My rear end was cemented to my seat.

"Valet?" he said again.

I nodded. Suddenly, I was sobbing.

He was too young to cope with me. I saw him signal a coworker. An older valet came over.

"Checking in?" he said.

I couldn't go into the inn. I couldn't go in because I knew that if I found Harvey with someone, anyone, we were over.

"Checking out," I said.

I steered away. I turned in to a strip mall and parked in front of Ace Stamp and Coin. I could see a couple inside behind the counter. I called Harvey.

"It's the anniversary of our first date," I said.

"At the steak place," he said.

"On Fiftieth."

"It's not there anymore," he said.

There were many things I had forgotten as I grew older, but not a single moment of that date. When Harvey and I had arrived at the steak house, the hostess said we would have to wait at least twenty minutes, but the maître d', in a tuxedo, greeted Harvey by name, ushering us immediately into a booth.

"That wasn't twenty minutes," I commented, glad we didn't have to wait.

"No, that was twenty dollars." Harvey was so well practiced at tipping his way about the city that I never saw him hand the money to the maître d'.

The waiter poured water from a pitcher. Harvey had insisted I tell him something, so I told him the truth—I was delighted he had called. He asked straight out if I was seeing anyone else.

I told him I wasn't, then changed the subject. "So, did your dad teach you the business?"

"No, my father died when I was a teenager."

"I'm so sorry," I said, feeling terrible for him while realizing I liked him a lot.

"Actually, he wanted to die. My dad jumped from Bear Mountain Bridge the day President Kennedy was killed in Dallas. And, yes, I remember where I was when Kennedy was shot. I was watching Walter Cronkite in a hospital lobby while my mother identified the body."

I leaned closer and spoke quietly. "Harvey, I'm sorry. That's a terrible story."

"It's a heartbreaker, all right. I rarely talk about it. But you asked."

The waiter delivered the menu. We both ordered the filet mignon special. Harvey insisted his steak be charred with a pink center, and asked for hot sauce on the side. He changed the lettuce wedge to coleslaw, and the potatoes to rice. He did this with authority, and I knew immediately he was a waiter's nightmare.

Then we talked about his mother.

"She lives in Scottsdale. For her arthritis."

"Did your mom work outside the home?"

He laughed. "Mom worked at Bountiful Bosom to keep tabs on my father. My father wrote a two-word suicide note. The note said *Good-bye, Gladys.*"

"Your mother's name is Gladys?"

"No. My father's secretary was Gladys, romanced under my mother's nose."

When the entrées came, Harvey said, "I'm sorry, but I asked for hot sauce, not cream sauce, on the side." He looked annoyed, but he forced a smile.

The waiter apologized, returning the meal to the kitchen. I didn't think returning the plate was a wise idea. I had heard from my friend Colleen, who had worked nights in a Chicago steak house through law school, that whenever a customer sent back a meal, the waiter spit in the replacement dish.

"Tell me about your family," he said.

"My mother worries about me constantly. She's always asking me what I need so that she can bring it to me, or telling me to go shopping."

"That's great. She means well."

"Yes, she does. There isn't a day that I don't know that I am loved."

"What about your dad?" Harvey asked.

"He was a good father. But Dad was strict. I would have had more freedom in a women's prison."

"Give me an example."

"He wouldn't want me to date you. He would have said you were too old."

"Old? I'm not old," he said squishing his brows and his lips together, nodding his head repetitively so he resembled a Floridian at an early-bird dinner asking that the air conditioning be turned off.

"Well," I said, "my father would have liked that you own your business."

"There's one point for me," he said.

⌒⊙

It had been easy to talk to Harvey that night. Now, decades later, in a strip mall parking lot, I was struggling with my words. "I was wondering," I said to Harvey over the phone. "I thought maybe we could get together, to talk."

"I'm not ready to talk," he said.

"I am," I said.

"I have to go. I'm waiting for a conference call. I will call you. I promise."

Like your promise is worth anything, you son of a bitch.

I had to know for sure if he was alone. Suddenly, I remembered that about a year before, there had been an intern at Guild for Good, a college girl who made jewelry, who also worked at Five Swallows. I reached into a crevice in my brain and came up with the intern's name—Liza Olivia.

I shut off the motor in my car. I scrolled through the contacts on my phone. There was her number. I hesitated. Did I have the guts to call?

"Liza, hi. It's Marcy Hammer."

"Marcy, it's been a long time."

"Are you still designing jewelry?" I asked.

"Yes, of course."

"Then why don't you promote it through Guild for Good?"

"You would help me promote it?" she said excitedly.

"I'd be happy to." Certainly I would help her, but I was feeling all kinds of guilty that this was not the reason I had called. "Liza, I was wondering, do you still work at Five Swallows?"

"Got to support my art habit somehow," she said.

I forced a chuckle at something I'd heard artists say about a hundred times a day.

I closed my eyes, feeling lowlier than an amoeba without a nucleus. "I was wondering whether you ever see my husband at the inn."

"All the time," she said. "He's in the Presidential Suite."

Bingo.

Now came the hard part. "I was also wondering, have you ever seen him there with someone else?"

Silence. Nothing.

"It's okay, Liza. You can tell me."

"He's alone. He sits at the bar a lot ordering appetizers. Your husband eats a lot of fried food. Honestly, he looks depressed."

That's fabulous, I thought.

"Marcy, I'll let you know if anything changes, but I've never seen him with anyone."

Inspired by the phone call, I started the car and headed for home, but then I decided I needed to witness Harvey's "aloneness" for myself.

∽

From a vantage point by the woods near Five Swallows, it was possible to look up to the fourth floor and into the wide windows of the Presidential Suite. The curtains were open. The TV glimmered. Then I saw Harvey, fully dressed, in a golf shirt and trousers, and I didn't see anyone else.

Based on the information from the intern and this newest, conclusive hard evidence, Sherlock Holmes rolled into one with Dick Tracy (a.k.a. Marcy) decided that Harvey was in fact, as he claimed, no longer involved with the model.

There was nothing more I could do. I would wait until he got his bald head back on straight. If Harvey was miserable, he would come home.

And I would take him back.

Chapter 9

It was my habit to bring food to shelters on holidays. On Labor Day, I decided to make chicken for Jaclyn's Place, a refuge for women. I slid four racks of coated pieces into the oven. Doing something for somebody else made me feel good. I thought about life. I concluded that health was the most important thing. And everyone in my family—including the Bastard in the Burbs, Harvey—was healthy.

While the chicken was baking, I checked my phone. My mother's neighbor, Lynne, had called. Her message was long, winding. Not like Lynne at all. She said that she was about to go shopping when she decided to drop in on Mom and ask if she wanted rye bread and some Italian cookies from Jack the Baker in Darcyville. When no one answered, she got worried and opened Mom's door with the key I had given her. Mom was sprawled on the floor in the kitchen. She had been there all night. Lynne said my mom was in an ambulance on her way to Saint Mordecai Hospital. Apparently, the end of my marriage wasn't enough; I now had a mother with two broken ankles.

I shut off the oven before the chicken was done and jetted into my car. I called Elisabeth to let her know what was happening, but I got her voice mail and rambled on. All I could think of was Mom lying on the floor, helpless, an entire night; I could only hope that she had fallen asleep at some point. I had implored her to order an emergency bracelet, but she had refused. "Collars are for dogs," she'd said. "When I'm a dog, I'll bark."

∼◑

By the time I got to Saint Mordecai, Mom was in an inpatient room. The elevator on her side of the hospital wasn't working, so I climbed the stairs, opened the door with *10* written in orange sans serif, and wiped my perspiring face with a crumpled tissue. In the corridor, swarming with visitors, a nurse was chastising a teenager for talking on his cell phone, which wasn't allowed. She wore a starched all-white uniform; no Mickey Mouse or Sesame Street patterns for her. Her breasts were two bulges attached to a double chin. In my head, I could hear Harvey: *"Bountiful Bosom Power of You, 46G."*

I look like my mother, and 46G recognized me. "Your mother is in 1010," she called out as she stacked a metal cart with an array of vials and pills.

"Thank you," I said as she approached me.

"Your mother keeps talking about your brother. Max? She says he owes money."

"Well, thankfully he owes so much my mother couldn't possibly help him."

My brother, Max, had sold commercial real estate in San Diego, then large homes, then small homes, then trailer homes, then cars, then nothing that was legal. He'd had a series of girlfriends—shapely women with helmet hair and ambitious plastic surgeons. He was single.

I walked into the room and was immediately overcome by the smell of antiseptic. My mother, in the bed near the window, was commiserating with her roommate's visitors—three women with black hair, charcoal eye makeup, and gold hoop earrings. She waved to me from her bed as though from a Ferris wheel at the fair.

"Mom, are you okay?" I said.

She pointed to her bandaged ankles. "Good news, Marcy—I don't have to worry about matching socks."

"No, you don't."

"Say hello to my roommate, Mrs. Cola. And these are her daughters."

Mrs. Cola was small, dwarfed by the hospital bed. Her hair was salt-and-pepper. She had dark skin, sunken eyes. "Quite a family," I said, jealous that her daughters had each other and all I had was scheming Max.

One of Mrs. Cola's daughters approached me as I passed to Mom's side of the room. She was the prettiest, in spite of her large forehead. She wore a black leather jacket with studs on the collar and black leather knee-high boots, and she kept walking toward me until she was just inches away. I've kissed people who didn't stand that close.

"Your mom told us about your brother," she said.

"I'm not surprised."

"I know someone who could lend him money."

"Thanks. Great. I'll let him know," I said politely, and then I went to Mom's bed by the window and kissed her hello.

"Do you think your brother will come?" My mother's hair was white, her voice full of gravel.

I had just arrived, and already I was sick of hearing about Max.

"I called and told him to come," my mother said to the room. "He has airline points."

"That's nice," I said without intonation.

"Don't say bad things about your brother."

"Can we change the conversation?" I asked.

"Harvey called," my mother said, straightening her body in the bed.

"Harvey called, and you're talking about Max? How did he know you were here?"

"Elisabeth told him," she said.

Elisabeth telling Harvey about my mother was irritating on a few levels. First, Harvey was leaving me, and he didn't get to keep my mother; my mother and I were a BOGO deal—buy one, get one free. Secondly, Harvey didn't deserve information about me, even if it was coming from our mutual children. Of course, I'm sure Elisabeth meant well and had no clue she had committed treason.

"He told me not to worry about you," Mom said. "That must mean he's planning to move back in."

I responded with a frown.

She patted my hand for further reassurance.

"Mom, what happened? How did you fall?"

"I was on the step stool."

"I told you not to use the step stool." I should have taken it from her house. Why was I always the one who had to be in charge? "What were you doing on a step stool at night?"

"I couldn't sleep. I needed more flour for the cookies," she whispered as though she had committed fraud.

"Cookies for whom?"

"For Max."

"You still mail cookies to Max?" It was unnecessary confirmation that my mother continued to treat Max as though he were ten and at sleepaway camp.

The nurse came into the room. "Want to keep your mother company tonight?"

"What about Mrs. Cola? Would she mind?"

"It's fine," her daughter the loan shark said.

"I'll order a cot," the nurse said.

There was no reason not to stay over. No one was waiting at home.

At ten p.m., my mother fell asleep and I retired to the cot between the clunky radiator and my mother's hospital bed.

∽

I woke at five a.m., attuned to the hospital sounds—health aides in the hall, phones ringing, carts moving, someone sweeping.

I thought about my mom. I remembered the time she'd watched Elisabeth so Harvey and I could go to Connecticut and look for our first home. Elisabeth was nine months old.

We had parked in front of Mom's only tree, an anorexic. Mom had rushed out of the house as though we were far-flung relatives she hadn't seen since before some war.

"The baby needs a sweater," she had said instead of hello.

I handed Mom a sweater, so that she would be happy and Elisabeth would feel like she was in Miami in summer, instead of Queens in the fall.

"Where are you going?" Mom said.

"Looking for a house," Harvey said as he kissed her on the cheek.

"There's a house for sale around the corner," she said. "Lucky house. The people who owned it had three sons, and three doctors came out of that house."

"We're looking in Connecticut," Harvey said.

My mother shook her head. "Connecticut is too far. Connecticut might as well be California."

"Connecticut is far from what?" Harvey asked.

"From me," she said, zeroing in on Harvey. She peered above Elisabeth directly into his eyes, and I was certain she could see his brain.

∽

I looked out the hospital window at the highway and the factory across the road. My mouth tasted awful, as though it were coated with sand. I pushed my hair off my face and longed to be at home, even though being home now meant being alone. I imagined opening my screen door to the fresh air, getting my mail from my country mailbox, perusing the police report posted on the front page, bottom half, of the *Town News*: *Daisy Alexander, 49, 210 Castle Corner, allowed her dog, a golden retriever, to roam without a collar.*

"Marcy," my mother said in a whimper.

I leaned toward her bed. I took her hand. I could see that her roommate, Mrs. Cola, was still asleep.

Mom wet her lips with her tongue. "You'll take care of Max."

"Mom, you're still on the planet."

"He needs family." She squeezed my hand to seal her deal.

I withdrew my hand. "You're talking about a man who is fifty-five years old. He lives on the other side of the country and dates women with plastic rear ends."

"One day he'll grow up. He'll find a wife. He'll have a family. Your children will have cousins."

෨

I slept in the hospital in Mom's room another night. When I awoke, a doctor was standing by the door. He was tan and dressed impeccably in a dark suit, a white shirt, and a maroon tie in a wide knot.

He straddled the doorway as though approaching me would be a commitment. "Are you *her* daughter?" The word "her" sounded accusatory.

I nodded.

"I need to talk to you," he said.

"I can be dressed in a minute."

"Go talk to him," my mother said.

I slung a blanket around my long shirt and underpants and followed him out the door.

"Dr. Morse, the orthopedist," he said. "I'll get to the point. Your mother has cancer."

"What?"

"Cancer, cancer."

To be honest, I wasn't sure whether he'd said the word twice or I'd just heard it that way in my airborne head. "But you don't understand—all she did was fall."

"The cancer may precipitate her propensity for falling," he said.

"She fell once," I said stubbornly, defensively, angrily. "Off a step stool."

"The elderly fall often. Some die within a year after such an event."

Cancer wasn't enough for one morning. He also had to mention she could die from a fall. A storm had blasted into the room, and I knew immediately I would need all my strength to be her advocate and live through it.

"You're not her regular doctor."

"Then I suggest that you speak to her regular doctor," he said, hands in his pockets.

"Believe me, I will," I said.

"Have a good day," he said.

And you, Dr. Doom, have a miserable day and a grueling, lonely life.

Back in the room, my mother wet her lips with a water-soaked cotton ball. I wasn't going to say anything until I spoke to her regular doctor. Besides, was this how it worked? Was I supposed to tell her she had cancer? What if this doctor was an imposter? What if this arrogant doctor was wrong?

She closed her eyes. "I didn't like that doctor at all."

"You're right," I said. "His shoes were too expensive."

"And so, tell me, what did he say?"

"He said you need some more tests."

"They took a thousand pictures already. And blood tests. Marcy, go shopping today. Buy a sweater. My treat."

✑

When my mother dozed off, I went to the entrance of the hospital, stepped out under the awning, and called her doctor. I left a message, then another message. I kept my cell in my hand. However, I wanted to keep the line free, so I went to one of the last pay phones in America to call Dana. But I was afraid to tell her the bad news, as if repeating it would make it true.

"How's your mom?" Dana asked.

"There seems to be a big problem."

"What happened?"

"I can't talk about it now. I'll tell you after I speak to her doctor."

"Any Harvey news?"

"He called my mother the second Elisabeth told him she was in Saint Mordecai."

"He misses you," Dana said.

Poor Harvey. He'd had endless years to dump me, but it was just his luck that when he finally did, his walkout coincided with my mother's hospitalization.

"I'll bet your mother fell down on purpose so Harvey would come around."

"I wouldn't put it past her."

"Harvey is such a good guy when it comes to family."

"Then why did he leave?"

"He's confused. His head was turned."

"I know," I said. "To tell the truth, I love him for calling my mother."

After hanging up with Dana, I paced in front of my mother's room, downed muddy coffee, and chewed on the defenseless paper cup.

My mother's doctor called back. "I'm so sorry, Marcy. But it's true," he said.

"Oh" was all I could muster. "Oh."

"I'll be there today, and an oncologist will see her. Take it easy. I know a doctor who told a woman she had months to live. She lived four years. Attended *his* funeral."

His feeble attempt at cheering me up, giving me hope, didn't work. In fact, it made me feel worse.

Later that day, a doctor stopped by the room and informed Mrs. Cola she would be moved to a hospice, and all I could think was *Couldn't he wait until one of her children was visiting?*

Eventually, the loan shark appeared, hugged her mother in the bed, packed her personal items, and said it had been nice to meet me.

Nice to meet you under the worst circumstances, I thought. A nurse wheeled Mrs. Cola out the door.

An orderly entered the room with Mrs. Cola's lunch.

"She went to a hospice," I said from my seat on the radiator.

He asked me if I wanted Mrs. Cola's meal. Apparently, my luck wasn't lousy enough. I needed to eat a dying woman's grilled cheese.

I didn't think my mother would enjoy hearing that Mrs. Cola had gone to a hospice, so when Mom woke from a nap, I said she'd switched rooms. I was standing at the foot of the bed with another cup of sludge. My mother looked me in the eye.

"I am so sorry for her children," she said.

"I know," I whispered.

"Her children," she repeated.

"She's the one who's going to the hospice, Mom."

"When she goes, she'll take a piece of her children with her. Her children will never be the same." A tear sat in the center of my mother's right eye. I believed it would never drop, but she blinked and it was gone.

Chapter 10

My mom had told me to go home. She'd said that sleeping on the cot was ruining my spine.

I took a long, hot shower, ate something that wasn't hospital food, and fell into my own bed. I made a round of phone calls to the kids and to Dana, to give them an update.

Elisabeth was so distraught that she had to hang up, calm herself, and then call back for the details she wanted as a doctor. Ben asked whether to drive up from Manhattan. I knew how busy he was, so I told him to stay where he was. He said he was coming anyway. He told me he was coming for me as much as my mom.

The following day, with framed pictures of my children on my front seat, I arrived back at the hospital parking garage. The ceilings were ominously low; I felt the need to bend my head down and forward as I steered through the entrance level. I sacrificed half an hour searching for a spot, riding up and down the cylindrical garage, disinclined to fight to the death with a white Buick, Florida plates.

As I entered the garage elevator, I noticed a petite woman with a lavish platter of cookies, heading toward the closing doors. I knew I knew her; I just didn't know from where. She was elegant and perfectly put-together, in a long-sleeve blouse and an ankle-length skirt cinched with a double-buckle skinny belt. Her hair was short, auburn, colored and foiled, dry-cut, washed twice, and blown to perfection by a Madison Avenue stylist.

"Candy?" I said when she entered the elevator.

Candace Knight wrote and illustrated picture books. Years before, she had been active in Guild for Good, spearheading a fund-raiser.

"Marcy," she said, "what brings you to the hospital?"

"My mother," I answered, like that was a complete explanation.

"My father," she said, then exhaled.

"She fell," I said. "Then they found cancer."

"My dad has cancer."

"Oh," I said gloomily. "I liked it better when people never said the word 'cancer.' My grandmother died from 'women's problems.' My great-aunt had a 'terrible situation.'"

I was pleased to run into Candy. I felt as though we were comrades on the same battlefield.

"My father has been here for over a month. He has transitional cell carcinoma of the bladder originating in his urethra," she said in one breath. "It's most common in men who have had contact with asbestos."

"Was your father near asbestos?" I said.

"No."

"Oh," I said as we exited the elevator on the same floor. We walked in step, me with my framed pictures at my side, Candy holding her cookies in both hands.

"It's also common in men who smoke," she said.

"Did your father smoke?" I asked.

"No," she said.

I decided not to ask any more questions.

Candy continued. "He's ninety-four. The doctors feel that something—some heart problem, a stroke, pneumonia, maybe a tsunami—will take Dad before the cancer does. My husband said the same thing the one time he visited."

Her husband visited her father only once in an entire month? Harvey and I weren't even communicating and I knew he would stop up to see my mother a few times—and bring her a robe or pajamas. Candy was beautiful and talented, and she was married to a selfish loser. Pain was everywhere.

"I'm to the left," Candy said as we reached a fork in the corridor. "How about coffee in the cafeteria at three?"

I was happy to say yes.

Candy was tucked into one of the booths for four, next to a window and in a corner, away from the technicians, nurses, and surgeons in scrubs, and the despondent visitors slouched over the daily special—fried chicken, peas, and mashed potatoes with gravy. This greasy special guaranteed that there would always be more patients at Saint Mordecai, most of them brought up from the cafeteria on a stretcher.

I poured a cup of coffee and walked to the far side of the cafeteria, where Candy was staring out the window and sipping orange juice very slowly, as if she had to save her supply until the Red Cross dropped juice boxes.

"So," I said, "what is it about visiting a hospital that causes healthy people to tank up on liquids?"

She laughed. "It's a time killer. I don't know how often I've told my father that I was going to get an orange juice. But sometimes when I get down here, I forget the juice and just sit in this booth and think."

"We should bring airplane bottles of vodka. For the orange juice."

"I'm in. How's your mother?"

"They're doing some tests."

"Every time I come to the hospital, I wonder one thing: How did I wind up here? How did I wind up the caretaker of the people who took care of me? Who put me in charge?"

"Is your mom sick too?"

"She's in an Alzheimer's facility," Candy said, shaking her head.

Nice day she was having.

"I'm an only child," she said. "And that was poor planning. If my parents were both going to be sick at once, they should have had more children." She sipped her juice carefully, a millimeter at a time, and it barely seemed to touch her lips. Her mauve lipstick remained perfect. She was just one of those women who always looked perfect.

"I have a brother, and I wish I were an only child."

"He can't be that bad," Candy said with the naïveté of a woman who'd never had a brother.

"My brother is my mother's magnificent obsession. If I had been the first woman to rocket into space, my mother would have pointed out that Max knew how to ride a bicycle."

"That's terrible," she said.

"Not really. I was the oldest, her responsible one, and the one who worked hard at school. But Max needed prodding, and the prodding came with her standing ovations for every little thing he did."

"Does your brother live nearby?"

"No, he lives on the other coast, in Los Angeles. But don't get me wrong. If my mother needed anything, absolutely anything—he'd call me."

We sat back, and I churned out several amusing stories about Max, which helped me take my mind off my problems. Candy laughed a lot. Her laughter had a pattern to it: one alto laugh, then one soprano. Even her laughter was organized.

"Well, I'm happy that you're not an only child. Your brother is entertaining."

I sat back in the booth, adjusting my legs under the table, and I would have been happy to sit there that way for much longer, especially since I was waiting for Elisabeth. But, too bad for me, Candy needed to go.

⁓

"Did you speak to the oncologist?" I asked Elisabeth as she approached me outside my mother's room. She had offered to call the cancer specialist to confer physician-to-physician about my mother's illness.

"Yes, tests are needed. He's not ready to decide the best course of action."

"What do you think?"

"Well, I'm not an oncologist," she said. "But I am beginning to wish I were."

"I can't think of a sadder profession," I said.

"Not if you can help people go into remission, to live longer, to get well."

"I always look at the downside of things."

"Yes, you do." She looped her arm through mine. "I know this is an impossible time for you, and I want to do everything I can to help. Not just as a doctor, but as a daughter."

"I can't lose Grandma," I said. My voice was cracking. I didn't want to cry. I didn't want to cause Elisabeth to cry.

"I know. Who will be left to drive you crazy?"

"Exactly."

"Whatever the treatment," Elisabeth said, "my guess is that it won't begin in the hospital. When she goes to rehabilitation, she can be transported for radiation or chemotherapy."

"That's what the doctor told me," I said, "but I thought he might reveal more to you."

"You thought they would tell me where the treasure was buried."

"No treasure?"

"Not a shilling," Elisabeth said. "Grandma is such an overachiever. It wasn't enough to break both ankles. She had to be diagnosed with cancer as well.

"There's Ben." Elisabeth waved to her brother. Then she poked me. "And there are all the nurses, male and female, taking a good look at good-looking Ben."

"Three-way hug," I said as I gathered my children around.

"I didn't have time to buy a present for Grandma," Elisabeth said. "I have to go downstairs to the gift shop."

"The gift shop is a horror story," I said. "The artificial flowers are blooming with dust."

"I brought her something," Ben said proudly.

"What?" Elisabeth asked. "And can I be your partner?"

He reached into his backpack and pulled out a huge bag of M&M's.

"Is that for her or for you?" Elisabeth asked.

"Let's just say I'm hoping she'll share."

Chapter 11

The next day marked the fifth day in the hospital for Mom. Cousin Leona came to visit, and I stopped by to say hello. Then, because I knew Leona would entertain Mom, I rushed off to meet Dana in our regular place, Francesca's Café.

The wicker furniture at Francesca's was white. The cushions on the seats were paisley. The plants on the mosaic floor, dangling from the raised glass ceiling and potted on the ledges of bay windows, were a glowing green. Repeat customers, day or night, were affluent women.

"I need a drink," Dana spouted the moment we took our seats.

She motioned for a woman in an apron embroidered with a basket of fruit and the Francesca's logo, but the woman was preoccupied with garnishing spinach salads. We waited awhile, then Dana tried again.

At last, a waitress acknowledged us.

"Grey Goose on the rocks with cranberry juice," Dana said. "Make that two."

"Two for you?" I asked.

"No. One for you and one for me. How's your mom doing?"

"We're waiting for tests." I didn't want to talk about cancer. I wanted to talk about Harvey, but Dana was entitled to her share of the conversation.

"Big news," she said. "Jeremy and his girlfriend drove down from Boston last night to tell us they are engaged."

"Congratulations! That was quick."

"He's known her a total of four months. Her name is Moxie. She's albino," Dana said.

"She's albino?"

"Yes. No. But she's extremely pale—and she'll look terrible in white. In addition, this Moxie person is very needy. I hate needy women. She was clutching his left hand all through dinner. Luckily, Jeremy is ambidextrous. And she said her parents are taking out a third mortgage to pay for their share of the wedding."

"What did you say to her?"

"I wanted to say 'I'm so sorry your parents are idiots.'"

"Her parents just want to give her a nice wedding," I said in the girl's defense.

"Then they should take out a mortgage to pay for the whole thing. I have two kids starting college next fall. My first wedding was in a church with white-bread sandwiches, cookies, and warm punch. There was a folksinger with long straight hair—and her name *wasn't* Joni Mitchell. They want the wedding at a country club in Massachusetts. What is more boring?"

"A country club in Connecticut?" I said.

Dana laughed. Then she imitated Moxie. "We want a very long cocktail hour. Don't we, Jeremy? We want tiny little itsy-bitsy lobster rolls and crab cakes. Don't we, Jeremy?"

"I love crab cakes," I said.

"I give this marriage two years," she said, swirling the ice cubes in her drink with a straw. "I guess my family is genetically predisposed for divorce. On the upside, he'll have gotten through his first marriage by the time he's thirty-two."

Maybe it wasn't a good idea to talk to her about Harvey when she was in this kind of mood. I decided I wouldn't bring him up unless she did.

"Harvey is still at Five Swallows," I blurted.

"And does he have company?"

"All evidence points to no."

"You checked up on him? I like that."

"What would you have done?"

"I would have divorced him."

"That's my last choice. But it's all on him. If he's not seeing her anymore and he promises to change, I want to salvage the marriage."

"Promises to change? What—the sheets?"

"Hilarious."

"Everything will be okay. This is not the end of the world."

"Then what *would* be the end of the world?" I said. "Oh, yes—it would be your son marrying a girl whose parents take out a third mortgage for the wedding."

"You're strong," Dana said. "You'll pick up the pieces. Take it from me. It can be done. And now I have Calvin. And he's great."

"But that's you. Not me. I want you to be honest, Dana, because you're the only one I can ask: Do you think the last sex I had with Harvey is the last sex I'll ever have? Because if I had known it was my last sex, I would have taken off my nightgown."

"Oh, stop. Remember those two built Navy guys the night we went to that crowded bar in Baltimore?"

"Yes, and what I remember is that they both wanted you."

"No. Only the good-looking one wanted me."

I ignored Dana's usual sarcasm.

"I know you hired the CIA and the FBI and the KGB to find out if Harvey was alone," she said, "but maybe it would be prudent to call an attorney. In case there's something else you should be doing or not be doing."

"Meeting with a lawyer seems premature, pessimistic, and overly reactive. And, most of all, greedy."

"Not to me. To me, it seems precautionary and smart. No commitments. Call Abby and Colleen. See what they think."

Years ago, we had met our lawyer friends, Abby and Colleen, when we served on the board of the Atherton Library. The last time I'd reached out for legal advice, a slither of a missionary in a black suit had stumbled on the ice in our driveway, shattering his right leg, and the Mormons were suing us. Abby had said to delay indefinitely, avoid contact with anyone from Utah, and flip the channel if Marie Osmond appeared on *Oprah*. Colleen had advised settling with the Mormons posthaste and obtaining a signed release before the missionary died of gangrene and I was sued for wrongful death. I went with Colleen's advice.

The waitress shuffled over, and Dana requested the check. She said she needed to go home and help her twin daughters with their college essays.

"Help?" I said, knowing full well that Dana's concept of help was standing behind the twins at their computers, then asking one at a time for each girl to stand up so Dana could write the essay she knew would be best, an essay sure to be heart-tugging enough to bring any admissions director to tears.

"Some parents call it helping," she said. "Others call it editing."

After two drinks and no food, Dana was in no condition to write an essay, unless the title was "My Tipsy Mom." I told Dana not to drive, to have a coffee first, which she did. Then she left—me with the bill.

I order another coffee and the veggie quiche special. Soon there was nothing but the crust remaining on my plate; there are two types of people in this world, and I am the pie-filling type. I noticed that all of the other tables were empty, except one with two women with sweaters on their shoulders, sleeves knotted in front.

I leaned back in my wicker peacock chair and called Abby. Since law school, Abby had worked at a big-name firm, becoming the first female partner. Recently she cashed in, then adopted a baby. Her law office was now in her house. She answered on the first ring.

I could hear the baby sobbing in the background. "Harvey moved out," I said bluntly.

"Why?" Abby asked.

"He was so happy he couldn't take it anymore."

"Get a lawyer."

"I don't think I need a lawyer."

"You called me." Abby must have picked up the baby, because the infant was now howling directly into the phone.

"I mean a real lawyer," I said.

"Oh, yes—someone who will charge you for advice."

"You know what I mean."

"Harvey may be gone a week, he may be gone a month, he may be gone a year. He may return. He may not return. Call Grace Greene in Stamford. They call her 'No Grace.' She's a ballbuster."

I looked down morosely at my crumbly quiche crust and called Colleen. Her paralegal, a stout megachested woman who could have benefitted enormously from Harvey's advice regarding bras, said Colleen would be with me in a moment.

"Harvey moved out," I announced as soon as she got on the phone.

"Grace Greene," Colleen said flatly, like there was no other possible response in the world.

"That's what Abby recommended." I had been hoping for a different answer, such as "I'm sure he'll be back."

"You called Abby first?"

I lied. "Your assistant didn't pick up."

"Is he having an affair?"

"Well . . ."

"Tell me," she said.

"I can't right now. I'll get myself all upset again."

"Listen up, Marcy. Get a lawyer. You don't know a man until he leaves you."

◦᥎

I sipped some lukewarm coffee and checked into Grace Greene on the Internet. She was the author of three books on matrimonial law, including a bestseller, *The Shirt Off His Back*. I called her office.

"I'd like to speak to attorney Greene," I said in a nerve-racked voice.

"Your name, please?"

"Marcy." Giving my full name seemed like too much of a commitment.

"Marcy . . . ?"

"Marcy Davenport," I said, misappropriating Dana's last name.

"This is in reference to . . . ?"

"My husband."

"And who referred you?"

I told her Abby Driscoll.

"Ms. Greene can see you for an initial consultation one week from today."

I'd thought it would take months to get an appointment. How good could she be if she could take me in a week? Besides, next week was way too close to this week. "That might be a little soon."

"Ms. Davenport, are you in an abusive situation?" The chipper voice was now low and dead serious.

"No, it's just that my husband left me."

"We have a cancellation one week from today at twelve noon."

I wanted the receptionist to slow down so I could gather all my thoughts between her clipped sentences. I was concerned that seeing a divorce lawyer was a show of no confidence that could never be taken back.

"I have placed you on the schedule. Thursday at noon." I swear she could have sold cookies to Nabisco.

"I don't know. We might reconcile. We'll probably reconcile."

"There is, of course, an initial fee for the consultation."

I was the damaged party in this soap opera, but calling a divorce lawyer—if only for information—made me feel like a traitor, for better or worse. I sank further back into my wicker chair and was stabbed in the rear end by a protruding piece of bamboo.

"Ms. Davenport?"

"Oh, there's my husband now," I said falsely, suddenly. "Maybe I should just talk to him first. You know, before I see the attorney."

Chapter 12

Three days later, my mother's medical problems were complicated by pneumonia. Candy and I convened in the cafeteria, where we met each evening. We sat in the same booth and ordered the same boring dinner. Candy ate a salad with balsamic vinaigrette. I had a hamburger with fries. Candy said she was too bushed to think about what to order. I felt the same.

She was a charter member of Guild for Good, and she liked to talk about it.

"The organization has done some terrific things," she said. "The Art Explosion over at the ammunition factory is probably the event I like the best. That was your concept, right?"

"The factory was empty. It seemed like the perfect place for the show. So many artists donated work. I can't take credit for it."

"How about taking credit for netting four times what we earned the year before? And for all the scholarships that were possible because of it?"

I felt uncomfortable being praised.

"You've brought the organization to a new level," Candy said.

"I'm only part-time," I said. "We need a real executive director. Someone with a lot of nonprofit experience."

"Come on now. Pat yourself on the back," she said. "So, what else do you enjoy?"

What else did I *enjoy*? I couldn't recall anyone asking me that ever. My conversations always seemed to focus on my children, or Dana's children—why our kids were wonderful and brilliant, or irritating, thoughtless idiots who never listened to a word we said.

"Do you have any hobbies?" Candy said.

Hobbies? What's a hobby?

"Well, of course I love art. I majored in art history."

"No one believes this, but I remember the first time I picked up a crayon."

"Crayola?" I said.

"No. It was this inexpensive brand, waxed like a candle. Even the brightest colors appeared faded on paper."

"I'm not an artist. I'm a fan. I feel the same way about modern dance. I love to see contemporary dance groups."

"What about opera?"

"I've been to the opera." I loved the costumes, the sets, the music, and the people-watching. It was the singing I couldn't tolerate.

"My mother loves . . . loved opera, until she became ill. Then she wouldn't allow it to be played in the house."

"What about your father?"

"He loved my mother too much to listen to it without her," she said.

How romantic, I thought. *How amazing. What would Harvey give up for me? Certainly not lunch.* "Did your father listen to something else instead?"

"Yes, the news. On Fox," Candy said with a grin and a shudder. She glanced at the time on her cell phone. She was a constant time-checker. I was sure that in the 1990s, before the smartphone, she'd had a chunky daybook in her bag, thick with notes to herself. "I hate to leave, but I have a meeting at the Alzheimer's facility, and it's an hour drive."

I wondered why she had placed her mother in a home so far away. Maybe it was near where her parents lived. I didn't ask. I looked out the wide cafeteria window. It was raining pellets. "Are you okay to drive that far in this weather?" I said, always the mother.

She stood and looked out the window with her hands on her hips. "I don't know. I am tired."

"Then you shouldn't go," I said, still in my seat.

"I shouldn't?" she said.

"I wouldn't."

"I never cancel an appointment," she said.

"A thrilling new experience," I said.

"I never cancel an appointment," she repeated.

"Live a little."

"My mother was brilliant, a history professor at Columbia, but she doesn't recognize me anymore. When I visit, she thinks I'm a famous person. Once, she insisted I was Jacqueline Kennedy. She whispered to me that Marilyn had been with my husband. And since she repeats everything she says, she told me the same thing from the moment I arrived until the moment I left."

The rain was beating against the window now. Candy looked out, looked at me, shook her head, and called to reschedule the meeting at the home. "Thank you for giving me permission not to go. As you see, I'm overwhelmed by my parents' situation."

"Isn't there someone in your family who could help?"

"I thought my husband would help. But I was wrong." The disappointment in her voice was palpable. Then she made excuses for him. "He's extremely busy, and he's on call every other weekend."

"What does your husband do?"

"He's a gynecologist."

Really? I thought. *My oldest daughter is seeing a gynecologist—a married one. It's a mistake of galactic proportions, but my daughter's gynecologist seems to have plenty of free time.*

"My husband is affiliated with Valley Hospital," she said.

"My daughter is a doctor at Valley."

"Well, then, she must know my husband. Brian Brownell?"

"I'll . . . ask her," I stuttered. But I didn't need to ask her. Brian Brownell was the name of the man she was seeing.

I couldn't speak.

I did not need news like this.

How many men were there in the world? Billions. There were at least 120 million in the United States, about two million in Connecticut. And my daughter had to be having an affair with the one husband of this one lovely woman?

There was no way I could live with the thought that my own daughter was seeing Candy's husband. Elisabeth had the night off and was coming to Saint Mordecai to see Mom. I called her and told her I would wait for her in the cafeteria and we could visit together.

She arrived in jeans that looked like they were sculpted to her body and a pullover sweater of violet angora. She was wearing fabulous lace-up black boots. Why did my beautiful, brilliant, and successful daughter need Candy's husband? Why couldn't she choose a young single man, or even an old single man—or a single woman?

"Sit for a minute," I said.

She sat exactly where Candy had sat before, across from me in the booth.

"Elisabeth, I want to talk to you about something."

"About Grandma?"

"No."

"About Dad?"

"No."

"Mommm. Don't even go there."

"Elisabeth, you have to stop seeing that married doctor."

"Mom, I'm not twelve. I'm old enough to do what I want. For crying out loud, I operate on people. People trust me with their lives."

"I know. And I couldn't be prouder of you. You're the daughter I always dreamed of."

"Then let it go."

"I can't, because now . . ."

"Is this because of Dad?"

"No, no. It's because . . ."

She held her hands to her head. "You know what, Mom? I know you're having a horrible time, the worst time ever. I don't know how you're surviving under all of this stress. And I so want to help. But I need you to stop talking about what's turning into your go-to subject. I know what you think, and I appreciate your advice, but I don't want to hear another word of it. Besides, I would think you have enough to worry about without throwing me into the mix."

"I'm a mother. I have an infinite capacity for worry."

"I love you, but you're impossible. Come. Let's go visit Grandma."

Chapter 13

When I got home from the hospital, I called Dana, confessing that I had become friends, accidentally, with the wife of my daughter's paramour.

"Are you nuts?" she had responded. "Cease and desist."

"I can't. She's my new friend."

"What are you, five?"

"She understands what it's like to take care of a parent."

"Oh, and I don't?" Dana said.

Dana's father lived in Deland, Florida. Deland not being near "de ocean." She flew down with the twins several times a year.

"I don't want to hurt her," I said.

"Then stop being her friend."

"I mean by telling her."

"Then stop being her friend."

"You already said that, Dana."

"But it's worth repeating."

"What if I tell her?"

Dana laughed. "*You* wouldn't tell her if her bra strap was showing."

"Yes, I would."

"Would you tuck it in?"

"Of course not."

"I would," Dana said.

"Okay, I'll tell her."

"No, you won't."

There was a real problem with someone knowing me as well as Dana did.

I was, at that point, one event away from uncontrollable hysteria. And this event could be as ordinary as somebody beating me to a parking spot at a strip mall or shoving me unintentionally on a movie line.

⁓♫

I took a week off from work, and, except for visits to my mother, I didn't leave the house. When my phone rang, I ignored it. When Elisabeth stopped by to make sure I was okay, I pulled it together long enough to make her agree that I was. I swigged nighttime cold medicine in the morning and slept through the day.

"Get out of the house," I repeated to myself one drizzling afternoon until I pulled on jeans and a polo shirt and a hooded yellow slicker. I convinced myself to drive to the grocery for more cold medicine. When I arrived at Big Buddy, my favorite supermarket and the largest one in town, I took a cart and began strolling down the shining wide aisles I knew so well. The Big Buddy jingle chimed over and over again.

It was two thirty, a short time before all of the kids hopped off the school bus, so the store was busy with shopping moms who knew each other from town, from the newcomers' club or the PTO, from church or the true religion—travel soccer. They clogged the aisles with flash discussions about the benefits of transitional kindergarten; why so-and-so was the worst math or science teacher at the middle school; which gymnastics center within an hour's drive was unsurpassed for training

Olympic-bound two-year-olds; and always some new revelation about college applications:

"Is your son taking the SAT course?"

"Yes. Is yours?"

"No. We hired a private tutor."

"Must be expensive."

"Not compared to college."

"That's so right, you're so right. What about the essays?"

"Oh, he won't even get started."

"We hired a retired admissions counselor to help him. Just to get him started. Suggest his theme."

"Marcy," a woman called from the far end of the pharmaceutical aisle.

Heading toward me was Samantha David, the mother of Amanda's nemesis in high school. I didn't want to talk to anyone, and I especially did not want to talk to her. She looked as though she had stepped out of a Talbots catalog—headband, pink oxford shirt, corduroy pants, penny loafers sans penny. But this wasn't what I disliked about her. What I really disliked about her was that she was the kind of field hockey mom who never cheered or clapped or arose from the bench for anyone except for her own daughter, the truculent goalie.

I pretended I didn't hear Samantha, but she scurried up the aisle. The store manager broke into the jingle to announce that ripe bananas were on sale for an hour.

"How *are* you?" Samantha said, placing her hand over mine, on my cart.

I slid my hand out from under hers. "I'm good, really good."

"Wonderful."

Okay, now go away.

"What is Amanda doing?" Of course, Amanda was working for Bloomingdale's, but Samantha would never ask what my child was up to unless she had Facebook evidence that her child was doing substantially better. "Karen Anne is in law school. She's first in her class at Penn. What about Amanda? She was always such a star."

What could I say to make her disappear? "Amanda just completed thirty days of house arrest," I said. "What a joy to have her at home."

"Oh no. Oh no. What happened?"

"You can read all about it on Facebook. I have to go. The bananas are on sale here. Did you know that bananas are the top seller at Walmart?"

I hurried past Mrs. She Was Always Such a Star, turning up another aisle. I stood face-to-face with an array of peanut butters, jellies, and jams. I wanted to slap my hand across the shelf and knock them all down. I closed my eyes, moving my fingers through my sweaty scalp. I had always and forever licked my wounds by pushing a cart through this market. But now it wasn't working. Apparently, I had too many wounds.

I went to the seafood department, thinking maybe I would feel better if I bought a large piece of fish. I thought about what Ben had said about all the food I'd been buying and decided I would buy the fish, but a small piece, six ounces. I waited my turn as a broad woman in front of me placed her order. She was wearing red pants adorned with minuscule pink whales, a canvas belt with dolphins, and a pink polo shirt with a goldfish logo.

Personally, I thought, *when I'm dressing, I never mix fish.*

She spoke to the counterman slowly, her words exaggerated. It was the way my mother spoke to anyone who was from another country.

The counterman had one lock of hair coming out of the top of his head. The shiny pin on his soiled apron said "Bradley."

"May I have a nice piece of swordfish?" the woman said.

Bradley presented the thick, meaty fish on wax paper, holding it up and outward so the woman could have a good look.

"A little bigger," the woman said, using both hands to indicate the desired size.

Bradley picked up another piece for her inspection.

She looked at it awhile. Was she memorizing it?

"It's too . . . I don't know," she said.

Quickly, he put it down. "How's this one?"

"A bit smaller, please. We're dieting."

This pain in the ass lived with someone, and I was alone?

She pointed. "No, no, no. Go toward the salmon. That's it—a bit to the left of the oily piece with the thick skin and the brown spot. That piece with the spot is terrible. You're not going to sell that piece. That piece will be here tomorrow."

I gave up on waiting for seafood. I rolled my cart to the bread aisle, where I considered a raisin loaf for Amanda and a forty-calorie wheat for Elisabeth. I passed Harvey's favorite, thick seven-grain—and thought how nice it would be if he choked on it.

I headed toward the cereal aisle, searching for granola without raisins. The backbreaker from the fish counter was now on my left, blocking the entire aisle with her loaded cart. She was yakking on a phone, asking her husband what kind of breakfast food to buy, rattling off the detailed name of every major cereal. She sounded like the sales director of General Mills.

What kind of wife doesn't know what cereal her husband likes? I thought. I knew everything about Harvey—cereal: McCann's oatmeal; orange juice: Tropicana; liquor: Macallan single-malt Scotch whiskey; fish: cod.

Thinking of cod made my eyes well up. I put on my sunglasses, and the tears ran down my face. About a year after our wedding, Harvey and I went fishing and brought home an ocean of cod. Each evening for weeks, we had cod for dinner, and before I prepared it he would say, "What's for dinner?" and I would respond, "We haven't had cod yet today." It was an endless inside joke, and the joke always made us feel closer. Maybe one day we'd share another joke: I'd say, "Remember when you had the affair with the twenty-two-year-old?" Then Harvey would say, "How old was she then?"

"Excuse me," I said to the fishwife blocking the aisle.

"I'm thinking," she said haughtily.

"I'm sorry, but there's no thinking in the aisle." *In other words, go to hell.*

"I will think in this aisle as long and hard as I please."

"Buy the Cheerios," I said, slamming a family-size box on top of the eggs in her overloaded cart.

"You'll crush my eggs," she said. "Remove that cereal from my cart."

"Remove it yourself."

"What is your problem?" she said as she jerked her cart around me.

"This is all on videotape," I said, waving a finger to the ceiling as though a camera were directly over us. "By tomorrow this incident will be on CNN. And then it'll be out there in the world forever, and everyone will know you don't know what cereal to buy."

"You're nuts, and I'm calling the store manager."

"Here—I'll call her. Store manager. Store manager!" I shouted, marching up and down the aisle, cupping my hands around my mouth.

Like she was being chased, the woman raced to the cash register. She put down her coupons in front of her groceries and waited for her turn.

I moved in behind her, my shopping cart almost touching her back. "You have to phone your husband to find out what kind of cereal he likes," I hissed, leaning toward her. "What kind of marriage is that?"

With her groceries still on the belt, she hurried out of the store, tripping at the door.

I was past reason. I yelled into the air, "That fool doesn't know which cereal to buy." The store was silent, customers watching me. I was a multiple-car crash on the turnpike.

The store manager, a woman in her forties with a warm heart-shaped face and pretty blue eyes, came up to me. Her badge said "Belinda." Even in my rage, I recognized that she was the good witch and that I'd had enough for one day. I wanted to go home. And never come out again.

"Please, please calm down."

I sniffled.

"You're on line, but your basket is empty," she said.

I began sobbing. "My basket is not empty," I said. "It's not. It's not."

The store was still silent, except for the wounded-animal sounds emerging from me. The manager and the cashier, a middle-aged woman in a store apron, exchanged looks as if to say "What now?" Then Belinda came closer to me and whispered in a soothing voice, "Is there someone we can call?"

"No," I said as I blinked back tears.

"Maybe your husband?" she said.

"My husband left me, and my mother has cancer, and she's in the hospital and I don't know what to do."

"Can I help you to your car?" Belinda asked.

I shook my head, but she pushed my cart to the side. She told me I should put up my hood because it was raining. I didn't react to her suggestion, so she pulled up my hood like the mother of a small child.

Belinda walked me to my car and waited until I was seated and reminded me to strap on my seat belt. I had never been a public nuisance before. Worst of all, I loved Big Buddy. I had so many memories of shopping there. Belinda lingered at my window, and I told her how my three school-age kids used to hang on my cart. I mentioned the game we had always played in the cookie aisle. Whoever found the Oreos first was the winner.

Belinda was compassionate. But I knew I would have to find a new site for my psychotherapy. Agitated and high on cold medicine, I started the car, then put it in reverse—without first checking the rearview mirror. I hit a mammoth tree, cursing the old oak for being in my way. I was startled but okay.

I got out of the car and checked for damage. My car was dented. I would have to take it to Barton's Garage, a place I had never been to because cars were Harvey's area of expertise. Harvey—CEO of bras, cars, and taking out the garbage.

∞

I didn't drive home. Instead, I swerved into the hospital garage, grabbed a ticket, and spiraled up to a compact space on the fifth level, facing the skybridge. I slumped back into my seat, eyes shut, until I was startled by knocks at the window.

It was Candy.

Oh no, I thought. I hadn't seen her for a week, the whole week I had taken off from work. Ever since I found out about her husband being my daughter's lover, I'd gone to the hospital to visit Mom at times when I knew Candy wouldn't be there. I knew I would have trouble looking her in the eye.

I lowered the window.

"Wow. You must be really tired. Your car was running."

"Does this mean you saved my life?" I asked.

"It could be."

"Are you coming or going?" I asked.

"Going. Dad's asleep."

"I like your coat." It was knee-length, taupe, and cashmere. Maybe I could compliment my way out of my guilt.

"That's what your mother said. I kept missing you at the hospital, so I went to her room and introduced myself. She explained that she wasn't really sick, that she stays at the hospital because she likes the man nurses."

"Male nurses?"

"No. She said 'man nurses.'"

"That's great. If only that were true," I said. "Was she wearing her oxygen mask for the pneumonia?"

"On the top of her head."

"Sounds like her."

"I told her that you'd told me you have a *wonderful* younger brother."

I laughed. I felt better.

"So why are you sleeping in your car?" she said.

"Just tired."

She nodded.

"I can't believe I'm complaining to you when you have two parents to care for."

"True. But that's why I understand."

"My life is in ruins," I said as I glanced in my rearview mirror and saw a Lexus waiting for my spot. I waved the driver on.

"Stay home for a day or two. I'll drop in on her."

"My husband moved out," I announced, omitting the part where Harvey, like Brian, had a younger woman. "He took a lot of clothes and left everything else, but I'm not sure he's coming back."

"Is there anything I can do for you?"

I wondered whether Candy's husband would ever—please, no—jump ship, go beyond this affair with my daughter, and actually move out. I felt sick. I hated the smell of a parking garage.

"Yes, there is," I said. "Refrain from saying anything positive. Do not be optimistic."

"What do you want me to say?" Candy asked.

"How about 'I am so grief-stricken that your one and only husband left you, and your one and only mother has cancer, and you went nuts in a supermarket and had to be escorted out, and you hit a tree with your car.'"

"You hit a tree?"

"That's what it gets for moving."

"And your husband?"

It was dead wrong to talk to Candy about my Harvey problems when her husband was probably sitting in the Valley Hospital cafeteria staring into my daughter's eyes.

Candy reached into her bag for a tissue. She was just the kind of woman who would have one. Dana never had a tissue. I never had a tissue.

"Good news," she commented as she handed over the Kleenex. "Your mascara isn't running."

"It's waterproof," I said. "I bought it before I flounced into my husband's office to give him the third degree."

"Do you want to get out of the car?"

I opened the door. Then I locked it as I stood beside her.

The sun was setting over the buildings beyond the open-air parking lot.

"He was seeing a young girl," I said. *Sort of like your husband seeing my daughter,* I thought sadly, hoping I didn't look as guilty as I felt.

"First time?"

"I think so, but honestly, I'm trying not to think about it. I mean, what if it wasn't the first time? In that case, I've been a chump for thirty-three years. So I'm going with 'it's the first time.' That's the story, and I am sticking to it."

"Then maybe you can forgive him . . . if you love him."

"I want him to come back."

"Then concentrate on that."

"But I called a lawyer. And I feel like a traitor. But my friends kept telling me I needed a lawyer, and then I thought I should call one . . . just in case."

"Just in case what?"

"Just in case *he* called a lawyer."

"Is he the type of man who would call a lawyer?"

"The best lawyer."

"So you did the right thing."

"But I didn't make an appointment."

"Because you're not ready for a lawyer. You want your husband to come back."

It all made so much sense—when she said it.

"He'll come back," she said. "You'll forgive him."

So she would forgive her husband if she found out about Elisabeth?

"Because you made a life with him, you have children with him, you love him," she said. "Can I borrow your cell phone?"

I searched my purse and handed her my phone.

She added her name and phone number to my contacts list.

"There," she said. "Now call me whenever."

It was terrible. Chilling. The nicer she was, the guiltier I felt.

"Thank you," I said as I dropped the phone back into my bag.

"For what?"

"For not saying 'No biggie. You'll live through this.'"

"You *will* live through it. But at times you'll wish you had died."

I wanted to hug her, but I didn't. I couldn't. Elisabeth was hanging over my head, a block of cement dangling from a chain.

"I have to go," she said. "I have a meeting about my picture book *Walter in the Water*. Walter is my father's name. In the book, he's a walrus."

"I know. My son, Ben, loved that book."

"Someone wants to talk about the possibility of a TV show based on it."

I waited until Candy had backed up her Mercedes, then I waved good-bye and walked to the elevator, holding her tissue tight in my hand.

Chapter 14

That Saturday, while I was at home watching television in jeans and an NYU T-shirt, Harvey called. Out of nowhere, he asked if he could come over or if I could meet him at Five Swallows. I said I would come to the inn, which seemed better than sitting at home, in the manse of memories, waiting for him.

I had no energy for changing clothes. I had already tried getting dressed and made-up for Harvey. It was futile.

I looked in the mirror in the living room. The mirror was a broad oval, centered on a wall with nothing beneath it, set in a smooth gilded frame. I stared as though I hadn't seen myself in years. I saw the reflection of someone who hadn't aged badly at all. I still had strawberry-blond hair, albeit through a monthly visit to a salon, and my wrinkles were for the most part limited to a few around my mouth. I held my hand over the wrinkles to conceal the offending lines. Then I used my hands to pull the wrinkles down on both sides of my chin. I took a few steps back so I could see more of my body. I was close to the same size I had always been, a major coup considering I'd lived with Harvey, whose concept of dieting was eliminating his fourth lunch. The jeans and the T-shirt took off twenty years. There was nothing wrong with me. In fact, I was still good-looking. He just wanted something new. Decades newer.

I considered what I would do if Harvey never came back, and it occurred to me that I could meet someone else. But I would never marry again. What was the point?

I conjured the anti-Harvey. A weathered physician without a border, traversing the earth, helping the feeble and needy. Or an actor, who would invite me to live with him in his house on a windswept beach. Or a contractor in a flannel shirt. My ideal contractor drove a pickup truck. He was hardly making a living, because he was too much of a perfectionist. He brought me a coffee every morning from Dunkin' Donuts.

I pulled my T-shirt down and smoothed my hair, noticing that the red had a touch of gray; I needed a salon. I headed out the door feeling calm and positive about myself, thinking that if I survived this difficult time I would make it to the other side.

The lobby of the Five Swallows was dark green and crimson. The wallpaper was patterned with hunting dogs. On the shelves next to the books—hardcovers and paperbacks that guests had left behind over the years—there were carved duck decoys, wooden thimbles, and other dust collectors. The lobby was awash with characters stolen from a '60s short story about a country club in Connecticut. There were thin, white, well-groomed blonds on club chairs and plaid colonial-style couches while others checked in at the front desk and low-talked to the alert bellmen, all of whom were wearing khaki pants and shirts with Five Swallows on the upper left pocket. Every person and pet looked like they'd escaped from a Tommy Hilfiger spread in *Vogue*.

Harvey filled an armchair in front of the fireplace, roaring even on this warm day. The fire was always roaring at Five Swallows. It completed the look. He was, naturally, on his phone. When he saw me, he poked up a finger as if to say "One minute."

I shook my head. I should wait for him to get off the phone? He was delirious. He snatched a butter cookie from a plate on a side table and walked over to me. I could tell from his appearance that he'd been socking away butter cookies at a rate the baker at Five Swallows had never seen before.

"Good cookies?" I said.

"My first one."

I laughed. "First one, eh?"

"Okay, so maybe I've had a few."

"Well, they look good on you," I said sarcastically.

He patted his stomach. "Elisabeth told me your mom needs to go to a rehabilitation facility, and that she'll be receiving radiation." His sport shirt was tucked into his pants, and he was wearing a canvas belt I had never seen before. I wondered whether he had bought the belt or she had bought the belt. *Did they shop together?*

"Yes," I said.

"So?"

"She'll be going to a rehabilitation facility."

"Oh, stop it, Marcy. You know how I feel about your mom."

True. But exactly how do you feel about me?

"Let's take a walk," he said.

"We can talk right here in the lobby."

Harvey cased the room. "I'd rather walk outside," he said.

Harvey was the great indoor man. He was either inside his office or inside the house. His idea of a picnic was eating off a paper plate in front of the TV. I decided he was afraid I would raise my voice in the lobby and create a scene that would result in the manager asking us to leave. It occurred to me that I might very well do that, so I headed for the revolving brass door.

We walked slowly on the jogging trail until we came to a picnic bench. That was far enough for me. I wanted to know why I'd been summoned. The bench had a plaque screwed into the top center: *In memory of Eunice P. Oakley.* I laughed.

"What's so funny?" he said.

I pointed to the plaque. "Ms. Oakley—the teacher. You told her I wrote Ben's paper. Remember?"

"Well, she didn't need a bench, because she will *never* be forgotten in our family. Do you remember that I took an afternoon off from work to go to school with you so we could be properly reprimanded? Then she insisted that Ben write two papers to replace the one you wrote."

"I didn't write it. I fixed up what he already had," I said.

Harvey started laughing. His eyes shone. "He had two paragraphs, maybe."

I loved the legends of my life with Harvey. I loved being married to Harvey. I loved being married, period. I had not one inclination to start over with someone else. I wanted so badly to believe his affair was over. There were few things worse than imagining him inside someone else.

"Do you remember that girl who busted Amanda's chops on the elementary school bus?" I asked. "What was her name?" I knew her name. It was Tory Regan.

"Something with a *T*," Harvey said. "That girl—"

"Tory, I think it was."

"That Tory didn't need cyberspace to be a bully."

"I know," I said. "After that, Amanda started calling the school bus the 'Loser Cruiser.' And she insisted that I drive her to school every day. I loved it—the Loser Cruiser. It figures that a kid who could come up with that name would be successful."

"We have three incredible kids," he said.

"Yes, we do." So there was something we could agree on. For all time.

"It's because of you."

Nice try at being nice, Harvey. "Why am I here?" I asked.

"I'm thinking that maybe I want to come home." Harvey spoke without looking at me, staring at the trees in the distance, as though facing me would be incriminating.

I felt the air slide from my lungs. I made mental notes of the gravel on the ground as I paced myself, waiting to respond. As much as I wanted my life back, I was not going to jump at his command.

"You want to come home," I said at last without any show of emotion, a statement not a question.

"I do."

"Can you look at *me* and say it?" Was I being too hard? I softened my voice. "I'd like it if you looked at me and said it."

He took my hand and looked hard and deep into my eyes. "I would like to come home."

I wanted this nightmare to be over. I wanted to feel whole again. I nodded. I cried.

He approached to enfold me. I shook my head no.

"I was thinking that maybe we should go for counseling," he said.

The problem was that he said it as though Feldman had told him to say it. *"Just tell her you'll go to counseling."* As far as I knew, Harvey had never been to a counselor of any kind. In fact, he believed that all psychiatrists had crazy children.

"Here's all the counseling you need: don't ever do it again," I said.

"It was the first time. The *first* time," he said. "It wasn't about her. It was about the business. About failing. About failing you, Elisabeth, Amanda, Ben."

"Sounds to me as though you've already been to a counselor," I said, holding my feelings of relief in reserve. "Or maybe a public relations expert?"

The nightmare was over, but victory seemed shallow, like winning a race because the other guy tripped. Now that Harvey had decided to come home, another devastating wound had opened: the realization that maybe I wanted my marriage back more than I wanted my husband back.

◟᷉

That night, Harvey returned home with the self-satisfied expression of a boy who had just scored a pile of prize tickets from an arcade game. As we stood in the doorway—Harvey with the first of his suitcases; me, relieved yet not glad—the look on his face made me think that he was expecting a stuffed gray donkey with a ribbon, from high on a prize display.

He suggested we call the kids to tell them the good news. But I didn't feel like calling.

"I think you should tell them," I said. I felt as though I had been in a great war and wasn't sure if I was safe from the enemy as yet.

"I'll call them in the morning," he said. "Let's just go upstairs."

I wanted to have sex with him to seal our agreement, but I couldn't do anything but lie in bed and search the ceiling. When he reached out, I cuddled into a ball on his chest. I put his hand in mine, indicating that I'd had enough for one day.

For days afterward, we hardly spoke. I was terrified that if I spoke, I would attack him with a rock-concert-volume soliloquy about what he had done. When Harvey began a conversation, it was always about one of the kids.

"Did Ben call?"

"Yes."

"What's going on?"

Then I would tell Harvey something I knew he already knew, because he spoke to Ben several times a week.

Harvey slept on his half of the king bed, and I remained on mine, the exact sides we had chosen so many years ago. He lay on the left, and

I was on the right, the same way we would be in the cemetery, once I died of disillusionment and Harvey succumbed to diabetes. Even when Harvey had moved to the inn, I clung to my side of the bed, never so much as nearing the middle, never so much as touching his pillows. When he came home, I placed a body pillow between us and faced the wall instead of facing him.

He waited a week before he reached for my arm again. I huddled closer to my edge of the bed. He turned on the light.

"You'll never forgive me," he said as he adjusted a pillow.

"It's going to take time, Harvey."

"I understand, but—"

I said I was too tired to talk. He reached out for me again. I didn't want to lose him, but I wasn't ready for this reunion. I grabbed my pillow and went to Elisabeth's old bedroom.

Then suddenly I returned, on a mission to question Harvey.

"Are you taking Viagra?" I asked. *Damn Dana for bringing the subject up and up and up in Starbucks.*

"Cialis," he said.

"Is that the one where you call a doctor if the erection lasts four hours or longer?"

I fell asleep, eyes wet, grieving, on Elisabeth's bed. I'd thought Harvey would come home and I would be exultant, but instead I was brokenhearted.

◔

The following Sunday, Elisabeth stopped by. Her hair was in a twist, and she wore a dress with a sweater over it. She didn't look like the kind of girl who was seeing a married man, a man married to my friend Candy.

She sat down at the kitchen table. Harvey was having lunch—tuna salad piled on a bulky roll, garnished with tomato and pickle. I handed Elisabeth a can of cranberry juice.

"I want you to know how happy I am—we all are—that you're trying to work things out," she said, like she was the parent and we were the kids.

"We live to serve," Harvey said.

Elisabeth asked Harvey if he wanted juice. He pointed to his glass of milk.

"Now that you two are copacetic," she said, "I have something important to tell you."

Why would she think that just because Harvey had moved back in, we were all copacetic or co-anything? It had to be because she was young. Harvey had been back a week, and a week for her was as long as a year for me. In fact, the passage of time was one of the worst parts of getting older. At my age, time traveled fast; winter came and went as though New Year's Eve and April Fools' Day had one Wednesday between them.

I was sure her "something important" was nothing I wanted to hear. Instinctively, I knew it was about Brian.

She took a breath.

Nothing good ever comes after a deep breath, I thought.

"Brian is planning to get a divorce, and then we're going to live together."

She said it proudly, like it was a major accomplishment, like riding a bike for the first time or getting a full scholarship to medical school. She said it like she had never been more certain of anything and it could never be taken back. She said it as though anyone who thought it was an unfortunate life choice should be terminated, like she was daring us to say something negative.

Harvey looked at her, then looked at me, then swallowed his tuna fish and took a swig of milk. I waited for him to speak. "I don't think so," he said.

"I can take care of myself," she said, turning toward me instead of him.

I didn't say a word. I was too busy reveling in the hypocrisy.

"No, obviously you can't take care of yourself," he said. "Because if you could, you wouldn't have gotten involved with a man who was married in the first place. And I think I will have some more milk."

Elisabeth went to the fridge and brought over a quart of milk.

"That's enough," he said as she poured.

She looked at the container. "Oh, this is skim," she said. "You like whole milk."

Interesting that she believed she could change the subject from Brian to milk. If only life were that easy.

"If you know what I like, why are you here telling me something I do not like, and won't accept? I want you to drop this phony no-good guy and get on with your life. You're too smart for this. Too smart."

I watched them go at each other, knowing well that Harvey the Hypocrite was on an express train to nowhere.

"When you meet Brian, you'll like him, Dad."

"I don't want to meet him."

"But you have a lot in common."

I'd say so.

"I can't like anyone who would leave his wife for another woman," Harvey said.

My cheeks were burning.

"Whoa," Elisabeth said. "Isn't that what you just did? I'm sorry, Mom."

"That Brian phony will return to his wife," Harvey said, "and then where are you?"

I clasped my hands, crushing my knuckles. I didn't want to interrupt Harvey's drop-Brian monologue to Elisabeth. *Don't do what I do; do what I say*—like there was a parent in the history of humankind who had accomplished anything with that line of reasoning.

"Don't compare me to you," Harvey said, "or bring up what your mother and I are trying to put behind us. You're a young woman. This decision will affect your entire life. And he has a child."

"He's hoping for custody," Elisabeth said confidently.

"So now you're going to be the wicked stepmother?" Harvey said.

"I hardly think I'm wicked," Elisabeth snapped.

"It doesn't matter," Harvey explained. "The kid will think you're wicked. You broke up his parents. You ruined his family."

Interesting how Harvey was putting the blame on Elisabeth, the young single woman, and no onus whatsoever on Brian. Wasn't Brian the one who was married?

"Find a young guy, your age, preferably one who has never been married."

"Dad, that's not—"

Abruptly, he pushed away from the table. Harvey had had enough. He stalked off to the family room with his remaining tuna salad sandwich on a plate.

"Dad is such a hypocrite," Elisabeth said.

"True," I said, "but I can't take your side. You are doing the wrong thing, making a mistake you'll never be able to take back. You're also inflicting pain on other people. Just think about Brian's wife and his son. Really think. You're not equipped to mommy a teenager—even if he is at a boarding school."

"How do you know he's at boarding school?" she said.

I scrambled for a credible answer. "Because Brian sounds like the kind of man who has a kid at boarding school."

"So, what's wrong with that?" she asked.

The tension, anxiety, and concern for Elisabeth, the devastation about my mother, the guilt about Candy, and the hypocrisy of Harvey simultaneously overwhelmed me. Silently, I cried.

Harvey stepped back into the room for more pickles. "What's the matter, Marcy?"

I stared at him in disbelief. Was his brain always this far up his ass?

Chapter 15

As my mother slept, I wandered about the hospital. Who planned hospital decor anyway? Walls as dull as gum. Linoleum floors speckled in tints of vomit. I found the bathroom, slurped at the water fountain, pumped the hand sanitizer, and stood at the door of the visitors' lounge, which was equipped with an aged television, a pair of couches heading south, and tattered magazines. A family was gathered inside—all average height, pug-nosed, and dressed in sweaters, except for a man in a jersey in the center of the room, with the build of a football star, who towered over everyone. He was telling a story. I knew it was legend, because the family laughed before he said anything funny.

I felt lonely. I found Candy's father's room and stole a look, hoping she was there. To my surprise, the room was decorated. A brown valance covered the top of the twisted hospital blinds. Photographs of Candy's son, Jumper, on skis and at the beach, were on the wall facing the bed. Clay pots on the windowsill were home to a variety of blossoming plants. A knitted throw partially covered the vinyl recliner. The bed was flat, and Candy's father was asleep beneath two down blankets. All I could see was a tuft of white hair. I turned to leave.

"Candace?" he whispered. "Candace?"

I was going to leave, but then I said, "I'm Marcy, Candy's friend."

"Come in," he said. "I can't see you over there. Come into the room." His voice was smooth. He reminded me of an announcer on a nighttime radio show.

I approached but stopped just past the door to the bathroom.

"A friend, you say? I've been here so long my daughter has made hospital friends?"

"I bumped into Candy while visiting my mother. We worked together a long time ago."

"You're an illustrator?" he asked, raising the bed.

"No. We volunteered together."

"Candace won't be here for a while. She had a meeting. I don't know if you know this, but she has written and illustrated many, many books. In fact, she won a prize for the finest picture book."

I loved how proud he was of her. The way Harvey was about Amanda. "Yes, I know. She won the Newbery for *Walter in the Water*."

"My name is Walter."

"In the water," I said.

He smiled—a room-size smile.

"As long as I'm here," I said, "is there anything I can do for you?"

"Yes. Could I bother you to turn on Fox News for me?"

I walked over to the bed, where the remote was hanging on a cord. "What channel is Fox News?"

"Look on this notepad. Candace wrote it down for me."

"Ten," I said.

"And we're on the tenth floor. You would think that would be easy for me to remember, but . . ."

"I wouldn't remember it," I said.

"Your mother is ill?"

"She fell," I said.

"Most patients on this floor have cancer."

"My mom has cancer," I blurted. Did I think he would feel better if he knew he had company? "We found out about the cancer because of the tests that had to be done when she fell and broke her ankles. At first, the doctor recommended radiation therapy, but now I'm not sure what the treatment will be. My eldest daughter is a doctor, and she's getting other opinions. My mother is a fighter. So that's very good." I said the fighter part for me, not for him.

"I'm sorry about your mother and her troubles," he said. "I was first diagnosed in 2008. I didn't tell a soul."

"You didn't tell your wife?"

"She was already in the home. She suffers from Alzheimer's disease. I told Candace when I started chemotherapy. Marcy, that's your name, right? Marcy, you should be relieved that your mom fell, because the doctors discovered her problem, and the result is it can now be treated."

"I hadn't looked at it that way," I said, realizing how much I missed having a father figure in my life. At that moment, I would have done whatever Candy's ailing father—"Walter Knight Jr.," it said on the door—instructed me to do.

"Everything happens for a reason," Walter said, nodding at the television.

On Fox, two Washington lawyers were chatting up and ass-kissing Bill O'Reilly. The women were almost identical—stiff, slim, standard white American turned-up-nose beauties with hair extensions—except one was blond, the other, brunette.

"I never talk about politics or religion," Walter said. "We can't discuss Obama, but what do you think of O'Reilly?"

"I'd have to watch the show regularly before I could decide that," I told Walter, because I thought it was what he wanted to hear. I hadn't had a television buddy since my daughters and I watched recorded episodes of *Sex and the City*. I turned up the volume on the TV.

"That's the spirit," Walter said. "You can learn a lot from O'Reilly."

When Candy entered the room, I was giving her dad a funnel cup of water and we were watching an analysis by a Georgetown law professor who had been an advisor to George W. Bush during Hurricane Katrina. Candy looked perfect in a suit with a mandarin collar, a scarf with a Chinese bird pattern, and black open-toe heels.

"Marcy, what a great surprise," she said, and her eyes brightened.

"My mother is asleep."

"I know. I looked in her room," she said. "Her dinner was delivered and getting cold, so I gave the tray to a nurse. She'll reheat it when your mother wakes up."

"Yes," I said. "It's appalling to eat ice-cold lobster bisque and filet mignon."

"Who had filet mignon?" Walter said jokingly. "I was served cottage cheese."

"But I bet it was epicurean cottage cheese," Candy said.

"Yes, Candace. It tasted just like Thanksgiving dinner," Walter said.

I was pleased to have my hospital friends and touched that Candy had looked in on my mother. Candy was in my boat—the boat with a mess of holes in the bottom.

～❦～

The following afternoon, as I stepped off the hospital elevator, wet from the rain, with flowers for my mother, I noticed Candy on one of two chairs stationed in the hall to the right. She had a cell phone in her hand and an art portfolio on her lap. I waved, and she hailed me over with an index finger.

"I'm trying to contact my dad's oncologist," she said, pointing to the other seat.

"Because you missed him when he made his rounds?"

"Because she called and left me a message."

She reached for my flowers and my umbrella, and handed me her phone. "I've lost patience. Can you redial it for me? Getting through takes forever."

I hit "Redial" and put the call on speakerphone.

"You have reached Connecticut State Health Partners and Practitioners Limited. Many of our world-class doctors and practitioners are associated with Saint Mordecai Hospital, a center of excellence, rated among the top one hundred hospitals in the United States. CSHPPL medical experts are wholly dedicated to your confidence and well-being."

If that's the case, I thought, *why doesn't someone pick up the phone?*

"Press '1' for directions to our offices in five Connecticut towns. Press '2' for questions regarding billing and insurance. Press '3' for prescription refills. To cancel or change your appointment, press '4.' To schedule an appointment, press '5.' For all other inquiries regarding CSHPPL, press '0' and wait to speak to our nurse manager."

"If you're dead by then, we're sorry," I said to Candy.

I pressed "0." That's when the commercial started. "Do you want to lose a hundred pounds or more? Do you suffer from life-threatening comorbidities, such as type two diabetes, sleep apnea, elevated blood pressure, or heart disease? Attend an evening or afternoon seminar at Saint Mordecai Hospital and hear how bariatric surgery can improve your life.

"Expecting a baby? Be assured that at Saint Mordecai Hospital, we welcome your doula.

"Impotence is a common problem for men. Our urologists—"

"Can I help you?" a live voice said finally.

"Dr. Indira Patel-Cohen," Candy said, and I repeated the name into the phone.

"Please hold for Dr. Patel-Cohen."

I handed the cell phone to Candy, and Dr. Patel-Cohen informed her that the cancer was now spreading in her father's brain. I closed my eyes. I didn't want to hear any more. What I wanted to do was stand up and race through the elevator doors, past the Au Bon Pain in the hallway, past the tacky gift shop with the shrinking heart-shaped Mylar balloons, the skimpy bouquets, the stale Russell Stover candy, and the faded cards with violets. I wanted to run through the revolving door to the hovering ceiling of the dark parking garage, then I'd crash my car through the narrow tollgate, because I forgot to pay the cashier in the lobby. Certainly there was an island in the Caribbean, lousy with tiny drink umbrellas, where I could avoid all of this heartache with one especially icy margarita or five.

"In the brain," Candy said for about the fifteenth time. "Yes, I see, I see."

I see what I don't want to see. I see the end.

"Thank you, Doctor," she said. "You have a good day too."

Just like a doctor to wish you a good day after telling you your father's terminal cancer has left the terminal.

"Marcy, I need juice," Candy said faintly.

"We can go to the place on the corner."

"No, no. We have to go to our place," she said as she stood. She pressed the elevator button as though the building were on fire and all of the stairwells were already burning.

I followed her into the hospital cafeteria, where we sat in our usual booth—far back, right corner—studying the fatigue of a young surgeon in faded green scrubs, his medical cap hanging from his bowed head. Our dumbfounded silence multiplied the sadness.

The sun was setting in the courtyard outside the cafeteria when Candy finally spoke. "There's a trial at Sloan Kettering."

"That's good."

"I would have to bring him to New York twice a week."

"I could help you," I said.

"Thank you. But I wonder if all the traveling would be too much for him. We could drive up and back all the time and he could end up receiving the placebo."

"What do you mean?"

"There's a control group."

"Oh," I said. "There's a lot to think about."

"Think about this—should I *tell* him how sick he is?"

I wasn't aware there was a choice in the matter. "Isn't it unethical to do otherwise?"

"He's ninety-four years old and extremely ill. His wife has advanced Alzheimer's disease. Certainly Dr. Patel-Cohen would understand why he doesn't need to know the latest bad news."

"I don't know. I don't know if that's how it works."

"You think I should tell him."

I thought about my visit to Walter. He was more than lucid. He was entertaining.

Candy began drumming her fingers on her cheeks.

When she spoke, she said, "This is too much. What should I do? What would you do?"

I spoke slowly. "I can understand wanting to spare him any more pain, but, honestly, I think he has a right to know. It's his life. He's entitled to the dignity of knowing. He's entitled to make plans, to live his days the way he wants to."

She stopped drumming. She looked out the window, thinking. "He'll want to visit my mother—if he can."

"Maybe you should have his doctor tell him while you're there."

"That's what I'm thinking."

Two women slid into chairs at a freestanding table for four. They were in blue scrubs, chattering about men. Since any diversion would do, Candy and I latched on to their conversation. The tall one, picking mindlessly at a salad, said that after e-mailing for weeks, she arranged to meet a man from a dating site. He was pleasant, sort of jovial, but she wasn't sexually attracted to him. She asked the other nurse if that mattered.

Candy asked me, "Would you marry a man if you weren't sexually attracted to him?"

"Sure. In thirty or so years, it won't matter at all."

"Let's just sit here," she said.

"Okay," I said.

And we sat there until the cafeteria closed.

Chapter 16

At the Guild for Good office, I walked in to find Jon London, vice president of the board, making copies for some other charity on our machine. Policy was a nickel apiece, but Jon never paid.

Jon smiled hello. He was tall, but compared to Harvey, everyone was tall. I'd say six feet, but maybe less. He had a charming, disarming, boyish manner about him. His hair was on the long side. His blue eyes were animated. His nose was large for his face. He got five-o'clock shadow at ten a.m.

An intern had dubbed him Jon Juan and said he was hot—for an old guy. *Great,* I'd thought. *Old.* I'd checked his birth date on the annual membership form. He was five years younger than I was.

When we were alone in the office discussing business, or a deficit of toner in the copier, I felt a pleasant chill. This had been easy to disregard, because previous to my husband's betrayal, I was a happily married woman giving a once-over to the local eye candy.

"I haven't seen you in a while," he said, looking at me intensely. The inspection was uncomfortable, so I moved toward my desk, at the rear of the office.

"I'm always glad when you stop by," I said. *And please be sure to wear that denim shirt whenever you do.*

"Any more copy paper?"

I pointed to a cabinet.

"Any ivory?"

"Getting fussy?"

He laughed as he filled the machine.

He pulled a slatted chair up to my desk. "I ran into Calvin Davenport, and he mentioned that you're having some problems." Jon was quasi-friendly with Dana's husband, Calvin, but why had they been talking about me?

"I'm fine," I said.

"If you say so," he said. He leaned forward and I could smell his cologne. I liked the earthy scent.

"What's up with the board?" I said, redirecting the conversation.

"Good news. We received the grant."

I clapped my hands together in delight.

"Thanks to you, of course," he said.

I shook my head as though to say "It was nothing," but I knew it was something. I'd never taken a class in grant writing, but I was adept at it. I had done an exceptional job on the one he was referring to, a grant application to the state of Connecticut.

"We're going to hire our first executive director."

"That's great," I said. All I could hope was that I didn't wind up the indentured servant of some neurotic bitch.

"I was thinking of recommending you."

"Are you serious?"

He smiled at me, as though he knew he was about to make my day. "Oh, come on, Marcy. You've been running this place on a part-timer's pay for years."

This was true, but I didn't say anything.

"The Art Explosion concept—start to finish—was all yours. And the results were phenomenal. We cleared two hundred thousand dollars for scholarships."

"Thank you."

"What I want to know, confidentially, of course, is would you be interested in the position?"

He had to be kidding. Would I be interested? Would I be interested in turning my part-time hourly gig into a fabulous full-time job with benefits? Would I be interested in being executive director of an organization that did so many awesome things for so many people?

"I understand if it's something you'd like to think about."

I tried to stay calm, but my eyes must have looked like I was watching fireworks.

"I'd be thrilled."

"Really?" he said, then paused. "In that case, I'm here to say that the vote of the board was unanimous. The job is yours."

I was overwhelmed with emotion. Dazed, amazed. My work had been recognized, and the new job would alter my life. "I don't know how to thank you."

Jon shrugged, then stood to leave. "I'm only the messenger. And the messenger is happy you're happy."

"Make all the free copies you want. Copy until the cows come home."

Jon shook my hand. "As soon as the board meets again, you'll receive a contract, all the details. No dental insurance," he said.

"That's a shame. I'm so excited my teeth are chattering."

"I guess my work is done here," he said.

I laughed. "For now."

As soon as Jon walked out the door, I kicked off my shoes and put up my feet. I toasted myself with a tumbler full of pens and pencils, markers, giant black clips, and scissors.

I was looking forward to telling Harvey about my new job. He had been home three weeks. I had worked my way over to the center of the bed. We had held each other. We had almost made love.

I thought that my new job would help a lot. It would take my mind off the past. It would give us new material to talk about. And I was hoping Harvey would be proud of me.

But Harvey didn't come home after work that night. Instead, he left a voice mail for me: "I'm meeting Ben for a drink in the city." When I heard this pathetic alibi, a bolt of anxiety coursed from my head through my arms to the tips of my fingers. *He's with her,* I thought. *And if he's back with her, it's over—for good.*

As I thumbed through the local newspaper, I came across a stress quiz. The test listed every conceivable life crisis—from losing your keys to losing your job to losing your mind. Each crisis was scored from one to ten points, based on the amount of stress it created. For example, scratching your car was one point. Escaping a grizzly bear was nine points. I received ten points, the highest attainable, for surviving my husband's philandering, then another ten for my mother's illness (an illness in the family was eight points, but cancer earned an extra two—and I should have gotten more because she was still in the hospital) and ten more points for a major unexpected life change. I was always good at tests. And now I was a National Merit Scholar of stress.

It was almost midnight when I settled under the quilt, but I couldn't sleep. I sat up in bed, surfing Harvey's flat-screen from channel to channel, pausing on a classic rerun of *Bonanza* as the map of Virginia City burned.

I considered calling my son, the alibi, and half dialed, but then I decided I couldn't get Ben involved.

"Ben, may I speak to Dad?"

"Dad?"

"He said he was with you tonight."

"Oh, yeah."

It would break my heart if he lied to me for Harvey. I twisted the wiry phone cord around my wrist, untwisted it, and flung the phone onto the French Provençal carpet Harvey had ordered from Paris. I heard the sound of the automatic garage door closest to the house. The door thumped down, and I was thankful I hadn't called my only son.

I assumed a fetal position on my side of the bed, sealing my eyes, feigning sleep, so I wouldn't have to talk to Harvey. He walked heavily into the room, like a fireman in galoshes. He switched on the light, shut off the TV, tapped me on the shoulder, and said he needed to talk.

"I'm sleeping," I said, punctuating my words with a cranky moan for effect.

"This is important."

I straightened myself out and rolled over on my back. Harvey's eyes were wide and bloodshot, as though he had witnessed horrific destruction—a wildfire, children swept up in a tsunami, the My Lai Massacre. He collapsed onto the tapestry chair that faced the bed. He grasped the lacquered arms tightly, and I could see his heavy knuckles turn pink.

My head jammed with fear and worry.

"Is Ben all right?" My voice cracked.

"Ben's fine." He stood to remove his trench coat and his sport coat. He unknotted his tie, unbuttoned his shirt, kicked off his Italian shoes, and leaned back in the armchair. He held the tie in his hand, twisting the ends into a noose. The few times he had ever been this upset about anything I had hurried out of bed, held his hand, and asked if he wanted some water, aspirin, or the expired painkiller I had received when I had tendinitis of the hand.

"Are you sure Ben's all right?" I asked.

"I told you, he's fine."

"Please say what's wrong. You're scaring me to death."

"She's pregnant," he said lifelessly.

"Oh no," I cried. I dropped the pillow, covering my face with one hand. *Elisabeth could have anyone she wanted. Why did she have to pick Brian? A married man. Candy's married man. And now she was having his baby.* I felt every particle I had eaten that day rise into my throat. I rushed into the master bathroom to vomit. "I need ginger ale," I called, waving, between throw-ups.

"Diet or regular?" Harvey asked as he stood in the doorway.

"Whatever people drink in this kind of situation will be fine."

Harvey rushed off and came back with a two-liter bottle. No glass. He passed the bottle to me with shaking hands. I sipped tentatively, wiping my lips with the towel Harvey placed on my shoulder.

"What kind of doctor can afford everything except a box of condoms?" I said, walking back into our bedroom with the enormous bottle.

"What doctor?" Harvey said.

"Elisabeth's doctor," I said as I thought of a thousand ways that Elisabeth's pregnancy would upheave her life, Candy's life.

"I'm not talking about Elisabeth. It's not Elisabeth."

Then the thunder struck.

"Your girlfriend is pregnant, and you moved back in here?"

I slapped him, once, hard enough for my hand to hurt, then backed away with my palms to my heart.

"I'm sorry. I'm sorry," he chanted. "I didn't know."

"What *do* you know? Do you know if it's yours?"

"Marcy . . ."

"Don't 'Marcy' me, you son of a bitch."

"It's mine," he said, plunging his bloody words not into me but through me.

My life as I knew it was officially over. From this day forth, my marriage, which I had tried to save, would be the greatest failure I had ever known. I loved Harvey, or once I did, but I'd never loved him enough to get through this scenario. We were done, destroyed.

"There will be a paternity test. I can assure you of that."

"I've *been* assured. I'm assured you're an asshole. I'm assured that my life is ruined. That I wasted thirty-three years. More, if I count time from the damn moment I met you. And stop talking. I don't want to hear one more word about that bitch."

"Her name is Madison," he said, looking straight at me.

Her name made her so exhaustively real I felt as though the letters were carved into my forehead. And once she had his child, no matter if I divorced him, she would be in my face, in my life, forever. Entwined in my family—him and her and the baby turning us into a soap opera without end.

"Take it back," I shrieked. "I don't want to know her name."

"But Madison—"

"Madison, Madison. Madison was fourth president of the United States. His wife made ice cream. Madison is a street. Is she a street?"

"She's a kid."

"I got that part, Harvey. I got it. She's a kid. She's pregnant. She's with child. She's got a bun in the oven. She's ruined my life. *You've* ruined my life."

Harvey wiped his eyes with his palms. At that moment, I detested everything about him—his bald head, his tortured face, his Rolex over a patch of freckles, his custom-made shirt, the paunch above his belt, a brand-new reddish-brown belt with a gold buckle. I wanted to wrap that belt around his neck. She was pregnant, and he'd had time to shop for belts.

"What are we going to do?" he said.

"Huh?" I wasn't sure I had heard him correctly.

"What are we going to do?"

"You're asking me what to do?" I said in disbelief. The son of a bitch wanted me to solve his problem.

Suddenly, I felt a surge of stealth strength rising from the floor, running through my legs, coursing into my heart and my pounding head. *What are* we *going to do?* I thought. *We are going to throw you out of this house. Then I am going to call a lawyer and take everything you've worked for, right down to the sticky shirt on your lumpy back.*

"I need *you* to get through this," he said. "She's a kid having a kid."

"Harvey, you're crazy!" I stared. Easily, my eyes could have popped out of my head.

"You mean you're not going to help me?"

"Huh?"

"I can't believe this. I'm always there for you—no matter what, no questions asked."

The thunder in my head crashed to a halt. I controlled myself with the fortitude a mother uses to lift an SUV off her child, and somehow, some way, I was able to calmly and sweetly say, "Of course I want to help. What should I do?"

He smiled. It was the biggest smile I had seen on his face since he'd sold his mastectomy division to Feminine Form. "I knew it," he said. "I knew you would help. Madison doesn't want to keep the baby. She said she's too young to be a mother."

"Of course," I said.

"You can understand that?"

"Of course I can. What about an abortion?"

"She doesn't want to have an abortion."

"Is she Catholic?"

"Argentine," he said.

I didn't want to know her nationality, or anything else about her this late in the game. I moved in for the kill. "I know—we should keep the baby."

"Are you serious?"

I nodded. Up and down. Up and down—with a sincere face—my eyes downcast.

"That's what I was hoping," he said in delirious amazement.

"I am a remarkable woman."

Harvey deserved to think this was going to be easy for him, that I was going to let him roll over me with an eighteen-wheeler, that I yearned to care for his blubbering baby.

"Feldman said you would never do it," he said.

"Our accountant knows about this? Our accountant knows her?"

"Of course he knows her."

He had probably been writing check after check to her. He probably did her tax return in Argentinian.

I wasn't sure I could hold it together much longer, but my need to extract further information while torturing Harvey was greater than my impulse to scalp him. After all, I'd have plenty of time to do that later. I was thinking about a Japanese knife, so I could slice his brain small as sushi—raw Harvey on a buffet. Actually, not sushi. Harvey sashimi. No rice.

"I think we should name the baby Lexington," I said. "In honor of Madison."

"Tell me something. You're joking about naming the baby Lexington, right?"

"I think Avenue of the Americas might be a better name."

He laughed with the abandonment of a drunkard in a bar on Saint Paddy's Day. I had a feeling I wouldn't laugh again for an exceedingly long time—if ever.

"How can I ever thank you?" he said.

I pretended to think for a moment. "Oh, I know, Harvey. You can thank me by dropping dead."

I handed him his trench coat and pointed to the door.

I poured a glass of Grey Goose in the kitchen, then washed down a prescription pain pill. Then I went to my bedroom and collapsed, cross-legged and shaking, in a dark corner. I was between my night table and the bookcase where I kept my favorite books.

The man was insane. I wanted him tortured, a filthy Harvey in tattered, sullied rags, in a decaying prison hell, a merciless dictator plunging his wild naked head under water. *Hold him down longer,* I thought. *Hold him down longer, until he chokes.* I imagined knives in a human chest. But it wasn't his chest. It was mine.

⌒

The sun came up. I had no idea how long I had been sitting on the floor, my eyes wide-open, but it was light outside. I glanced at the clock across the room on the night table. It was eight.

I heard the landscaper shouting to his helpers, then the jarring noise of the tractor. That's what my entire situation felt like—a grating lawn mower rolling over my body, starting at my feet, crushing every part of me—my thighs, my back, my shoulders, my neck, my head. I felt literally mowed down.

Slowly, I stood up and walked down the stairs. In the kitchen, I managed to dial Dana but clicked off before the call went through, before I would hear "Dana Davenport. Leave an interesting message."

There was no one in this world I wanted to know about this. Ever. I collapsed onto the floor and crumpled into a ball.

I called Dana again fifteen minutes later.

"His girlfriend is pregnant," I said, mortified as I heard the words come out of my mouth for the first time.

Dana had no comeback line. Things were worse than I imagined. "I am devastated for you," she said. "What can I do?"

"Throw her down a long flight of stairs?"

"Done."

"She's twenty-two," I said.

"They're all twenty-two, except when they're twenty-four."

"She doesn't want the baby."

"Who told you that?" Dana asked.

"Harvey."

"Now, there's a trustworthy source. What else did he tell you? Did he mention that the government planned 9/11? Of course she wants the baby."

"I don't know. Maybe she realizes she's too young to take care of a child."

"You're endowing her with intelligence? She's not a brain surgeon. She's a model. And not even a real model. A fitting model."

"That's what my mother said."

"You told your mother she's pregnant?"

"No, of course not. She said it when I said Harvey was having an affair. I told him to leave." I blew my nose and wiped my eyes with a pink oven mitt shaped like a pig. I knew exactly when I'd bought it. It was one winter day I'd planned to bake brownies with the kids when school was out. I bought a pig mitt, a turtle mitt, and a snail mitt—one for each child. Ben was whining because Amanda snatched the turtle; he wanted it because he'd once had a real turtle and his imaginary friend was named Turtle. I separated the two and told Amanda to give Ben the turtle.

That was eons ago. When I was actually alive.

Chapter 17

The law firm was located on the top floor of an office tower with the architectural design of oddly stacked boxes. The reception area was filled with Oriental rugs, brass-trimmed armoires, and trinkets from all over the world. An Asian bookcase showcased a collection of elephants— wood-carved, stuffed, painted, ceramic, silver, and brass.

The receptionist was on the phone with a person clearly in distress. I stared out the enormous window into the wet, dreary morning sky, studying the private helicopters landing on the building to the right. I was considering hailing one of the whirlybirds and taking off, without destination, when a slender woman, older than I was, emerged from the corridor and laid claim to the reception area.

"You must be Marcy Hammer," she said, as though never happier to meet anyone.

I nodded as I took her in. She was glamorous, long and lean. Her hair, streaked gray and white, was tucked into a bun.

"Grace Greene," she said with authority, extending her hand to me.

No Grace, I thought, remembering what my friend Abby had said.

I followed her into a grand office. She pointed to the conference chair opposite her desk. I sat down, my pocketbook—more of a sack—in my lap. I smoothed my suit and shifted in my chair. I had never seen a lawyer about anything in my entire life.

I glanced at the diplomas framed in tortoiseshell on her wall, a degree from Yale Law School and a BA courtesy of the University of Pennsylvania.

"What can I do for you?" Greene said as she lifted a teacup to her lips.

"I guess that's what I am here to find out," I said with a weak smile.

"Touché," she said. "Please tell me what is going on."

"My husband had an affair with a twenty-two-year-old and now she's pregnant," I said in one breath. I had never said it like that, all at once, the entire story in a sentence. And when I said it that way, the choice seemed clear. I had to divorce him. How could I stay with a man, even one I loved, who was having a child with another woman? I would be a total dishrag.

Greene sighed, shaking her head in concert, as though she had never heard a more pathetic outpouring. "How devastating. How shattering for you."

"He told me about her when he moved out, then we reconciled, then he told me she was pregnant, and it was too much for me."

"How long have you been married?"

"Thirty-three years."

"Men are unbelievable," she said sympathetically.

"Where do I stand?" I asked.

She leaned forward like she was confiding in me. "I'm sorry to tell you that whether he had an affair, and whether she's having a baby, will not weigh much in a divorce settlement."

"But he cheated," I said petulantly. "He wrecked our marriage."

"No matter. Maybe it's worth a few points in the allocation."

I was outraged. "But how can that be?"

"That's the way it is," she said. "Besides, and it will hurt to hear this, we don't know what claims he will make about you, true or false. So tell me, what would he say about you?"

Me? Why did she want to know about me? I hadn't caused this misery.

I thought for a moment. "He would say I wear a 36C."

"That's what he would say?" She stopped sipping her tea and laughed.

"He's in the lingerie business. I guess he would say I was a good mother. We have three grown children—twenty-nine, twenty-six, and twenty-four."

"And your financial situation?"

I told her about the bounty of Bountiful.

"We'll need a forensic accountant to audit your husband's business," she said.

Feldman would not be happy about this.

I told her the house was in my name, because Feldman had told Harvey to put it in my name. I told her we had investments in the stock market, but I didn't know much about it or all the names of all the stocks. Then I remembered a conversation between Harvey and Amanda, when Amanda was fifteen and we went to Orlando, and I said that I knew we had shares of Disney. I said Harvey liked mutual funds.

"And do you work?"

"I work at an arts organization, a nonprofit. I just got promoted."

"It's critical that you keep your job. We don't want you to appear lackadaisical."

Lackadaisical? I had worked my entire life, raised three children, ran a home, served as PTO president for four consecutive years, and volunteered until I needed a calendar for it. I had just accepted a job as executive director at Guild for Good, and I was caring for my mother, who was still in the hospital with broken ankles, cancer, and pneumonia.

"Have you always been in the nonprofit arena?"

"No. I started out in advertising."

"I'll bet you were good at it."

"I was very good." I blushed. I was bragging in a futile attempt to compensate for not being secretary of state, and for not knowing exactly how much money we had and exactly where it was planted.

She leaned back in her chair, folding her arms over her stomach, as though she had just finished a seven-course Italian meal. "As I understand it, you, like so many well-educated, ambitious women, forfeited your tremendous career to have his children."

"My children too," I said.

"Are you sorry you gave up your career?"

"Yes, of course."

"What a loser," I could hear her thinking. Greene was a powerful attorney, and I had spent my life playing second fiddle to Harvey. I wondered if she had children, and if so, how many, boys or girls.

"You said your husband earns into the mid to high six digits? From my experience, that means it could be more. Here's what I think. I think you deserve the chance to earn what you're worth. A chance you passed on to take care of him and his children. This is it. This is why I handle divorce."

"What I want to know is what I should do," I said.

"Well, first you have to be ready to do what you should do. Are you ready?"

I nodded. But I wasn't sure I meant it.

"You have to be ready to assault."

"I can't assault," I said from my alternate universe.

"Why?"

"We have three children together. Lovely children. If I attack, he'll counterattack. Then it's warfare. Besides, he hasn't done anything yet."

"You just told me he has a pregnant girlfriend. It seems he has done something."

"I meant financially, in terms of money. I'm living as usual—in my house. With Visa and American Express. Terrible as all this is, I want to take the high road."

"Marcy, I have practiced matrimonial law for forty years. If you find the high road, I want you to let me know." She finished her tea and moved the cup to one side.

"I have to think about this. I don't even know if Harvey has a divorce attorney."

"Of course he does," she said with a smile.

"Well, then what if I wait to see what his plan is?"

"Not a good idea."

I held my hands to my head.

"I am the child of divorced parents," Greene said. "I am divorced as well. I know how tough this is. Dissolving a marriage is devastating. I believe you should think long and hard before arriving at a decision about divorce. That said, I am here for you. And down to the shirt off his back, I am ready to do whatever it takes."

She stood to shake my hand.

Initial consultation over, I went to the ladies' room and looked in the mirror.

"Who are you? Who are you?" I asked my face.

Why was I asking? I knew who I was.

I was a woman who had been married to Harvey Hammer for thirty-three years. I could stay married to him until my mother got well. There was no way I could deal with a divorce now. When I was ready, I could find a lawyer with some grace.

Chapter 18

My mother was ready to be transferred to Valley Care, a top-notch rehabilitation facility that Candy had recommended. There, she would be well taken care of, and able to stay off her feet. The facility would provide transportation to and from her cancer treatments.

When I went to the hospital to make arrangements, Candy was in the main lobby. Her flawlessness in the face of her parents' story was awe-inspiring, as well as completely depressing to me.

"I ran into your husband going into your mother's room," she said.

"You did?" Was that his penitence? Visiting my mother?

"I told him you were on your way, but he said he couldn't wait. He had a meeting."

"Yes," I said. "That's him all right."

"I thought he'd be tall and dark," Candy said.

"Instead of short and red?"

"Red?" she said.

"Before he was bald," I said.

"Marcy, he's not bald. He's just missing some hair."

"Yes, the hair on his head."

"He's considerate. That's a wonderful trait."

"Harvey loves my mother. The problem is that he's not so fond of me."

"But you told me that he came home. That he asked to come home when you met him at Five Swallows. I'm sorry if it's turned out badly."

I could see she was pained, sincerely pained. I was not entitled to unload on her. Not while carrying the secret that could destroy her. Besides, once I told Candy about Elisabeth and Brian, our friendship would be terminated, the whole subject of Harvey and his progeny, moot.

"My mom is waiting," I said. "I brought hot soup." I handed a takeout container to Candy. "And here's one for your dad. I hope he likes corn chowder."

"He's sleeping. I'll be in the visitors' lounge."

⌒☉

I spent about an hour with Mom, who said she had told Harvey not to visit her if he was once again living out of the house.

I had to change the subject. "Mom, we need to style your hair before we go."

"Just getting out of the hospital will make me look better," she said. "Of course, I could have done without the rehab."

"Not if you want to walk again."

"True," she said, picking up a mirror to take a look at her hair. "Candy is so nice. She offered to wash my hair. But the nurse is going to do it. When the nurse comes, you take Candy and go for a nice lunch in a nice restaurant. It'll be my treat. Have coq au vin. I love coq au vin. It's what I ordered whenever your father took me to a French place."

A nurse appeared. I went to the visitors' lounge, where I found Candy on her cell. She was telling Jumper that she had mailed a care package to his school. I imagined the package—each item tagged with a calligraphic note.

"I liked your husband," she said when she got off the phone. "But I don't think I would have picked him for you."

"Then I should have let you pick," I told her.

"That sounds as though things aren't good."

"Not good would be an improvement."

Thoughtfully, she moved on. "I'm planning on redoing this visitors' lounge."

"Maybe you should ask first." It was a joke, but it went right past her.

"I loathe that we are waiting in this repugnant lounge, and that when people are going through the worst times of their lives, they have to congregate here."

"You would be doing a good deed."

"I'm also going to donate new wallpaper to the Alzheimer's wing at my mother's home."

"Whoa on that one. Save your money. It's an Alzheimer's wing—just *say* that you changed the wallpaper. That's good enough."

A volunteer poked her head into the lounge. "I'm looking for Marcy Hammer," she said tentatively.

I raised my hand.

"We're releasing your mother soon. Would you like to travel with her in the ambulance?"

"I would, but if I leave my car here, I have no way to get back."

"I'll follow the ambulance," Candy said.

"No, no. I couldn't ask you to do that."

"You're not asking. I'm offering."

◯╲

I crouched inside the ambulance. My mother nodded off and snored while I made small talk with the EMT.

When the vehicle reached Valley Care, I spotted Elisabeth, in pants and a toggle coat, standing by a sign that said "Rest, Recover, and

Renew." I had called her to tell her that Mom was being admitted, but I had no clue she would show up.

The thought of Elisabeth meeting Candy while my mom was being hoisted out of an ambulance on a stretcher was enough to make me wish I hadn't eaten breakfast or lunch, or anything ever.

I looked back. Candy was parked in her Mercedes, a few yards away. I watched, relieved, as she leaned her laptop on her steering wheel. She was working, maybe answering e-mails. She was not getting out of her car.

I needed Elisabeth to go before it became necessary to introduce her to Candy. I knew all her buttons, and the only way to facilitate her departure was to annoy her. "I can't take care of my own mother because I don't have a medical degree?" I said.

"That's what I get for leaving an emergency room packed with sick people?" Elisabeth said.

I had gone too far. I was throwing over Elisabeth, my own blood, my baby.

"Who's that?" Elisabeth asked.

I pretended I didn't hear.

"Mom, who is the woman sitting in the Mercedes and looking at us?"

"Just an acquaintance, someone I met at the hospital. She followed the ambulance. She's going to take me back to my car."

"That's really good of her. Tell you what. I'll admit Grandma so your friend doesn't have to wait. Go get your car and come back."

"Do you think Grandma would mind?"

"Mom, she'll totally understand."

I looked at Candy looking at us. Did she recognize Elisabeth? Could she tell she was my daughter? Maybe Candy thought she was a physical therapist at the facility. I could hope.

"Candy, soon-to-be-abandoned woman, I want you to meet my eldest daughter Elisabeth. She is having sex with your husband and there's a solid chance she will be his next wife." The thought of Brian dumping Candy

to be with Elisabeth was upsetting on so many levels I wanted to jump off the highest one.

As the attendants moved the stretcher from the ambulance to the ground, Elisabeth told Mom she would stay while I retrieved my car.

～

I fastened my seat belt in Candy's car.

"Who was that?" Candy asked.

"My daughter," I said.

"What a great-looking girl."

The last thing I wanted to do was hear compliments about my daughter from Candy.

"She's a knockout," she said. "She's young and beautiful, with all of her wrongheaded decisions in front of her."

Not so far ahead of her, I thought. "Thanks for this favor," I said.

"It's my pleasure. After all, you've helped me enormously."

"You badger a nurse for my parent, and I'll badger one for yours," I said.

"It's more than that. No one cheers me up like you do," she said as she steered left onto one of the most heart-clogging roads in America, a carnival of fatty meat and fried carbohydrates—starting with two McDonald's, a Burger King, and a Wendy's.

"I'm happy when I make people laugh," I said as we drove past a Taco Bell and a KFC. I felt guilt-ridden and shameful, and what I was really thinking was *You won't think so much of me once you know the truth.* Carrying around the secret of my daughter and Candy's husband had become a load that was breaking my back.

"Brian made me laugh. Until I married him—then he made me cry. I guess we know each other well enough for me to tell you that my husband and I are on the edge."

So she knows her marriage is in trouble. Maybe she knows Brian is sleeping with a younger daughter—I mean, woman.

"Actually, it's been over a long time, but I can't bear to tell him."

I was surprised that she was unhappy in the marriage, and shocked that she would reveal any of this to me.

"Eventually, it became seasonal," she said.

"What do you mean 'seasonal'?"

"I wanted to separate in December, but it was before Christmas, and it's our favorite holiday. I decorate everything. Our tree is always in the center of the living room, ringed with presents all around. I couldn't ruin Christmas for my son. So I decided to wait until after New Year's, but then I didn't want to spoil Jumper's birthday—which is later in January. Valentine's Day seemed too cruel, so I gave him a bottle of his favorite Scotch. Then in March, there was a father-son scuba trip to the Bahamas. I thought about after Mother's Day, but Brian's father, who he's very close to, was diagnosed with Parkinson's disease. Jumper goes to a sleepaway camp in northern Maine for July and August, so I decided to wait until he left for camp—that was the ideal time to confront Brian—but he slipped on a dock while mooring his boat and broke his leg, and I couldn't strike while he was miserable and hobbling around on crutches. Just the other day, I decided I would tell him in November, but then I realized that would destroy Thanksgiving. We go to Plymouth every year, and I paint there. I love the color of the cranberry bogs."

"What about Martin Luther King Day?" I said it as a joke, but I was sure of one thing—the holidays were all excuses. She loved the man, and there wasn't a date on the calendar she wouldn't utilize to procrastinate about the inevitable—choosing to live in hope, not separate in despair.

"Now I have to deal with two ill parents," she said, "and I can't deal with anything else."

In my own sick way, I was relieved to hear her marriage was falling apart. Elisabeth was not the cause. Elisabeth was merely the effect. I wondered whether Harvey had been thinking of separating from me for months on end. Whether maybe he would have left me earlier— sometime in January—but had hesitated because he'd realized it was approaching Groundhog Day.

Chapter 19

Immediately, Mom liked Valley Care—especially one of the nurses, Jazmin. She was a single mother who had helped every one of her five children through a four-year college. Jazmin had a grandson who was a doctor. My mother had Elisabeth. It was kismet.

I decided that Jazmin was the best thing that had ever happened to me. My mother *liked* Jazmin. I *loved* Jazmin.

One night when my mother was asleep, I told Jazmin about Harvey. I left out the part about the baby, a little detail I had also still never told my mother.

"You need to get on with your life," Jazmin said as she handed me a can of ginger ale and a vanilla pudding.

"Too much going on," I said.

"There will always be too much going on."

I knew Jazmin was on duty a couple of days later, so I spent a morning with Dana. We were sitting in the club chairs stationed by the piano in Nordstrom, waiting for the twins, who were trying on clothes.

"My mother's nurse gave me a pep rally," I said.

"What did she say?"

"Get on with it."

"You should go on a date."

"Are you nuts?"

When I thought about going out on a date, I thought about my shortcomings. I was older than I had ever been. I was saggy at the knees, sad in the brain, and out of practice. I was too chewed-up to be charming for an evening. I was too hurt to be hurt again.

I had no idea what it would be like to kiss someone other than Harvey. And sex? The concept of taking off all of my clothes, of complete nudity, was overwhelming. Once I was freed from the mortification of the high school locker room, I'd never stood fully undressed in front of anyone but Harvey again.

My friends didn't know I felt this way. Sweetly, they had been looking out for me. When Colleen called to check if I had seen No Grace, she told me I should bring my car to the town garage, because the new mechanic was hot. Then there was Abby. She had called me with the most promising news of all—her dermatologist had just lost his wife.

I listened as Dana talked up dating like she had minutes ago invented it herself. But I was not Dana. I was not a former cheerleader with long blond hair and a track record for man-hunting. I'd had one serious boyfriend before Harvey. What's more, Harvey and I were still legally married.

Right now I just wished Dana would hand over the American Express to her kids, which was the entire reason they had invited us along.

Dana stood up, hands on hips. "I'll bet Arlen knows someone. A starter. You have to get started. A journey of a thousand miles begins with a single step."

Arlen was an account executive at Dana's advertising agency. He was about our age, handsome, and personable. Always when he smiled, I thought his mother had taken him to a good orthodontist.

The girls approached, ponytails swinging, piles of tops and bottoms and dresses in their lovely young arms.

"Cull," Dana said. "Four items apiece. No butt cleavage, please."

⌇

Dana worked fast. That afternoon, someone named Peter shot me an e-mail and asked if I would like to have dinner. No precursory quips. No introductory coffee. No clumsy "Let's meet for drinks, then we'll see." Peter started with the main meal.

I called Dana.

"Who is this guy? He wants to have dinner right up front?"

"And that's bad because . . . ?"

"I don't know if I can do a whole dinner. I don't know if I can do a handshake."

"I've never met him, but Peter is Arlen's brother. And Arlen is a great guy."

"So what? In every family there's one winner brother, one loser brother. Every man who has ever been president has an alcoholic, drug-dependent sibling who plays guitar in a tone-deaf garage band for a living."

"He's never been married."

"So he's gay."

"Marcy."

"What does he do?"

"He was in the appliance business."

"Fascinating—he sold washers and dryers all day."

"Harvey sells bras all day."

She had a point, but I wouldn't let her score. "That's different."

"So don't go. Sit in your house and have pizza delivered. Better yet, date the delivery guy from Papa Antonio's. He's the person you see most often."

I considered the pizza comment the lowest of blows, subterranean. But it was the truth. And I had the empty pizza cartons piled in my garage to prove it. I had to do something. And this Peter was making it simple.

"His last name is Lerner," Dana said, "but don't bother looking him up. I tried. There's nothing."

"Nothing about him online? That means he's definitely a loser."

"There's almost nothing about *you* online."

The Won Ton was in a shopping plaza with a Goodwill store, a dry cleaner, a bagel place, a pizza parlor, and a shuttered barbershop with a busted pole. We met insanely early—he wanted to dine no later than five thirty. I drove once around the busy parking lot but didn't see anyone waiting outside the restaurant. No way was I going to arrive before Peter.

I parked inconspicuously, facing the restaurant head-on, between a turquoise Camaro on jacked-up wheels and a Honda with Democratic bumper stickers from three presidential elections. I saw a tall, solid older man, with graying hair and bushy eyebrows, coming out of the restaurant, adjusting his belt, and glancing around the lot. He was in an open brown coat, white shirt, and pants I call "daddy Dockers." He checked his watch and paced, as though he had no patience for someone who was late.

He looked around some more. I could see that his face was as wrinkled as a linen dress crammed in a suitcase for two weeks, but he wasn't bad-looking.

I couldn't believe my life had come to this.

But I managed to take a breath long enough to recognize that he wasn't the full-tilt disaster I had expected. *Just go eat Chinese food with him,* I told myself. *Share an egg roll.* What a thought. *Then you will have gone on a date—and then you can decide, based upon brutal experience, never to date again.* Then I could tell Abby I didn't care if her dermatologist's wife was alive or dead.

I had dressed conservatively—in my navy peacoat and navy slacks and a French blue shirt. I wore a silver necklace, two rings, my watch, and a bangle. I gathered my withered forces and walked directly up to him, my bag in hand.

"You must be Marcy," he said.

"And you're Peter." *Petered out,* I thought as I shook his creased hand.

As he released my hand, he looked not at me but into the restaurant. "Ready to eat? It's a buffet on Thursdays. That's why I said we should go tonight. Also, we need to be seated by six."

Who makes a reservation at a Chinese restaurant in a shopping plaza?

"It's six-fifty more a person after that," he said.

It was too late to turn back. But if I kept refilling my plate, I could limit my time at the table.

He held open the smudged door to the restaurant, revealing vinyl booths and large round tables, a cloudy tank with whale-size goldfish, most probably considering suicide, colored umbrellas in the drinks, a studded bar favored by slumped-over middle-aged boozers, white—as in Caucasian—waitresses in washed-out, worn-out Hawaiian shirts and miniskirts.

An actual Chinese hostess, however, showed us to our seats. I sat down in the booth facing the buffet, anticipating a go-ahead from a waitress, and/or some introductory chatter from my first-ever blind date. Peter remained standing. "Let's get it on," he said, pointing to the buffet.

Not sure whether to stay seated forever or follow Peter to the buffet, I chose the latter. A waitress stopped me and asked if I would like soda. "Diet Coke," I replied.

"And what about your father?"

I bit my hand so I wouldn't laugh.

I walked two stretches of hot Chinese foods gone cold, with some American mixed in—French fries, barbecued wings, salad, red gelatin, cans of whipped cream.

Peter tapped me on my shoulder.

I shuddered.

"Get a load of these ribs. From the pig that ate New York, right?"

I looked at the spare ribs lacquered with sweet-and-sour sauce. I made my way past a young family of five and an elderly couple holding hands while ogling the food as though it were Michelin five-star, and walked over to the cauldrons of soup. I was spooning egg drop when I felt Peter come up behind me. He was standing way too close.

"Great choice, right?"

"Very nice," I said.

"I know restaurants, right? Ask me about any all-you-can-eat in any town."

"Atherton."

"That la-de-da town?"

"I live there," I said.

"The Sunday brunch at Five Swallows, right? But I don't go there. You should see the blowhards."

I thought of Harvey, and my sense of humor was back.

I carried my soup to the dim booth. Peter arrived with two plates. One plate was overwhelmed with ribs; the other, with an epic supply of cashew chicken, egg rolls, and pork fried rice. *It's a buffet,* I thought. *You can go back.*

"My favorite restaurant," he said, lifting a rib to his mouth and yanking off a chunk of meat.

This will be over soon, Marcy. Enjoy the duck sauce.

I tried to make conversation. I brought up Dana's coworker, his brother, Arlen.

"Arlen's my boy, right? He's like a son to me. I guess he told you that there's a fifteen-year age difference between us, right? My mother was pregnant in high school, right? Much later, she married—and that's Arlen."

When he had eaten his last lychee nut, Peter paid cash from a wad of bills in a rubber band. He insisted on walking me to my car. He said he'd like to go out again.

I said, "That's nice."

He suggested a baked-bean supper. Baked-bean suppers were held at his fraternal order on the first Wednesday night of the month.

I said, "That's nice."

Then I hit myself over the head for going on a date when I wasn't ready to date. I had enough to deal with, without having to immerse myself in a ritual I hadn't experienced since John Travolta had Saturday night fever.

Chapter 20

My cell was ringing. I sat up in bed. It was dark outside. It was six o'clock on a January morning.

I answered the phone.

"Your mother has had a heart attack," a man said.

Still in pajamas, I rushed to put on my snow boots.

In a panic, I got into my car with no coat on. The streets were empty, and the lights turned green in my favor. I clutched the steering wheel, my hands sweaty and my knuckles white. I wiped tears running, flooding, down my face.

I screeched into a parking spot at the rehab facility. I raced inside.

I ran into Mom's room. She was in bed—a pillow under her head, a blanket to her chin. Medical equipment was in the way. I put my cheek to her cheek. Her skin was soft, baby-soft, as though she had just been born.

"Let her rest," a nurse said. "She's sleeping comfortably."

The nurse left. I pulled a chair up to the bed and held Mom's hand. "Mom, Mom." No response. I tried her name. "Lila, Lila."

She was wearing the necklace my father had given her when I was born. I stared at it. Never before had I noticed the thickness of the gold chain, the scalloped edge of the heart. It was so pretty. I kissed the necklace. I kissed her head.

"I'm here. I'm here," I said, as though my words would make her whole again.

I wanted to pray, but my mind went blank. *Say something. Pray something. Pray anything,* I told myself. I couldn't think in English, much less Hebrew, but then I remembered a Hebrew prayer my mother had said when I was growing up. I said it aloud, even though I couldn't remember all the words.

No, no, I thought, *that's the prayer for lighting the Sabbath candles.*

My mother was dying, and all I could come up with was the prayer for lighting the candles.

Then suddenly, another prayer came to mind. And another. It was like a prayer book had opened in my head. Suddenly, I remembered the prayer for bread, the prayer for traveling, the prayer for rainbows. I recited the Shema, the most important prayer of all, completely, rapidly, from beginning to end.

I felt my mother let go of my hand. Something was wrong. I ran into the hallway. A doctor appeared. He bent over my mother. No breath. No pulse. Her pupils were fixed.

"Resuscitate her, resuscitate her," I shrieked, but the shriek was mostly in my head.

He said she was gone.

No, no, no. Not now, not yet.

She'd once told me she wanted to live to be a hundred. And I was stupid enough to ask why.

Oh no, oh no, I heard my heart say. *I don't understand.* She was fine when she got here. She had broken both of her ankles. She had cancer. But she was fine. After this, my mother was going home or to my house. Whatever she needed.

"Mom, Mom, Mom," I repeated, I chanted, I cried.

"Take your time," I heard a voice say.

I sat there, on her bed, staring at her face, memorizing it, memorizing her lips, her lines, with no idea what to do next.

∽

I was shaken by sounds in the hallway. *Show some respect,* I thought. *My mother just died. How could the world go on? Why didn't it stop?*

I took my cell phone out of my pocket. It was then that I realized I had run out of my house in nothing but pajamas and boots.

I stared at my phone as though it had fallen from outer space. I looked at the first name on my "Favorites" list. I had never moved Harvey out of the top spot.

I wanted to call him, but I couldn't. I wouldn't. He should have loved me through this.

I called Elisabeth. Number two.

"It's Mom," I said.

"I'm in the middle of something. Can I—?"

"Grandma is gone," I said.

"What are you talking about?"

"She had a heart attack," I said.

"Oh no. Oh no," she said. "Where are you?"

"At Valley Care. In her room."

"Alone?"

"Yes," I said. "I am alone." I had never been more alone.

My husband was gone. My mother was gone. My whole life had been filled with people. And now I was alone.

"Elisabeth, I don't know what to do."

"Mom, I'm coming. I'll be there in half an hour."

"But what should I do?"

"Is there a chair?"

"Yes, there's a chair."

"Sit down in it."

"I'm sitting. I'm cold. I ran out of the house in my pajamas."

"Ask for a blanket. I'm calling the desk. A nurse will come in."

"I need water," I said. "Something to drink."

"Tell the nurse you need ginger ale," she said.

"I need ginger ale," I said slowly. "Elisabeth, I want you to call Daddy."

"I will. I'll call Daddy and Amanda and Ben. Dana too."

"Thank you, sweetheart."

"If you want, I'll try to reach Uncle Max."

"No. I'll do that."

"Are you sure you want to talk to him now?" she said.

"I have to. Grandma would want me to."

I got off the phone. In a few minutes, a nurse came into the room. She gave me a blanket and some water. She didn't stay. I wanted her to stay.

I phoned Max.

Maybe once, just once, I thought, *he'll act like the brother I always wished for.*

"Who is this? It's the middle of the night." He was on the West Coast. I had forgotten about the time difference.

"It's Marcy," I said. "There's terrible news, the worst. Mom passed away."

"Oh, geez. Geez. The cancer?"

"No, a heart attack."

"Huh?"

"It was sudden," I said.

"Oh, geez."

"I'm sorry, Max."

"I have a plane ticket for the red-eye on Thursday," Max said.

"You were finally coming in?"

"What does that mean?"

"Mom prearranged and prepaid the funeral. It's all planned—you know a Jewish funeral has to be in twenty-four hours, and I know Mom would have wanted her service to be in twenty-four hours. Can't you please get on a plane now?"

"My flight gets in around nine in the morning, and I got an aisle seat."

"Change the flight," I said.

"There's a one-hundred-dollar change fee."

I'm sorry, Max, I thought. *I didn't realize you had so many mothers.*

I didn't want to argue. Besides, maybe there were other people who needed a little extra time to come in for the funeral.

"Fine," I said to my brother. "I'll see you on Thursday."

Just then, Harvey called. I hadn't spoken to him since he'd announced the pregnancy.

"Hello, Harvey," I said, trying not to cry.

"Your mother was a wonderful woman."

"Yes."

"You are the best of her," he said.

"Thank you."

"Do you want me to come to Valley Care?"

"No," I said, realizing it was true. I didn't want him to come.

"Okay, then," he said.

"Thank you for calling," I said. Then I hung up the phone.

Dana called.

"Oh, Dana, this is unbearable."

"Elisabeth said she's coming for you."

"Dana, don't say this is going to be okay. This will never be okay."

"I know."

I wandered into the hall. A lot went by me. A man griping to his wife, some crackling announcements I couldn't decipher, a volunteer turning over a book cart somehow that caused a spill of water, a lot of mopping. I couldn't get a grasp on any of it.

"Oh, Mom," I said out loud. "I'm so sorry about the piano." My mom had insisted on piano lessons until I was ten, when the music teacher, a woman who smelled like decayed eggs, mailed Mom a note saying that I was disinterested, wasting her time and mine. My mom had been mortified. But the truth was that I was disinterested. I could have easily chopped up the upright and chucked it out a window one piece at a time. But now, now, I wished I could play the piano. I wished I could do everything my mom had ever wanted or asked me to do.

I was weeping so vociferously people in the corridor were staring at me and then turning the other way, pretending not to hear, not to see.

"Is there a chapel here?" I asked a nurse who came by to comfort me.

"I'll walk you," she said.

I sat staring at the stained-glass windows high above the mahogany walls. Was she in the sky yet? Was she in the sky?

The next morning, when Candy called in response to the message I had left her, I asked if she would come over and keep me company while I made calls to family and friends about the time of the funeral service.

She arrived bearing herbal tea from the natural foods restaurant on the road to town. It was the first time I had seen her dressed casually—if you can call black pants, a white shirt, and jewelry casual.

"Would you like me to make some calls?" she said, passing tea and a paper napkin to me.

"You would make calls?"

"Of course I would," she said.

I scribbled a list of second-string friends and relatives she could call.

"What day, what time, and where?" she asked.

"It's Thursday at one o'clock." I passed her a business card with the address of the home in Flushing, Queens.

"There's actually a place called Flushing?"

"I grew up there. On 170th Street."

"I lived on Canterbury. Then when I was ten, we moved to Devon."

"Devon Road?"

"No. Just Devon," she said. "After this, I have to call Jumper. He's receiving an award at school on Thursday, but I'll be at your mother's funeral. He's not going to be happy. His dad can't make it either."

"Candy, you should go to the school."

"No, no."

"You should go," I said. One less thing to worry about—I wouldn't have to introduce Candy to Elisabeth.

"Are you sure?"

"Go be with your son," I said.

She pointed to the paper I handed her. "Is this Uncle Toby or Uncle Tubby?"

"Uncle Toby, but on second thought, don't bother calling him. My dad had an argument with him and his wife, about a wedding gift—money—and civil war broke out."

"Our family never gives money," she said.

"I think I knew that."

"Are you making fun of my culture?" she said, smiling.

Joking around made me feel better, so I called Dinah, my mother's lifelong friend. She wasn't at home, but I left a message saying I had called, and since I never called Dinah, I knew that message would be code for "My mother died."

I turned to Candy. "I can't do this now. Am I a bad person?"

"No, but don't you want to get it over with?" she said. Candy was the kind of person who had never shirked a responsibility in her whole life and never procrastinated.

Truth was, my mind was on other things. For one, I was obsessing over what I should wear to the funeral service. I don't know why I was concerned with funeral attire. After all, anything black would do, and since I went into the city often, I owned plenty of black pants, skirts, long and short, and dresses. I had a hanging shoe bag full of black shoes. If you checked my closet, you would think I was a witch.

What's more, it was cold. I'd be wearing a coat, so why did it matter what I wore under it? It was my mother who always gave me the once-over at family events, and she certainly wouldn't at this one. I recalled the black jumper over silk blouse with limp bow I'd chosen for my father's service. There was no actual burial. My father had requested that his body be donated to the Yale School of Medicine, making Dad the first person in my family to go to the Ivy League.

After Dad was cremated, we scattered his ashes on Houston Street in New York City, where he had grown up. As we stood in our coats, hats, scarves, and boots, Mom made me promise I would bury her in the plainest pine coffin, with a rabbi speaking plenty of Hebrew at the service.

"This is pretty shallow," I said to Candy, "but all I can think about is what I'm going to wear to the funeral. Do I think I'm going to the prom?"

"Black," Candy said.

"I know black, but what black?"

"Do you have a suit? You need a suit, a classic. Let's go shopping."

"I can't go shopping. My mother died."

"How do you feel about mandarin collars?"

"I was thinking of having my hair blown at a salon, but I was afraid that if I looked too good my mother's friends would think I wasn't grieving enough."

"Let's go. There's a boutique in Westport that has just what you need."

"I can't go to Westport. My mother died."

Candy drove to Westport, where the saleswoman greeted us as though Candy was the second coming of Princess Diana. She showed me a rack of black suits in my size. I took the one with the mandarin collar and the large black buttons that Candy liked. Afterward, Candy insisted that I buy new black shoes. She pulled me into a shoe store, and I bought a pair of pumps.

I was sad that my friendship with Candy was going to end when I told her about Elisabeth. She would have no use for me after that. Who wants to befriend an absolute fraud? This would all end—like everything else—horribly.

There was a coffeehouse next to the shoe store. As we waited on line, the student in front of me—with a monogrammed L.L.Bean book bag, the Connecticut book bag of choice—ordered several drinks with long names. When we'd received our coffees, we sat down on brown velveteen armchairs in front of a fake brick fireplace.

"I bought a coffin," I told Candy. "It's plain pine. Jewish people tend to like fancy cars and plain coffins."

"Is your brother attending the funeral?"

"Yes. And, no matter what Max says or does, I am going to get along with him. It's what my mother would have wanted."

"There is a possibility he won't act the way you think he will," Candy said. "On occasion, people surprise us."

I welcomed such an occasion.

Chapter 21

A Rabbi Horowitz officiated at the funeral. I had received his name from a haggard woman in the cemetery office, who most likely was wearing the same cardigan she had thrown around her shoulders on her way to vote for Richard Nixon. Her glasses dangled on beads that stopped at her chest. Harvey would recommend a contour bra with comfort straps.

The funeral chapel was serene, though densely packed with black auditorium-style seats divided by a middle aisle. I had respectfully asked the rabbi to perform the service in Hebrew, my mother's wish. Besides, I didn't need a pat, meaningless speech from a rabbi who'd never met my mother.

I sat in the front left row surrounded by Elisabeth, Amanda, and Ben. Dana and Calvin and the girls were seated behind us. Dana tapped my shoulder. I turned. "Love pat," she said.

I squeezed Elisabeth's hand. She squeezed mine. Ben leaned his head on my shoulder.

"When I visited her, I needed a caravan to bring home all of the things she bought for me," Ben said. "She will always be with us. I'll think of her every time I witness an act of generosity."

I turned my head as Harvey entered the chapel. I hadn't seen my husband since the day he told me about his impending fatherhood.

Harvey greeted Leona's husband, Steve, who was in an aisle seat. Steve and Leona and their children scooted over to make room for Harvey. It was my mother's funeral, and my husband and I were separated by rows.

I spotted Roslyn, Mom's oldest friend, who had moved to Florida years before, and she saw me. I turned and faced the casket, which was under a velvet cloth. My entire childhood was behind me in rows.

The rabbi, in a fresh suit, was at the podium. He pulled his goatee and adjusted his white yarmulke over a bald spot in the center of his head, apparently his signal that he was about to begin. I heard mumbles and looked back. Max was walking down the aisle. He was tan, sporting sunglasses, a beige poplin suit, and Nikes.

"My brother," I mouthed to the rabbi.

The rabbi waited for Max, recited a Hebrew prayer, and then continued the service in English. *Kill the English,* I thought. *What part of "No English" didn't he understand?*

"I didn't know Lila, but I know that Lila would want me to talk first about her children, Marcy and . . ."

"Max," I mouthed to the rabbi.

"Max." He moved the yarmulke over his bald spot again. "And about her fine husband, Murray—may he rest in peace. From everything I have heard, I know Lila was devoted to her family, loving generously and selflessly. Family was her bedrock.

"She adored her wonderful grandchildren, Elisabeth, Ben, and Amanda," he said as he glanced at an index card on the podium and smiled at my children. "I learned a lot about Lila by talking at length with her dear devoted sister, Dottie."

Oh no. The rabbi must have spoken to Aunt Dottie. There was a lot to say about my mother, but I knew that Aunt Dottie had dwelled exclusively on what Mom did for my father, which in her era was to cater to his every need.

"When Lila's husband—of blessed memory—came home, a dinner was always waiting—a brisket and a noodle pudding, warm with apples—the way I myself like it."

The rabbi patted the podium and moved closer to the microphone. "And when Murray, may he rest in peace and be remembered for a blessing, woke up in the morning, his shower was hot because Lila turned it on and tested it. 'Murray,' she hollered, 'the shower is perfect!' Later, she'd prepare his breakfast, always an egg, scrambled with sweet red onions, and always a toasted bialy."

"A woman of valor, who can find?" the rabbi said. "Her price is far beyond rubies."

When the service had concluded, I saw Harvey helping Mom's friend Dinah into his car for the ride to the cemetery. I hated that he was being gracious. I wanted to roll down the window and shout, "Don't go with him. His girlfriend is having a baby."

I traveled to the burial in a stretch limousine with my children and Max. I wondered if he was shaken by our mother's death. Although Mom was always telling me to be good to him, she'd spent her time advising him about things he wanted no advice about.

He had gone to college as far away as he could get while still having her pay for tuition. He transferred around, always choosing a school that had a mountain to ski or a beach to lie on. He took six years to graduate at a time when more than four years of college was unheard of. He was a conniver, a gambler, and a party boy. I knew he loved me, but he'd always thought my state in life—married to a workaholic like

Harvey, living in the suburbs, staying home with kids, playing by the rules—was beneath him.

I was sure my mother had informed him that Harvey had left me, because he never mentioned anything about Harvey arriving alone, not sitting with us, and not being in the limousine.

Max shrugged off his jacket and loosened his tie. He cackled at the sight of the premium liquor in the well-stocked limousine bar and poured Scotch into a glass.

"I told the rabbi to give the eulogy in Hebrew," I said, annoyed about the service. But really, what service would have been good enough for my mom?

"Too bad he didn't," Max said, settling in with a drink. "Then we wouldn't have known what he was saying."

"I think 'bialy' is 'bialy' in any language," Ben said.

"Dad hated those red onions," I said.

"He did?" Max added an ice cube to his Scotch.

"Yes, he did. He always said, 'Lila, stop with the red onions.'"

"Sometimes I wonder if we grew up in the same house."

"I wonder if we grew up on the same planet," I said.

Ben poked me in the side lightly, as if to say "Don't let him upset you."

"Uncle Max, when was the last time you came home?" Ben asked, trying to save me.

"Early 1800s. When your mother got married."

Max turned on the television in the limousine. He flipped channels until he came to *Jeopardy!*

"What is 'syphilis'?" Ben said, responding to the TV show.

"Is the box with the safe deposit key still under the kitchen sink?" Max asked.

I ignored him.

"What is 'gonorrhea'?" Ben called out.

"Ben, what's the category?" Amanda asked.

"What do you think? Venereal diseases."

I kicked off my pumps. There was a run in my stockings from big toe to thigh.

"If you don't mind," Max began, so I knew I'd mind, "I'll drive Mom's car back to Los Angeles."

Fascinating what was on his mind.

"Who is 'William Shakespeare'?" we all said at once.

Max continued. "I think we should dispose of the house immediately. You can sell the furniture on Craigslist. Amanda, would you like to buy Grandma's so-called antiques from the estate?"

"As a matter of fact, I would," she answered as she rolled her eyes. I knew Amanda didn't want anything; Amanda was into new. And if she did want something, she wasn't giving Max a dime for it. "I want everything."

"That's not happening, Amanda. The living room is mine," Ben piped up. "But I will remove the plastic. It sticks to my ass. What is 'the Louvre'?"

"I like the plastic," Elisabeth said. "I'll fight you for the plastic."

How much did I love my children, my heroes?

"Uncle Max," Ben said, "is it okay if we divide the estate later? Some of us miss Grandma, loved Grandma. What is 'the Museum of Modern Art'?"

～◎～

Out of the heated limousine and into a cold day. I squinted as I looked back and saw car after car, headlights on, behind our limousine. Uncle Sidney and a few longtime friends of my mother's inched down the slope to her grave site. Harvey held Dinah's hand and helped her down the hill. He came up behind me and stood next to me. I wanted to walk away, but I didn't want my children to see me do it. Was Harvey solicitous, or did he believe all was forgiven because Mom had died? I hoped he was leaving right after the burial. The mere sight of him brought me grief, and I had grief enough.

I reached for Elisabeth's hand as the rabbi swayed back and forth, head down, praying rapidly from memory, without a prayer book. Max grasped one of the shovels, straight and tall in a high pile of dirt. The ping of loose earth striking the casket ripped through my ears, as shattering as the wail of a mother who's lost a child. Max handed his shovel to me. I lifted dirt slowly seven times, because seven was Mom's favorite number. Then Amanda and Ben took over, and Ben shoveled so steadily, so furiously, I thought he was going to finish the job without handing the shovel to anyone else. Suddenly he stopped short, straightened up, took a breath, turned around, and handed the shovel to Steve as Amanda passed hers to Elisabeth. It was Steve who passed the shovel to Harvey, directly across from me on the left side of the grave.

I could hear Harvey thinking, *"Should I pick up the earth or put down the shovel? Pick up or put down?"*

Was he irrational enough to think it was okay for him to place one speck of earth, one solitary pebble on my mother's grave?

Then I heard my mother say, *"Let him do it, Marcy. It's only dirt."*

Waiting and watching, I covered my mouth with my hand and felt my breath through my fingers. Harvey glanced at the remaining pile of soil and handed the shovel to me. It was all too much, too painful and overwhelming. I passed the shovel back to Harvey and he lifted a great heap of dirt.

Chapter 22

As I pulled onto my street, a bundled nanny waited for the school bus at the end of her icy driveway. A neighbor, the wire-haired shrink, was putting mittens on her toddler. Mom was gone, but the world went on. Not a soul missed a beat, and it felt more disrespectful than I could have imagined.

I had asked a neighbor to stay at my house during the funeral in case there were any deliveries. In my kitchen, there was a Luigi's lasagna from Dana; a casserole from Colleen; baskets of fruit blessed with kiwis; the leaning tower of condolence candy; and floral arrangements I didn't need. I read the card on a dozen roses:

> *Our prayers are with you.*
> *—Shapely Woman Inc.*
> *We support you.*

The doorbell. A short man stood next to a tall floor plant with a pot wrapped in foil and a ribbon:

For Harvey Hammer
In memory of your mother-in-law
—From your friends at URA
Underwear Retailers of America

I collapsed in my bed fully clothed.

⁓

The following afternoon, I was putting a black *X* on the date on my calendar, January 25, when I heard a car pull into the driveway. I thought it was Dana. Then there was a knock, one knock, and I knew it wasn't Dana. At a time like this, Dana would never knock on a door just once. Dana would pound on Harvey's brass Buddha knocker from his trip to China, ring the matching bell, and call my name.

I went to the door. The sun was bright for winter in Connecticut, reflecting on the snow. I put up my hand to block the light from my eyes. Candy was at the door.

"Oh, Candy, thank you for stopping by."

"I hope it's okay that I dropped in without calling first."

"It's a relief to see your face."

She was carrying a plastic bag, the kind with a drawstring. She placed it on the floor next to the door without saying a word about it.

She followed me into the kitchen, where several pints of ice cream were melting on the counter. She studied the containers but didn't say anything to embarrass me.

I grabbed a can of diet something from the refrigerator and offered it to her.

"Diet soda causes cancer in mice," she said.

"What are you worried about? You're not a mouse."

Candy said something else, but I didn't hear. My thoughts were rampant neon headlines popping in my head. Times Square had nothing on my brain. Every revolving flash had the word "Mom" in it.

"How are you feeling?" I finally heard her say.

"Sad. Lethargic."

"You should go for a long walk. You need to exercise. It will help you through this. After you get settled, and I know it will take a very long time, I want you to meet my personal trainer, Leonardo."

"Da Vinci or DiCaprio?"

Candy pointed to her shopping bag. "I washed and ironed your mother's laundry, the clothes you left in my trunk the day we followed the ambulance. I thought you might want to donate them."

"Thank you," I said. I couldn't think of another friend who would have laundered the dirty, rumpled garments I'd left in hospital bags in the trunk of a car, especially clothes my mother was obviously never going to need again.

"Are you going to your mother's place to take care of her things?"

"What?" I was having a hard time concentrating on what Candy was saying.

"Do you need help with anything—maybe your mother's house?" She was amazing. She was offering to help clean out my mother's house. Did she do this kind of self-sacrificing favor for everyone?

"No," I said at last. "I'm going to do it when my daughters can help."

"I wish I had a daughter. Maybe I'll adopt one of yours."

I can think of one you don't want to adopt, I thought.

I heard three rings and someone knocking loudly. Dana was at the door. She was carrying a bag of groceries, with family-size potato chips and a baguette poking out of the top.

"What a loss," she said as she hugged me, the bag between us. "The end of an era."

"I remember the first time your mom invited us to dinner. Jeremy was ten, and he had never seen such largesse. Your mom called to ask him what he liked for dinner. And there it was—fried chicken and mashed potatoes with chocolate chip cookies for dessert. Also, she gave him a present, a Papa Smurf. The boy was in love." Dana looked down the hall. "Who's here besides me?" she said.

"Candy. Come in and meet her."

As I introduced the two in the kitchen, I could hear Dana thinking: *"Oh, yes. What a pleasure to meet you. You're the woman who's married to Elisabeth's boyfriend."*

"I'm a great fan of your children's books," Dana said as she unpacked the baguette and the sour-cream-and-onion potato chips, along with a Nestlé Crunch bar, Hostess cupcakes, Brie cheese, Vermont cheddar, and a liter of Diet Coke.

At the sight of the diet soda, I was sure Candy was conjuring a laboratory full of mice chasing each other, dropping dead from a disease brought on by artificial sweetener.

Candy stayed a while, then said she had to get to the hospital to see her father.

"Thanks again for the laundry," I said.

"I know you would do the same for me," she said.

But of course I wouldn't. Candy was a much finer person than I was, and she was also fastidious. For sure, she ironed her dish towels. I was low-life enough to dump her mother's soiled apparel in a garbage bin and never mention it.

After Candy left, Dana waited at least three seconds to say, "Did you tell her about Elisabeth?"

"No."

"You have to tell her the truth, or you have to end your friendship."

"Are you the ethicist for the *New York Times*? I don't want to total my friendship with her."

I was drenched in melancholy, and any thought of eliminating a relationship with Candy was enough to sink me. I knew that much.

"You always do the right thing," Dana said. "This is not the right thing."

"She washed my mother's laundry," I said.

"She did?" Dana said as she opened the chips.

"Candy wants me to meet her personal trainer, Leonardo," I said as I reached into the family-size bag.

"Is that DiCaprio or da Vinci?"

$$\sim$$

That evening, I was about to go to sleep when Candy called me. "How are you feeling?"

"Like a bowl of liquid green gelatin."

"You should go for a long walk."

I took a walk to a fruit basket and extricated a bar of Godiva.

"Exercise would help," she said. "Leonardo is away now, but he returns next Friday. Can you come over and meet him?"

"I don't know," I said, even though I did know—I was not up for exercise. I wasn't even up for standing. I had turned into a vegetable, and my body was crying out for the old Marcy, the one who enjoyed a walk almost anywhere.

Why did loss have to be fattening? I knew there were other women in distress nauseated by food, not even real food, just the word "food." In my next life, I was coming back as a woman who became queasy at the thought of eating between meals.

"I'm not sure anything could make me feel better," I told Candy.

"Give it a try." She wasn't about to surrender.

"If I don't feel better, will you give me a refund?" I joked, aware I should at least feel grateful and comforted that someone cared about my latent physical decay as much as Candy apparently did.

When Harvey left (the first time), I could feel my most reliable clothing tightening, but I'd attributed this to the Tri-Town Cleaners, who were suddenly shrinking every article of clothing I brought there. I was so bothered by the shrinkage I had gone to Tri-Town and asked whether they had changed cleaning fluids. The answer was no. When I left Tri-Town, I had crossed the street to Kenny's Deli, my mouth watering for a corned beef sandwich. Now I had a horrific, overwhelming thought: *What if while I was gaining weight, Harvey was losing weight?*

Candy was right. I needed to exercise. "What time?" I asked her.

"Six," she said.

"Do you mean at night?"

"In the morning, before you go to work."

"That's nuts," I said. "I can't exercise at six. I can barely find my face at six."

"If you do it in the morning, it's done for the day."

"No, *I'm* done for the day."

"If you like Leonardo, you can hire him to come to your home and you can choose the time."

"Okay, maybe next week, or next month, or next year. Just in case, how do I get to your house?"

"All right turns. Go right out of your driveway, right at the McCourt apple orchard onto Pine Turn. You'll see River Run. Turn right again, and follow it to the end."

⌒

Two weeks later, just when I was looking myself over with disdain in the mirror, Candy called with purpose. She said she thought it was time for me to meet Leonardo. My reflection told me she was probably correct. I had put off her proposal long enough. I agreed to show up the next day.

Chapter 23

I turned right at the apple orchard onto Pine Turn, a curving two-lane road with an array of clapboard Capes and colonials set back just enough and spaced well apart, the front yards shaded by oaks. There were gray mailboxes on the road. The driveways were gravel.

One of the Capes had white ruffled curtains, except one window had gingham—blue. It was the kind of house I would have chosen when Harvey and I first moved out of New York—before we bought the house I didn't want, in the place I didn't want to live, so Feldman could bill Harvey for a strategic tax plan.

I had assumed River Run was the name of a street but when I came upon the words on a boulder, I realized River Run was the name of Candy's property. Her house was on a hill, overlooking a valley.

Her country mailbox was hand-painted with characters from her book *Walter in the Water* and set in a stone post. The driveway was cobblestone and wound its way to a gracious farmhouse, an all-white Southern-style home with a broad porch, the windows as large as doors.

Candy greeted me in casual clothes. I was wearing the sweatpants from the bottom of my closet and a sweatshirt with a hood that

Elisabeth had sort of bought for me when she was a college senior. She'd picked it out in the bookstore. I'd paid the account. Even so, it was good to be given a gift. I looked at my watch. Was I late? It was impossible to be early at six in the morning.

"Marcy, I left a message for you. Leonardo had to cancel," Candy said as I stepped onto her porch.

"I usually don't check my phone before daylight," I said.

She patted the rocker next to her, an invitation to sit down. "Leonardo apologizes."

"Do you have any coffee?" I asked. This could all be made better with a cup of coffee.

"Herbal tea?"

She was fully dressed and all chatty—without caffeine?

While Candy brewed chamomile, I wandered into the room next to the black-and-white kitchen. "This is fabulous," I called out from her great room.

"Oh, thanks," she shouted back.

The great room was stark white, but from the ceiling to below eye level, there were amazing paintings, contemporary art in riotous colors.

She handed me a cup and saucer.

"I love that one," I said, pointing to the picture closest to the French door that led to the back porch. She provided an exhaustive history of the artist, and how she had come into possession of the work.

"How long have you been collecting?" I asked.

"The day I sold my first illustration, I bought someone else's painting," she said. "I do that every time something good happens, buy a painting. I bought the last one two years ago."

"What was the occasion?"

"My most recent picture book, *Wonders of Walter*, hit the bestseller list. It was only for a week, but I thought that counted."

"Absolutely," I said.

"This is my favorite," she said, pointing to an abstract.

We reclined on the spotless white couch on the spotless white rug. There was a tri-level coffee table in front of the couch with enormous art books and a marble vase with flowers. There were open white armoires, and books stacked this way and that—as though placed randomly, instead of carefully, one by one, by Candy.

"This room is perfect."

"The room, the whole house, was featured in a few magazines."

"Well, I'm glad I got to see the house," I said.

"I want to give you a tour," she said. "You'll love our attic."

"Why? Is it messy?" I laughed, then sipped my tea. It needed sugar, of course.

I considered Leonardo's absence a signal. It was meant to be.

I could now confess to Candy in her own home. She could chuck me out onto the cobblestone road. If I ever saw her house again, it would be in a magazine. I decided I would tell her when I finished my chamomile.

I didn't. I decided I would tell her when she returned from the kitchen with more tea.

But I wasn't sure how to say it. I could just say it straight out: *"My daughter is having an affair with your husband."* Or I could back into it. Talk about Elisabeth first, and then tiptoe through her latest activities.

"Brian adores that painting," Candy said as she pointed to a skier in blue snow. "He says snow should be blue, and the sky should be white. The way the picture is."

"If the sky were white," I said, "we wouldn't be able to see the clouds."

"Exactly," she said.

"I see Brian's point." I couldn't believe I had said his name. I had to tell her. I was going to tell her. "Candy . . ."

"He filed for separation," she said, staring at the blue snow and the white sky.

My face dropped. "When did you find out?"

"Yesterday," she said.

My fingers were pacing on her coffee table. Was Brian leaving Candy for Elisabeth? Never did I think this would happen. Why hadn't I told her? Why hadn't I spoken up before he filed? I was a coward, immobile on her couch.

When she turned toward me, I was sure she could see the guilt in my eyes. I looked ahead at the fireplace. A forest could burn in that fireplace.

"I should have divorced him years ago, but I kept hanging on, hoping he would change. He's a player."

So Brian was playing with Elisabeth. I felt so bad for my daughter. *Why hadn't Elisabeth listened to me? Oh, yeah, now I remember—because no girl listens to a parent when the subject is a boyfriend.*

"I didn't want to admit Brian was a fool's choice," Candy continued. "You need to understand that my parents never liked him, never trusted him, and my father said he was not an honorable man. I guess I didn't want my father to be right."

"I know your father. He'll be beside you no matter what."

I had to come clean about Elisabeth before she found out another way. It was the right thing to do, and it had been the right thing all along. I wished we were sitting farther apart. Slowly, a little at a time, I moved to the other side of the couch. But that wasn't far enough. I stood and walked away from the couch, and then to the couch—pacing until Candy knew something was very wrong.

"What?" she said.

Think of something, Marcy. Permeate the air with nonsense.

"What?" she repeated.

"I don't know. It's so sad."

"Well, it's over. And I have to go on, and I will."

I looked out the window. But the truth was in the room. I tried to speak, and then I did. "Candy, I have something to tell you. I should have told you long ago. But we both had so many problems. My daughter Elisabeth, my oldest daughter, the one you saw at the rehab facility, the doctor—she's seeing your husband, and I didn't know how to tell you. I mean, I didn't want to tell you. Because I didn't want to hurt you, and I thought I could convince her to give him up. After all, he's an old man. I didn't mean that. He's old compared to my daughter. First, I didn't tell you because I felt that I needed you, and you needed me. Then you washed my mother's laundry, so I loved you for that, and I didn't want to hurt you."

"You didn't want to upset me because I was your washerwoman?"

I shuddered, shaking my head, as I rushed desperately to explain. "I didn't mean it that way."

"What way did you mean it?" she asked sternly.

I was cold. I was shriveling, shrinking. I had never felt more shameful. I had never felt smaller. There were dust mites bigger than me. I had to respond, but I knew whatever I said, it was going to be the wrong thing. There was no right thing. I was in a disaster movie. The ship was going down. And I deserved to be on it. There was no lifeboat for me.

"I just meant that I value your friendship." It was honest. I meant it wholeheartedly, but it sounded like a ninety-nine-cent birthday card from Walmart.

"This is what you call 'value'?" she said.

I had never seen her angry, and it was transforming her face.

"You're important to me," I said, stopping myself from crying. What right did I have to cry?

"And what—if I wasn't important to you, you yourself would have had an affair with Brian? I'm so glad I'm important to you."

I stopped talking, because I couldn't think of a thing to say that she wouldn't turn into venom. Not that I blamed her. Why hadn't Leonardo shown up? I would have been out of breath, and this conversation would never have happened. On the other hand, the truth was out at last.

Candy stared at me in silence. Her face became pale and pained. I wanted her to say something. Anything would do.

"Candy?" I said, as though questioning whether she was in the room. "Please say something."

I deserved her rage and fire, but her silence was death. I was unaccustomed to a person who was silent when vilifying me. I faced an intimidating force I'd never encountered before. Silence was her artillery. The lack of sound was deafening.

"I'm sorry," I said again.

She walked to the door and opened it without saying a word. The cold February air rushed in.

"I apologize," I pleaded, like that was sufficient. "I didn't want to add to your problems. I told her to stop seeing him—over and over—well before I realized he was your husband, and after. Harvey begged Elisabeth to stop seeing him. Candy, I don't know what else I could have done."

Still holding the door, she spoke. "So if she'd left him, then what? You would never have told me?"

"I don't know."

"Would you have told me, or wouldn't you?" She swatted the door back and forth.

"Eventually I would have told you," I said as I approached the door. "I would have told you," I repeated. But I knew it was hopeless, and worst of all, unforgivable.

Candy shut the door behind us. We were face-to-face on her porch. I was no longer good enough to set foot in her house. "Don't tell me that your daughter is serious about him."

Candy was steamed, as steamed as someone like Candy could become, but she was calmer by a long shot than I would have been had the situation been reversed. Maybe she was medicated. She lifted her arms, and then rolled her neck back and forth. "I needed Leonardo today," she said. "My life is better when I work out."

"I didn't know when to tell you." The more I spoke, the more loathsome and despicable I felt.

Then she knocked me over completely.

"You had news for me, and now I have news for you. The woman my husband is leaving me for is a forty-year-old large-animal vet."

"What do you mean? A veterinarian? Like a vet who takes care of dogs?"

"No, not dogs. Horses and cattle."

"My daughter is a *doctor*."

"She's a vet, and she's moving to Colorado to open a practice."

"Oh no," I blurted for Elisabeth, wishing instantly I could take it back for Candy.

"Brian will be chief of staff at the hospital in Vail. He loves that hospital. And he also loves skiing."

My heart was somewhere near my ankles as I thought how painful this was going to be for Elisabeth. She would be devastated. On the other hand, she wouldn't wind up with Brian, dismal and divorced. Brian was going skiing. I was rid of him. Maybe he would be trapped in a Colorado blizzard and die.

"Elisabeth fell for a player," Candy said. "If you'd told me, I could have told you who she was dealing with. When it comes to women, Brian is the busiest doctor at the hospital. I'm sure he hurt your daughter, and sadly that's your punishment for being no friend to me."

"He convinced her he's in love with her," I said. "Whatever that means these days."

"That's how good he is," she said like she was bored.

"I told her she shouldn't be with him."

"You should have said it louder. And you should have told me sooner. Brian has done every doctor, nurse, therapist, you name it, between here and Cedars-Sinai. His nickname at the hospital is Dr. Bang."

Elisabeth was seeing "Dr. Bang"? She was too smart not to know this. Either she didn't care or she really thought that she was his final affair. It had to be the latter—that Brian was a cheater but not when it came to her.

"I thought he would stop playing around when we married, after I was pregnant, after my son was born. After, after, after," Candy said, sobbing. "The worst part is, Brian wants custody of Jumper, which is ridiculous. I'm the one who brought him up. Brian was always missing in action. One Christmas, he left two gifts under the tree—one for me and one for Jumper—and a note that said he would be back before New Year's Eve. If not your daughter, it would have been someone else's daughter. I wish you had told me. We've known each other a short time, but we've shared so much. I deserved to know."

"She was seeing him long before we met," I said. "When I realized the connection, I should have spoken up, but I couldn't."

"Would you have told me if you knew Brian was having an affair with someone who wasn't your daughter?"

"I don't know—maybe not, with all of the problems you're having."

"Do you know if your daughter has been tested?"

It was possible for this situation to become worse?

"She should be tested," Candy said when I didn't respond.

Elisabeth had made a foolish choice, but she was mine. I could feel my daughter's anguish coursing through my veins, and from the way Candy was speaking, I knew there was a lot more fallout to come. I was at my limit, and I knew I needed to leave Candy's house; all of this truth serum in one day was paralyzing. But I had no right to leave until I was dismissed.

"I think it's time for you to go," Candy said.

Thank you, I thought. "Please don't hate me," I said.

"I don't hate you," she said. "You've helped me more than you could ever hurt me. And I will always remember that."

I was broken. And the worst part hadn't even started yet. I had to go talk to Elisabeth.

Chapter 24

Elisabeth lived in a former factory town transformed by local artisans. The town had gone from old and decrepit to young and desirable. On the main street, banners touted the next church event—a vegan supper. There were funky names in jiggly fonts on store windows. There was an abundance of bicycle racks and unmetered diagonal parking.

The center of town—one stop sign, no traffic lights—had all the necessities required for twenty-first-century survival, including a fresh bagel bakery and a pizza joint. The movie theater had a kiosk, and a marquee requiring the owner to climb a ladder to change a letter at a time. There was also a laundry, a nail salon, an organic hair salon, and the obligatory food co-op.

I found a spot in front of the laundry—All Washed Up—walked half a block, past pregnant mothers with baby buggies, climbed three flights, caught my breath, and rang the bell. Ringing was a formality. Elisabeth kept her door unlocked.

To my surprise, Harvey bellowed, "Come in."

At the sound of his voice, my impulse was to hurry back down the stairs. I faced the unlocked door, deciding whether to enter or flee. I hadn't seen Harvey since my mother's funeral.

I hadn't contacted No Grace Greene again. Nor had I reached out to any other attorney. If there was a chance that Harvey and I could settle fairly and proceed with our lives amicably, I wanted it to happen. Despite my hurt and the hell I was going through, we had three children, and it wasn't as though I would never see him again. Another thing: my vanity was in play. I wanted Harvey to file first. *I* didn't rear-end our marriage on a cliff. *He* did.

"Who's there?" he shouted. "It's open."

Obviously, he was sitting, relaxed and comfortable, with no intention of moving for anyone. I wondered why Elisabeth wasn't coming to the door. I turned to leave, and then I turned back. I had to face the facts—visiting my children would on occasion mean being with Harvey. Might as well start getting used to it.

Harvey was splayed on the couch, wearing a cashmere sweater and khakis. His loafers were brand-new. We always went shoe shopping together, and the sight of the shoes threw me off my game. I might as well have been playing tennis with a basketball. I'd lost my mother, and he was out shopping for designer shoes.

"Harvey," I said, "you're wearing loafers with tassels."

"I thought I would try something new."

Hadn't he already done that?

"Do you like the leather? I went to Eagleton's."

We always bought his shoes at Eagleton's. I bet Mr. Eagleton knew something was awry the second he saw Harvey enter the store on his own. Often, we went shoe shopping on a late Saturday afternoon, then to Luigi's for dinner. Harvey loved their spaghetti and meatballs. Their meatballs could sink a ship.

I had to ask. "Did you go to Luigi's?"

"Didn't you hear? Luigi's is closed."

"But Dana sent a lasagna from Luigi's when Mom died."

"Must have been their last lasagna."

"Oh," I said, thinking, *Another day, another tragedy.*

"Elisabeth went to get a bottle of white wine," he said.

What was Harvey doing at Elisabeth's apartment? Was she confiding in him, or was he confiding in her? Either way, it felt like a conspiracy.

"Wine?" he said, offering me a glass. "This red is from Mendoza."

What was this passion for all things Argentine? Next he'd be dressing like a gaucho.

"Try some," he said.

I was not going to drink the wine, on principle. I shook my head and dropped my shoulder bag on Elisabeth's desk.

"So what brings you here?" I asked Harvey. Why wasn't he scouting Manhattan for a couture breast-milk pump?

"She invited me over."

If Harvey had said those words before he took up residence at Five Swallows—back when I was his concierge—I would have been proud that Elisabeth relied on him, grateful he was spending time with her. Now I was every shade of green.

"I want you to know that no matter what," he said, "family comes first."

Family comes first—unless something else came first. Who was this twisted person? Not anyone I married. Was this the man I chose as my health advocate in case I lost my mind? I could hear a doctor saying, *"Your wife is sneezing. She has a cold."* And Harvey snapping, *"Do not resuscitate."* If I couldn't trust Harvey, was there anyone I could trust? Did trust exist? I gave this man my entire life, and now I was alone— without a husband to be notified in case of emergency.

I was about to leave when Elisabeth came through the door with a brown paper bag.

"Elisabeth, could I speak to you—downstairs?" I said.

"Absolutely," she said, passing the bottle of wine to Harvey.

On her stoop, Elisabeth glanced up, extending her palm, checking for raindrops. "It's starting to drizzle."

"We can sit in the laundry. I'm parked in front of it anyway."

We sat side by side, the washing machines chugging—clothing, towels, and sheets whipping around. A girl in leggings and a striped tube top folded laundry while listening to music through her pink earphones, stretching a chartreuse pillowcase above her head, dancing with it side to side. *Was I ever that happy?*

I wanted to come back in my next life as the kind of girl who danced in a tight top in a laundry. I couldn't dance in a laundry even if I was pumped with drugs.

"How are you doing, Mom?"

"Missing Grandma a lot," I said.

"Me too. I keep thinking she's going to call me and tell me I'm her queen. Remember how she used to say that when I was little?

Elisabeth pushed the lever on the wall-mounted detergent machine. A box of Tide fell out. She looked at me. "I'm rich!"

"You are rich. You're young and healthy and beautiful."

"Mom, what's up?"

"I need to tell you something."

"About Dad?"

"No, something else."

I took a breath. Then another. "Elisabeth, Brian is seeing another woman."

"What?"

"Just what I said."

"What is this, Mom? Your last stab at convincing me to break up with him?"

"He's moving to Colorado—Vail—with a woman who is a veterinarian."

Her eyes seemed to roll back in her head. I reached for her arm. She snatched it back.

"Wait," she said. "Exactly how do you know this?"

"I know his wife," I said, and it was a relief to finally say it.

"What?" she said incredulously.

"I met her in the hospital when I was taking care of Grandma. She was there because her father—he's in his nineties—has cancer. I recognized her from Guild for Good. We started talking. We became friends. She told me her husband is leaving her for a vet. She told me this morning, but it was too early to come over here so I waited until the afternoon."

"If you knew his wife," she said angrily, "how come you never mentioned it to me?"

I threw up my hands. "I don't know. It didn't matter. It only matters now."

She leaned back against the detergent machine, absolutely aghast, like she was about to pass out. Then, she stood straight up and breathed heavily, in and out, with her eyes closed. When she opened her eyes, I thought she was going to explode at me, cursing wildly, and I wasn't sure I could take it, but instead she said, "I have to admit that it bothered me some that he was married. But cheating on me with *another* woman?"

I swerved into the disbelief lane. *It's fine he has a wife but not fine that he has another girlfriend?*

"Does his wife know about me?"

"Now she does."

"I can't believe that the entire time I've been comforting you about Dad, being the daughter of the century, you were poking around behind my back. You'd never do this to Amanda. Never. But how could you, since she hardly comes home. You wouldn't know her boyfriend, Arnold the Famous Producer, if you fell on him."

"You really need to grow up."

"I don't want to, Mom," she said sadly.

Then she sobbed—in the laundry, on my shoulder.

⌒

"Can't you pick up the phone?" Dana asked when I answered my door a few days later.

"I'm averse to human contact," I explained. "The more people I meet, the more I like man-eating sharks."

"But it's over. So get over it. Candy knows about Elisabeth. Elisabeth knows about Candy. They'll both realize how much you mean to them, and everything will be fine. Well, maybe Candy won't realize."

Thanks, Dana.

"What kind of pizza?" She lifted the top of the box I had scavenged the night before.

"It's meatball."

"Open it. I'll pick the meatballs off. First, what do we hear about Harvey?"

"Besides that he was at Elisabeth's drinking Argentine wine? Let's see. Ben said that he had met Harvey for dinner at a restaurant that required reservations months in advance. Harvey had phoned in as Rabbi Harvey, and the respected title of 'rabbi' resulted in a table that evening—an old trick of his. He told me Harvey was on a long-term rate at Five Swallows."

"You saved the headline for last."

"No one wants to read bad news."

"Is that bad news?"

"I guess it doesn't matter where he stays. I'm done. I'm not taking him back."

Dana plucked the meatballs off her slice. Then she went back into her own world. "I found out today that I'm supposed to wear gray to

Jeremy's wedding. Isn't that appalling? Have these people never seen the color wheel?"

"My understanding," I said, wishing to discuss anything but my own life, "is that a groom's mother wears beige and keeps her mouth shut. And knowing Jeremy as well as I do, I'm sure he would agree."

"Yes, I remember. You were the one who watched Jeremy for a week when he was five and I went on a much-needed sure-to-lead-to-marriage vacation to Nantucket with that guy I never saw again."

"Among other times," I said.

She knocked my shoulder as she laughed, then bit into the pizza. "Now, about the twins. New college discussion at my house."

"Dana, is there anything that hasn't been discussed about college at your house?"

"Well, this subject *has* come up, but we're revisiting it," she said. "Do you think the twins should go to the same college or different colleges?"

What an obsession. I forced myself to respond, but I was uninterested in the conversation. "I don't know."

"You must have some opinion."

"I used up all of my opinions on *my* children," I said.

"My CFO knows the dean of admissions at the reach school, and he called about the twins."

"Does he know the twins?" I chose a slice of pizza, the largest remaining in the box.

"Not really. I told him to mention that the girls were altruistic scholar-athletes. Altruism is very big right now."

"Earth to Dana. You might be carrying this college thing too far. I'm sure they'll be happy wherever they go."

"Of course they'll be happy, but what about me?"

If I heard any more about higher education, I would deserve a degree. I closed the pizza box on two slices—tomorrow's cold breakfast.

"I miss my mom's phone calls," I said. "I've been playing back messages I saved on my cell. One was 'Harvey paid a visit today. He's not a bad man.'"

Dana laughed. "Harvey robbed a bank," she said. "He's not a bad man."

∽𝓞

I was thinking about my mother as I spent therapeutic time in Food Kingdom. Donation notifications came every day—mostly from my mother's friends. For the most part, my mother's departure had benefited an orphanage in Tel Aviv. What tie did she have to that orphanage? Was I adopted? Maybe that's why she always let Max sit in the front seat of the car. As I wheeled my grocery cart past the frozen food, my cell phone went off.

"Mom," Ben said, "Elisabeth called. She's in a Denny's in New Haven. Hysterical. She was supposed to meet Brian at a conference and spend the weekend, but he never showed up."

"Oh no," I said. I felt my shoulders collapse, and I leaned over my cart. I hadn't spoken to Elisabeth since the awful reveal. She had refused to answer my calls.

"She's been there for hours. A waitress saw her sobbing, brought her a Grand Slam."

"What did she say?" I said.

"The waitress?"

"No, Elisabeth."

"She said she's wiped. She is not leaving Denny's."

"Okay, so call the police," I said, obviously not thinking straight.

"What do you want me to say? 'My sister is sitting in Denny's'?"

"I'm overreacting."

"She asked me to come to New Haven and pick her up. She said she would wait in the Denny's. She said she couldn't get on the train alone."

"I'm going with you." I checked the time on my cell. "Ben, I'll drive. Take Metro-North, and I'll be out in front of the station. Call Elisabeth and tell her you're on your way."

⁓

When I got to the station, Ben was waiting there.

"Here's the address for Denny's," he said as he climbed into my shotgun seat in the pelting rain.

"She's still sitting there?"

"Yes, but I think she's settled down. She's talking to a waitress. Apparently, the waitress went on break and is in the booth with her." He pulled off the hood of his winter jacket. He mopped his face with his sleeve.

We shook off the rain as we entered the restaurant and found Elisabeth in a booth at the back, listless and leaning. She was staring at her plate like a woman who'd just seen a vision of the Virgin Mary in her pancake batter. Her table was heavy with dishes—eggs, fruit salad, a basket of rolls, and a turkey club sandwich on burned toast run over by fries.

Ben slid in next to Elisabeth. I sat with my coat on, my bag in my lap.

"I didn't know you were coming, Mom," Elisabeth said without intonation. She wasn't crying, but I could see from her face that she certainly had been sobbing.

"Well. I'm here."

"Talk about 'I told you so,'" Elisabeth said, looking at me.

Ben took a bite of the turkey club. "How long can you sit here before rent is due?"

"Let's go," I said.

"I have to pay," she said.

A waitress was taking an order at a raucous table of mothers and toddlers. When she finished and was nearing us, I asked her for the check.

"Sheila, this is my mom," Elisabeth said to the waitress, seventy pounds with her shoes on. "Sheila's been cheering me up."

"Thank you," I said.

"You're lucky," she said to Elisabeth. "There were eight of us in my family. I think that's eight more than my mother should have had."

How did anyone care for eight children anyway? I took the check. Ben took the rest of the turkey club.

Elisabeth said she was too miserable to go to her apartment. She came to my house. I couldn't remember when I had seen her so bereft. Without a word, she went upstairs to her room. Although I had begged her to clean it out, the room remained exactly as it was the day she left for college. Maybe the mementos on the walls would be soothing. She had done the wrong thing, seeing a married man, but I felt her suffering. Her misery was my misery. That's the way it is with mothers and daughters.

I considered going to her room to console her. When I reached her door, I listened. Not a sound. Maybe she was fast asleep. In any case, she had probably had enough of me.

I changed into pajamas and got into bed. There was a knock at my door.

"Mom?"

"Come in."

Elisabeth came into my bed. She hugged a pillow and snuggled up.

"Men," she said.

"Men," I repeated.

She put her head on my shoulder.

We cried ourselves to sleep.

Chapter 25

Harvey remained at Five Swallows. Neither of us had made a legal move toward separation. Therefore, I considered the two of us "illegally separated."

As far as I could see, there was only one part of my life that was going right. And that was Guild for Good. I liked the full-time salary and my new title. My box of one thousand business cards too.

The Monday after Denny's, I walked through the office door in a heavy parka, black trousers, and a tailored shirt. I had forgone makeup for a while now, because I had been weeping on cue at any thought of my mother. I couldn't stop dwelling on the fact that I was an orphan now, even though I was an adult with three adult children.

As I removed my coat, I thought about inventing a new brand of makeup. I would call it Traumatic. That's when Jon showed up—in a barn jacket, boots, jeans, and a navy crewneck sweater without a shirt underneath.

"Hey, director," he said. "I brought the mock-up of the poster for Art Explosion. And, as long as I'm here, I need to make a few flyers for a kid in my building. The kid runs a fair in the spring at the community center in Blake to raise money for leukemia research. Each year I walk around on stilts, and he bills me as the tallest man in the world."

"You walk on stilts?"

"Doesn't everyone?"

"Would you rather use color instead of white?"

"Thanks," he said as I handed him a package of blue.

"I don't think I've ever seen you without makeup," he said.

Makeup, no makeup—there's something Harvey would never mention.

"You look sort of bushed," he said. "Sad about your mother?"

I considered whether I had the wherewithal to discuss my bereavement.

"Yes," I said. "We were very close—like a mother and daughter."

He laughed. It cheered me up that I could make him laugh so easily. What's more, I felt lonely, and I was happy to have someone to talk to.

"Losing a parent is tough. It's a tough one," he said. "I am truly sorry."

"Thank you."

"How old was your mother?"

He put the flyer into the machine, and a pile of copies came out.

"Eighty-five."

I had come to the conclusion that people asked me about the age of my mother in order to gauge how sad to be for me. My mother was elderly, so no one took her death too seriously.

"What happened?"

I decided to become open, the Wikipedia of my own life. "The short answer is that she had a heart attack. The long answer is she fell off a stool, broke both ankles, went to the hospital, found out she had cancer, went to a rehab facility, and had a heart attack. My daughter says that my mother was an overachiever."

"What an ordeal."

"It was. And I miss her terribly."

I handed him a brown envelope to put his copies in.

"Was your husband with you?"

"Somewhere on the planet." I hated how sour I sounded at that moment. "My husband and I, well, we aren't officially separated or anything, but it looks like that's where it's going."

"Mutual decision?"

"It was mutual—after I found out he had a relationship with someone else." I stopped myself from telling him the whole sordid story. I had some restraint.

"You really are having quite a time."

"Well, if I were planning it, I wouldn't have had my husband check out just when my mother checked in to a hospital. Maybe I would have put a year between the two happy occasions."

"How long were you . . . I mean, have you been married?"

"Not long," I said sarcastically. "Just thirty-three years. I'll save you the math. We got married when I was ten years old."

He laughed. "I was married twelve years."

"Harvey and I had fights that lasted that long."

"Great line," he said.

"It's not true," I said.

"You know what, Marcy?"

"What?"

"It seems to me that even though you're holding a cup of coffee, you need a cup of coffee. Would you like to take a break?"

"I would."

○

We strolled over to the Starbucks down the street. Jon drank his coffee black. I added some whole milk and one blue Equal to mine. Most often, I used three Equals, but I didn't want to do anything embarrassing. I followed as Jon headed toward armchairs by the front window.

As he set his coffee down, I noticed how well his jeans fit—no daddy Dockers for him.

"I'm sorry to hear that you've been through so much recently," he said.

I hoped Jon wouldn't ask me any questions about Harvey. He didn't need to know more than what I had already told him—that Harvey had had an affair.

Jon is a man, I thought. *Men don't ask a lot of personal questions.* I changed the subject anyway.

"My new job is helpful. It keeps me busy," I said.

"So what's your plan?" he said.

"My son, his name is Ben, believes that my husband gave me a pass, and it's now the time to do whatever I want."

"Smart son. What does your son do?"

"Ben is looking into law schools."

"That's his job?"

"For now it is."

"They didn't have jobs like that when I was in my twenties."

I smiled at him.

"People do seem to do everything later," he said.

"Yes. Maybe I should have done some things later. At thirty, I was lodged in a house in Connecticut. My deck was outfitted with a Weber gas grill and Brown Jordan deck furniture."

"That's a sad story," he said, pretending to wipe his eyes with his knuckles.

"And, what about you? I know so little about you."

"You know I never pay for my copies."

"That's okay, because they're always for some other do-good organization."

"Less well off than Guild for Good—with no copy machine."

Jon told me that he grew up in Portland, Maine. He lived in an old brick house near the waterfront, a waterfront now saturated with bustling bars, well-rated seafood restaurants, and independent retail stores, even some thriving bookstores.

He received a scholarship to the University of Maine. He majored in English, earned a PhD at Boston University, came to Connecticut as a lecturer. Now he was a tenured professor, and his specialty was the twenty-first-century American novel, a topic that he liked because he updated the curriculum constantly with literature by new writers. He painted in his spare time. He had a well-known rep, and he sold a lot of his work.

Jon was easy to converse with. There wasn't one stagnant pause. I'd ask a question, and he'd roll on.

"Any children?" I said.

"No kids of my own. The boy who runs the fair lives with his grandmother, my neighbor Rose. I like to take him places—ball games, movies. I took him to New York last week."

"Where did you go?"

"Museum of Natural History. So he could see the dinosaurs."

"What did he think?"

"They were big."

We both laughed.

"Do you have a brother or a sister?" I said.

"My older brother, James, still lives in Maine. He's a marine biologist. He has five daughters—seventeen, fifteen, thirteen, eleven, and nine."

I was impressed that he knew their ages. An uncle who had that information on recall was an attentive man.

"It's easy to remember their ages," he said. "No mind-bender. They're all two years apart."

I was no less impressed.

"Also, I have a younger brother in Maine, Allen, a character, chronically unemployed. When I visit Portland, I cook a big Italian dinner."

"And clean up?"

"And clean up."

I imagined Jon removing dinnerware from the table, loading the dishwasher, and pulling the start knob.

I wanted to know more. I wanted to know what brand of cereal he preferred. Eggs poached or scrambled? Whether he'd opt for a weekend in the city, in the country, or at the beach?

"I have an apartment. I found owning a house time-consuming. Finished raking, had to start plowing. Put on a magnificent new deck, needed a new boiler. I'm sure you know how it is. I'd rather paint. I'd rather be here talking to you."

Go ahead. Warm my heart. I glanced at his watch. I had to get back to work. "I'm happy we did this," I said as we exited.

He agreed. Then he ran his long fingers through his sandy hair.

Jon Juan, I thought. *The intern was right.*

⌒⑨

Jon started calling me, asking how my day was going. He'd drop by the office often, even if he had no reason to be there. Most board members showed up only for events and meetings. Often, he would say something about my mother, as though he knew her, but of course I knew he didn't.

One day, out of nowhere, he said, "What was the best food your mother ever made?" I told him about the turkey with cinnamon-apple stuffing she made ages ago for me to take to my friends.

"What a woman," he said.

"A lot to miss."

"You know, Marcy, I don't make turkey, but I'm a great cook."

Was that an invitation?

"That's an invitation," he said.

⌒⑨

I drove to Jon's apartment complex in Blake, two towns away from Atherton. His building was four stories and a currant shade of concrete.

Once a bustling candle factory, it had been emptied, ignored, condemned, and then converted into apartments.

I took the elevator to his floor, four. Jon answered my knock and, as he held the door ajar, shooed away a tabby the color of delicatessen mustard. I heard a meager meow, but it was from a different cat.

"That's Peek-a-Boo," he said. "She meows but she won't come out to meet you. My tabby is the friendly one."

"What's her name?"

"Tabby."

"A lot of thinking went into that."

"There's also Hubert. But you don't want to meet him. He's a wild man."

I felt that I looked good, but I was nervous. I had done my hair up in a loose way, but I could feel the tendrils tightening up. *This is ridiculous,* I thought. *You've known this man for years. This might not even be a date. He may simply feel bad for you because your mother died recently. Bingo. This is a pity party. Poor Marcy.*

Calm yourself, I thought. *Buck up. He's been dropping by the office on a regular basis. He already likes you.* I adjusted my turtleneck, pulling it over my pants.

In the midst of Jon's living room—statuesque windows, smoky wooden floor—was a canoe, crafted of beautiful burled wood. Polished to a shine. Perfect. There was space around the canoe, a walkway, but backed against every wall were art supplies and easels. Books were piled high. It seemed he had every novel ever written. There was a recliner in a corner with a pharmacy lamp near a window. The open galley kitchen had a granite countertop. Two wicker stools, reminiscent of bars in France, were tucked under the counter.

I handed him a bottle of classic Chianti in a silver gift bag. I had bought Chianti because he had mentioned he was cooking an Italian meal. I stood idling about, not sure whether to stand or be seated on a stool.

I wasn't much of a cat person, but I needed activity, so I plucked Tabby from the floor and scratched her head. She scratched me. I put her down gently, as though I adored her. "Tell me about the canoe," I said.

"I made it."

"Like with your own hands?"

"That's usually how you make things."

"Can I sit in it?"

"Yes, but don't go too far out in the water."

I laughed as I took a seat in the canoe facing the wall full of easels.

He brought over two wineglasses—one metal, one crystal—and the bottle of Chianti, and sat down next to me. I was extremely close to Jon. A man who wasn't my husband. *Close, close.* I shifted, uneasy. But the boat was a canoe, not a cruise ship.

"Dinner is ready whenever you're hungry," he said.

How many times had I said that to Harvey?

"I'm not used to this," I said.

"Canoeing?"

"No. Sitting in a boat with a man. As I told you in the office, my husband left abruptly months ago. Then he moved back in. Then I told him to leave. It's a long miserable story. Began in the '70s, actually. I made the mistake of attending my cousin Leona's engagement party, and my mother pointed him out. She admired his sport coat. It was from Barneys."

Stop talking, Marcy. Cease and desist.

"Is he coming back again?"

"No."

"You never know."

"I know. There's a young girl, and she's pregnant."

"I had heard."

That really stung. "People knowing about it all—that's one of the hard parts."

"No secrets in a small town."

"I wish I lived in New York City."

"Then your doorman would tell everyone. Calvin mentioned that she's Colombian."

"Argentine."

I sipped, but I wanted to gulp the Chianti. I was screaming to be tipsy, to loosen up. I had to stop reciting my miserable story. But the missing man was the father of my three lovely children, and he had chewed up decades of my life.

I scanned the ceiling from the canoe. There was an endless number of souvenir key chains hanging from a rod. "Tell me about the key chains," I said as I pointed above.

"Been collecting them since I was a kid."

Done. I had changed the subject. "Have you ever counted?"

"Hundreds. From places I've been, places my friends have been."

I studied the mementos. "You must have a lot of friends. So tell me, what's your status on Facebook?"

"I'm not on Facebook, but if I was, I'd say sort of a widower."

"Sort of?"

"My wife died."

I had assumed he was long divorced. That was what everyone at Guild for Good assumed. This news was startling, unsettling. "That's not sort of."

"My wife passed while making love."

I was speechless, blown away. It took a few minutes for me to imagine him in bed with his wife. He's on top, or worse yet, she's on top. In the case of death, which would be worse? And suddenly she has a heart attack.

Even though I hated Harvey for wrecking my life, I couldn't imagine what I'd do if he dropped in the act, something that could very well happen to him now, because I'd read that a side effect of Cialis was stroke.

It was too forward to ask, but I couldn't help myself. "What did you do?"

"I wasn't there."

She was masturbating? She had a heart attack and died while masturbating? I scrunched my forehead.

He threw up his hands. "My wife was with another woman— her lover for years. I thought they were friends. I thought we were *all* friends. 'Girls' weekend,' she would say. 'Ladies' night out.'"

I refilled his glass, hoping he had a wine cellar in his fourth-floor apartment.

～

Jon served dinner at the galley counter. Not one of his plates matched. I liked that. It seemed freeing. And it looked attractive. I had bone china for eighteen.

There was a caprese salad and delicious meat lasagna, and cannoli for dessert, but my mind was on two lesbians in full swing and one of them, suddenly, shockingly, dying. How could I get past that? Certainly, he hadn't.

I was enjoying the amazing chocolate cannoli cream, but the story about his dead wife, and my own nervousness, made me feel like I wanted to leave. I glanced at his watch—there was a speck of paint on the leather band. It was eleven. If I left, I could still catch a late-night talk show.

"I think I should go," I said.

"Marcy," he said, swiveling on the stool. "Can I share?"

"Of course."

"I'm not ready to date."

I swiveled. *No kidding.*

"So let's get to know each other," he said.

"That's perfect," I said.

"No hurry," he said. "We're young. We have plenty of time."

Chapter 26

In March, for my birthday, my children bought tickets to see modern dance at the Joyce Theater on Eighth Avenue in Manhattan. I loved the Joyce. Harvey enjoyed musicals and plays but was not a fan of dance. The one time we had gone together, Harvey left at intermission and spent the second part of the performance in the lobby, on a business call.

I could have been blindfolded that day, and it wouldn't have fazed me. I was getting together with all of my children for the first time since my mother's funeral.

I desperately needed the distraction. According to information slipping from Amanda, and my obsessive calculations, Baby Oops, son or daughter of Harvey Hammer and Madison Avenue, was due any day—maybe this week, maybe next. I was calculating the days as though I were due myself.

I pushed the baby out of my mind by thinking of my own babies, grown babies, and steered into the city down the West Side Highway. I found a parking spot on Twentieth Street, and knew immediately that this spot was just another part of how pleasing my birthday was going to be. It was big enough to pull in forward, which was perfect, because I'd forgotten how to parallel park while living in Connecticut.

⌒

The kids met me at Cleo's, one of Ben's favorite restaurants in Chelsea, before the matinee. It was warm out finally, and some patrons were seated at outdoor tables, reminiscent of an Old World café, but I went inside.

The restaurant was swarming with the usual Saturday crowd, mostly men in their twenties and thirties who were eating breakfast at noon. Sadly, my belief that noon is the time for lunch was the equivalent of flashing my AARP card. It went along with considering one a.m. too late for a drink, or agreeing in advance on a place and time to meet a friend instead of texting en route.

I drank in the sight of my children, standing in front of me greeting one another. My marriage was over. My husband's baby was due any day. But look what I had.

"There's the birthday girl," Ben said, then hugged me.

I kissed my daughters.

Cleo, about forty, welcomed us, and considering his toned body I was surprised he had any time after working out to actually work. His T-shirt was a second skin, his muscles ready to pop. He picked up menus, and we trailed behind him to a table in the center of the room under a replica of a Calder mobile, red and black.

I pulled out the chair opposite Ben. We ordered chardonnay. The waiter, a young man with spiked hair, asked me to taste the wine first when Ben mentioned it was my birthday.

"Perfect," I said. If it had tasted like gasoline, I was too happy to care.

"Here's to Mom," Amanda said.

"Hear, hear," Elisabeth said, lifting her glass and clinking mine.

I felt embarrassed by the attention.

Amanda clinked my glass, then Ben's, then Elisabeth's, glancing at Elisabeth—in an odd way. As though they knew something I didn't know. And I started to wonder what it was.

"What's going on?" I asked.

"What do you mean?" Elisabeth said.

"Something is up," I said.

"It's your birthday," Amanda piped up.

"Just tell me," I said.

"Mom, enjoy your day," Elisabeth said.

"I can't enjoy anything when I know there's something going on I don't know about. Tell me now what it is."

"Okay, I'm waiting for a call," Ben said.

"From Dad?" I said.

"Yes," he said. "And believe me, I am not happy to be waiting for it. But it's just the way it is, I guess."

"Ha. The way it is?" Amanda rolled her eyes at him. "Ben, for once quit being so accepting."

"What would you like me to do?" he said.

"Bitch and moan," Amanda said.

"It's Mom's birthday. We don't have to discuss this now." Elisabeth opened her menu, as if to say "Let's call this quits."

"Discuss what?" I said, although I knew it was about Harvey and the baby.

"Case closed," Elisabeth said. She tapped me. "So, Mom, what are you ordering?"

In minutes, my happiness factor had swerved on the meter from one hundred to minus one. I wanted to know what exactly was going on. On the other hand, I didn't want to turn my birthday into a WWE event.

The rest of us rolled our eyes as Amanda ordered lunch. She had learned crazy ordering from Harvey, and she requested the Cleo salad, chopped, no romaine, just field greens; extra chicken—moist; balsamic dressing on the side. And please add diced apples. She also wanted breadsticks instead of bread.

"That was *so* Dad," Elisabeth said. Then she reverted to middle-school-level teasing of her sister, which took the edge off until lunch arrived.

At the adjacent table, a young couple in black requested a high chair for a one-year-old. I turned the other way and concentrated on my stuffed artichoke, plucking one lightly breaded leaf at a time. *Harvey will need a high chair for his baby,* I thought. *He's in his sixties, and he's going to need a high chair.*

We were finishing our meals when Ben's cell phone rang. I felt a stab in my groin, my lower back ached, and suddenly I knew as sure as I was lunching in Chelsea that it had happened. A baby had been born.

Ben removed his cell from his pants pocket and glanced at the incoming number.

"Oh," he said. "It's Dad."

Elisabeth slumped in her seat. Amanda's eyes were glazed, wide-open. All the air had gone out of my party, the restaurant, Chelsea, the world.

In the words and tone of a businessperson receiving a call about the sale of real estate, Ben said, "Excuse me. I have to take this."

"Tell me," I said to my daughters.

"She went into labor last night," Elisabeth said.

"And to think I was hoping she would be in labor for a month," Amanda mixed in.

"We didn't tell you because we didn't want to ruin your birthday," Elisabeth said.

Ruin my birthday? My birthday had now been ruined forever. Baby Oops and I were practically twins . . . fifty-nine years apart.

As Ben walked swiftly to the front of the noisy restaurant and maneuvered out the crowded doorway, the waiter hailed a busboy to remove our dishes. The teenager, about an hour out of a rural town in Idaho, bustled about our table.

When he asked nervously if he could remove my stuffed artichoke, I snapped at him. "Stop," I said. "That's enough with the dishes."

The waiter signaled the busboy to leave the table. "It's his first day."

So in addition to being a woman who was cold enough to despise the birth of an innocent baby, I was a heartless bitch to a young man on his first day at work.

"How did we get into this soap opera?" Amanda said. "How could this happen to us?"

"You're not helping," Elisabeth said. "Let's just wait till Ben gets back."

Ben approached the table with a slow gait, dragging out the inevitable.

I wondered if Harvey had gone to Lamaze class with her. He came with me one time—to the film about C-sections—but partway through, he rushed off to the men's room to vomit his steak, charred with a pink center, hot sauce on the side. As it turned out, Elisabeth was a C-section, then Amanda, then Ben—Harvey waited in the visitors' lounge each time, appearing after I was rolled into my room.

I imagined Harvey at Lamaze with Madison. I envisioned some pregnant girl in a red leotard stretched over her belly complimenting Madison by telling her how wonderful it was that she'd brought along her grandfather. At Lamaze, Harvey would need to sit on the floor. Harvey abhorred the floor. There was a reason chairs were invented, he always said.

Ben stood and looked around the table at each one of us.

Amanda gave Ben the eye.

He nodded.

"I don't want to know," I said.

"Okay," he said as he sat down in his chair.

My daughters were silent.

"Don't tell me," I said, shaking my head, putting up my hands to block any information.

"Isn't it better to hear it while we're with you?" Ben asked.

"Why? In case I have a little breakdown? I'm not having a breakdown. I haven't had one thus far, and I am not having one now. I will not crack up under any circumstance. I am not an egg. Do you hear me?"

The waiter came by the table. "Everything all right today?"

"Delicious," Elisabeth answered instantly to ward him off.

The artichoke and baked chicken dish with a side order of asparagus had tasted fine when I'd devoured it, but now both my lunch and my emotions were wedged in my throat. I could have swallowed a soccer ball with less effort.

Now the waiter was facing *me*, asking, "Is everything okay today?"

I meant to say "Couldn't be better," but instead I said, "Could be better."

"Oh," he said. "What's the problem?"

My husband had a baby with another woman, I thought. *He had three babies with me, but this baby is the baby of an old man, and old men are always on television saying how much better it is to have a child at a later age. How rewarding it is to coach Little League at seventy.*

"The food was fine," Ben said when I didn't answer.

"Can I bring you anything else?"

"Thank you. But we're fine," Ben said.

The waiter smiled and headed toward the kitchen.

I wiped my eyes with a napkin and threw up my hands. "Just tell me."

"She had a boy this morning."

"She had a boy this morning," I repeated, stammering.

"We knew it was a boy," Amanda said. "What else did he say, Ben?"

"You knew it was a boy?" I said in confusion.

"Mom, there was an ultrasound," Elisabeth said.

I visualized Harvey and Madison smiling at the black-and-white fuzzed-over picture.

"Oh, Harvey, those are the legs," I could hear her say.

"Beautiful," he would have said.

"And look, the head."

I still had the ultrasound pictures of my three kids—among the souvenirs of my life, stored in a file cabinet. And when Harvey had seen them, the first time he saw them, he'd pronounced, "Beautiful" about each one.

"How long have you known it was a boy?" I asked my children.

No one answered.

"What else, Ben?" Elisabeth said. "Does the baby have a name?"

"Not yet," Ben said.

"That's it," Amanda said. "No name, no height, no weight?"

"He said he would call me later when he saw the baby."

"When he saw the baby?" Elisabeth said.

I was dumbstruck. He had been there, at least in the hospital, for the birth of our children.

"That's all he said," Ben replied.

"And what did you say?" Elisabeth asked.

"'Congratulations.'"

"Well then," Amanda said, "he's lucky he called you and not me."

"You're all talk," Elisabeth said. "When you start working for Dad, you'll treat that baby like it was born in a manger."

⁓

We trudged four city blocks to the theater. There was mostly silence, except for the endless noise in my head. *Why did the baby have to be born on my birthday? Why did I have to share my birthday in perpetuity, forever, for all time?* Elisabeth, Ben, and Amanda were upset now, but once they were back in love with Harvey, they'd be with him at Chuck E. Cheese or McDonald's each year on *my* birthday celebrating the baby's birthday. *Happy birthday to me—for I'm a jolly good fellow.*

I imagined Harvey with the blanketed baby in his hands, the tiny blue- or pink-striped hospital cap on the baby's head. *Did the baby look like Harvey?* I wanted the baby to look like his mother. Whatever she looked like.

I held myself together behind my sunglasses until the theater usher ripped my ticket in slow motion. I was about to start sobbing, so I rushed downstairs to the ladies' room. There was a line. I'd known I was going to have a reaction to the birth of the baby, but I didn't think I would be tormented on my birthday, my special day with my kids. *Shut up, Marcy,* I told myself now. *Suck it up.*

Elisabeth tapped me. "Mom, are you all right?"

"Fine, fine. What about you?"

"Ben's right. It's not the baby's fault. We can't fault an innocent child."

"Amanda is upset," I said.

"Amanda is Daddy's girl. She's worried the baby will take her place."

"And you're not?"

"What can I do? Dad fell into a trap. But, Mom, you need to know—Dad isn't living with her. She makes him miserable."

"Somehow there's no solace in that."

"There's a line," a middle-aged woman with the body type of a dancer said to Elisabeth with the verve of a native New Yorker. "No cutting."

Did she think my daughter was intrepid enough to cut a line in Manhattan? Cutting in the city could result in homicide—or worse.

"I'm just checking on my mother," Elisabeth explained.

"Fine," the woman said. "But don't cut."

Elisabeth smiled at me and walked away.

"That was my daughter," I said to the woman and the people waiting behind her, who all seemed to know one another. "She's a doctor, seeing if I was all right."

"Oh, please," she said. "That's how everyone cuts."

I needed an argument to relieve my tension, and this woman was about to oblige. "She wasn't cutting."

She didn't respond, staring at the metal doors to the individual stalls.

A woman came out of a stall. I went in, but I didn't sit down. I stood in the stall as though it were a tiny jail. Two women with thick New York accents were discussing how rude I was.

I heard the five-minute-warning bell. The kids were waiting for me. The show would start, and I would be stranded in the lobby, alone with nothing to think about except whether Madison was breast-feeding. *Pull it together, Marcy. Is this how you want your kids to remember you when you're gone so long no one visits the cemetery anymore, a crumbling weak loser who couldn't take a hit? Do you want Amanda to tell Harvey that you imploded at the mention of Baby Oops, that you're now in a psychiatric clinic outside of Boston that's famous for famous patients? That you're in there humming "Fire and Rain"?*

I went to the mirror, fixing my eye makeup with the corner of a paper towel. I wanted to splash water on my face, but then I would need to scrub off my makeup, and the warning bell rang again.

I hurried into the dimmed theater as the announcer cautioned the audience about candy wrappers. Amanda waved to me from the fifth row. My empty seat was dead center. Half of the people in the fifth row rose as I shimmied to my seat. I was an annoyance to everyone.

A male dancer entered from the left, a sprite of a woman from the right, both in bodysuits, appearing to be nude. The woman, nipples at attention, had flaxen hair in a high ponytail that touched her waist. Their dancing simulated a love affair, a brilliant spotlight tracing their movements across the stage. The spotlight procreated—two, then four, and then eight—and I envisioned round baby faces flashing on the stage. I forgot about the performers. This was the torturous dance of the baby face.

When we'd brought Elisabeth home from the hospital, my mother was there to help. Harvey dropped us off at the house, puttered about for an hour, and then was off to the office with boxes of "It's a girl" cigars.

And what about Madison? Was she going to give the baby up, as Harvey had told me when he asked for my assistance? Or was she keeping the baby? If she was keeping the baby, did she actually think Harvey was going to help with the daily care?

I imagined Madison calling Harvey's office, the receptionist telling her that he was in a meeting with the advertising agency, and even though the baby had crawled out of the crib and onto the road, Harvey could not be interrupted, Madison should call back later—when the baby reached the interstate.

I blocked my thought pattern. I was too vindictive. Harvey had been a superb father once the children were able to converse. I'd enjoyed when he held court, commandeering the kitchen table at dinner and Sunday brunch. He loved his children. And once upon a time, he'd loved me.

I guess I didn't fool the kids very much, because Ben offered to drive me home in my car. I wondered if he wanted to drive to Connecticut to visit the hospital and see Baby Oops. If that was the case, I wasn't interested in helping him get there. If Ben wanted to see the baby or stop in on Harvey, he could ride the train. Or walk.

I couldn't help myself, and as we hugged our good-byes next to my car on the side street, I said to no one in particular, "Are you going to the hospital to see the baby?"

"Are you kidding?" Amanda snapped.

"No," I said weakly.

"I don't care if I never see that baby," Amanda said.

"Well, he is our half brother," Ben said.

"The son of a fortune-hunting bitch," Amanda replied.

"So she's after his money," Elisabeth said. "That's not the baby's fault."

"I told Dad I wouldn't let her use my employee discount to buy baby clothes."

"Ooo, you're tough, Amanda," Ben said.

Amanda dressed him down. "That bitch wrecked our family."

"Give me a break," Ben said. "Like none of this is Dad's fault."

"Oh, please, she was stalking him in his own office. And I bet he isn't the first old guy she tried to fleece with her rock-a-bye-baby story."

"Well, she did have a real baby," Ben said. But Amanda wasn't interested in reason.

"Sugarcoat it all you want, Ben."

"He's our half brother," Elisabeth said.

"Then *you* go to the hospital," Amanda said. "But I want nothing to do with her or Dad's drooling, breast-fed midlife crisis. And I think we should cease all discussion of this, because we're getting Mom upset. Dad thinks he can buy his way out of this mess, but he wrecked our family, and I have no plan to make nice anytime soon. And FYI, Ben, I told Dad that for now I'm staying at Bloomingdale's, away from that bulimic bitch. If I join Bountiful, it'll be long after she moves back to Argentina."

We all looked at her as though she had said the earth is flat.

I broke my silence. "Bulimic?"

"And one more thing," Amanda said. "As long as we're talking about how she looks—"

"Oh, stop," Ben said. "Elisabeth and I are going to be kind to the baby."

"Of course," Amanda said. "As long as everyone here knows that the thought of that baby makes me want to heave."

Ben caved in. "So much for half a brother being better than none."

I had done the best I could not to be the one who caused a rift between Harvey and the kids. If they were angry with him, thought Madison was a bitch, and didn't want to bond with Baby Oops, I hadn't said a nasty word or done a vengeful thing to provoke their unpleasant feelings. I removed the car keys from my bag and released the automatic locks. I was about to get into the car when I turned and called each one of their names.

"What, Mom?" Elisabeth asked.

"Thank you for your support," I said.

Amanda broke in. "I wasn't shooting off my mouth just to make you feel better."

"Ben is right. Be kind to your dad and your little half brother." It was the most difficult, generous sentence I'd ever had the responsibility to say.

Chapter 27

I missed Candy, and often I wondered how Walter was doing. So one day I called Saint Mordecai and asked to be connected to his room. I wasn't going to talk to him; I simply wanted to see whether he was still in the hospital.

When there was no room number for Walter, I started to worry that he had died. Was Candy so angry that she wouldn't have called me if her father were gone? I couldn't tolerate that thought.

I had to make amends.

I went to her house, off the beaten path, a place no one could visit with the excuse "I was just driving by."

Candy was out front, planting March bulbs, in a cardigan, old overalls, and a floppy woven hat almost bigger than she was. Crouched on her knees near the buckwheat that abutted her grass, she looked up as I shut my car door. When she saw the likes of me, she turned back to the bulbs.

"It's me," I said.

"I'm gardening," she said.

"I see," I said. "Do you want help?"

"From you?" She was irritated.

I looked around. "Don't see anyone else."

"Have you ever gardened?"

"I hate gardening."

"I'm sure you do, but have you ever gardened?"

"Of course not."

"I see. You're not only dishonest and callow, but you are also intrusive and useless."

I didn't even know she had it in her to talk like that. "Guess so."

"Here," she said handing me a bulb. "Plant one. In case you're wondering, which you're not, it's a tulip. Very dramatic. So dark a purple it appears black. By the way, tulips are perennials in New England, but I like to refresh every few years."

I glanced into one of the eight-inch furrows that were about six inches apart. I held up the bulb. "Which side goes up?"

"You're kidding." She pulled the poor tulip bulb out of my hand.

"Another bulb, safe at last."

She rolled off her knees and sat with her legs crossed. She patted her forehead with a neatly folded tissue she took from a pocket in her overalls.

I knew my only chance was to make her laugh. "Missed a spot," I said, pointing to her head.

"I'm not going to laugh, Marcy. Not happening. We're through. Leave before my bulbs expire from the fear of having you around."

I decided I had no choice but to plow right in. "Candy, what would have been accomplished if I had come clean with you? I begged Elisabeth to stop seeing him, not to see any married man, but no one ever listens to a mother. I don't have to tell you that."

"Do you put any value on the truth?"

"I do."

"I had lunch with your daughter," she said.

"You did not," I said.

"I did."

Fabulous. Now they were gal pals, best friends forever, lunch buddies. Like a pomegranate martini wasn't enough, they'd had a whole luncheon special. I could hear them, could hear Candy say politely, *"No dressing on my salad, please."* Then Elisabeth's snarky response: *"My mom orders extra dressing. She might as well eat a steak."* Thank you, planet Earth, for crumbling on every side.

Truth was, I didn't care if they ate tree bark; I just wanted to know what was said. Was it worse than their bonding? Had Candy beaten up on Elisabeth? Reduced my daughter to pulp—purposefully, eloquently, without once raising her voice? Told her how insipid she was, falling for a man who was playing her all over the medical world—the hands-down Nobel Prize winner for womanizing?

"I called her at the hospital and introduced myself. She was baffled. I asked her to meet me, away from the hospital, at the Myron, on East Center Street. For some reason, she agreed. She told me you told her repeatedly to break up with my husband."

"That's what I tried to tell you. But Elisabeth wouldn't listen. Your mother tells you to act a certain way, so you have to do the exact opposite thing . . . It's a law of nature."

"Uh-huh."

"How many times do I have to apologize?"

"We're not even close."

I got down on my knees in the garden. "I was wrong. I will never do it again."

"Oh, yes, I forgot. You have another daughter." She stood up and brushed off her overalls. "Honestly, Elisabeth is a wonderful girl. Lucky for her, she resembles you. I regret that she became ensnared in this. No one ever said it was easy to be young."

That was Candy. Being kind when she should be the angriest, meanest person in the pack. That's what I loved about her. Her fairness. Her evenness. The way she saw the other side of things.

I wanted to say "Please, can we be friends again?" but I wasn't thirteen years old, so I nodded in agreement.

"I need time," Candy said. "To think about this, to think about you. Can you understand that?"

"Can I stay around for a while and help with the gardening? I promise I won't plant anything."

"That's right," she said. "Because there is no chance I'll let you."

"There must be something I can do to help."

"Make me laugh," she said.

Relieved that I had made headway, I asked her about Walter.

"He's in a home right now. Mom is in one home, and he's in another."

"I'm back," I said. "I'm here for you."

Chapter 28

I had seen Jon at a meeting or two at work. We were warm to each other but businesslike. After all, he had told me that night in his apartment that he wasn't ready to date.

So I was pleased when, for no apparent reason, he turned up in my office a few days after I had been to see Candy. I tried not to light up, but I was glad to see him. Yes, he had problems. But I had problems too. To my surprise, he asked if I wanted to meet him at a local art gallery. There was a show opening the next night.

I was very familiar with Gallery Leftkowitz, owned and curated by a munchkin of a socialist from the Upper West Side of Manhattan. He had replanted himself in Connecticut in an attempt to replicate the happiness he had known as a boy, when he'd gone to sleepaway camp there.

∽

Upon entering, I spotted Jon in a small group, talking to Ronald Leftkowitz, who had grown frail, sickly, since I'd last seen him.

Jon and I were accidental twins in our faded jeans, black shirts, and black boots.

"I like what you're wearing," Jon said.

"I had thought about a skirt, but then I thought you'd be wearing pants."

"I know you know Ronald."

"Naturally. How have you been?"

"Great," Ronald said. "I hear you were promoted. I hope those tightwads at Guild for Good gave you a raise. But as you know, I'm an old socialist—so not too big a raise."

Jon interceded. "And this is the artist, Godfrey Paine." Jon stepped back so I could greet Paine, a bear of a hairy man, in his forties, in the nubby dark suit I guessed his family had bought for his high school graduation. Looking into his big eyes to say hello, I wondered whether his face could be mowed.

"Pleasure to see you," the artist said. He would have been pleased to see Joseph Stalin, as there were only a handful of people at the showing.

I gazed around the room. The paintings were huge, and Godfrey Paine was the phallic Georgia O'Keeffe.

"I am so excited to see your work," I said. A white lie. Always tell the bride she looks beautiful.

"They're almost all self-portraits," he said.

◦つ

"Penis paintings," I said to Jon when the artist had left our side.

"I'm sorry. I had no idea he did this kind of—what should we call it—work. We'll slow-stroll once around, admire, and go."

We walked over to the portable bar, where champagne had been prepoured into plastic glasses.

"I like the one over there," I said, raising my eye toward an outsized canvas with three objects.

"Oh, yes, that one," Jon said, pointing with his plastic glass of champagne. "Parrot, peony, penis."

"My husband has a parrot." Harvey had rescued his pet from the good life at Dana's. Ben had mentioned that the parrot was residing in Harvey's office. I imagined a new repertoire: *"B cup, B cup, B cup."*

"My wife and I liked cats," Jon said.

"Would one of your cats like to eat my husband's parrot?"

⁓

When Jon thought we had stayed long enough not to be rude, we went to the bakery next door. There were sunny yellow tables and airy white wire chairs. At the counter, he asked, "What do you think?"

"Chocolate," I said.

"I never met a chocolate I didn't like," he said.

We agreed on chocolate croissants.

"Interesting that the artist paints his own body parts," I said as I ripped a piece off my croissant. Happily, the chocolate was oozing.

"Augmenting reality," Jon said.

"I like *your* work," I remarked.

He smiled. "What's your favorite?"

"Hands down, your paintings of Maine by the sea. I love pictures of New England."

"But you're a New York City girl originally, am I right?"

"I moved here years ago when my husband insisted on it and I relented. Would you believe I had never heard of lacrosse?"

"Such a sad story."

"It's okay now. All of my children played at some point."

"You're still in your house?"

"Yes, I am."

"Loneliness is the same no matter where you live."

"I'm thinking of moving. Actually, I've been thinking about it for a while."

"Where would you go?" he asked, his look forlorn.

"Oh, I would stay in Atherton, maybe find a small Cape."

"I'm glad to hear you're not moving far."

I liked that he said that.

"So what's the problem?" he said.

"Problem is that moving is traumatic. Lots of memories—especially about my kids. I think they would miss their rooms. Of course, there's the kitchen—which is where we spent the most family time. And there's the finished basement—fondly known as the Make-Out. It's also about my mom. She'll never have been in the new house. And I need her karma. If you had met her, you'd understand."

"But your kids are grown-ups with their own places."

"True, but I tend to forget that. I enjoyed their growing up so much that even though I know they're adults, I cling to whatever I can. Besides, it's tough to think about only yourself when you've spent your whole life thinking about everyone else. Until a few weeks ago, I still went to the supermarket and bought their favorite things. But I have to say, I'm trying to get over that. I restrict myself to the ten-items-or-less checkout."

"Let me guess. Skim milk, low-fat yogurt, skinless free-range organic chicken, decaf coffee."

"Try Pepperidge Farm Milano cookies, Diet Coke, Cape Cod potato chips . . . I consider a slice of apple pie a portion of fruit."

"You surprise me. You look great."

Thank you, I thought. It was such a great thing to hear, and he had said it like he meant it.

"As you know, I like to cook. Back in the day, I went to the farmers' market at the old fairgrounds on Sundays when my wife went to church."

"You didn't go to church with her?"

"Marcy, I'm Jewish."

"Maybe we're related," I joked.

"I must admit that I enjoyed celebrating Christmas," he said.

"Did you have a Christmas tree?" I asked.

"Of course. I made all of the decorations."

"That's wonderful," I said. "Did your Christmas lights get all tangled? I always thought that if I had a tree, that would be my big problem."

He shook his head. "The lights were Amy's job. I mean, my wife's job. Her name was Amy. Amy Vogel."

"Well, as long as we're coming clean . . . my husband's name is Harvey. Harvey Hammer."

"I know. I buy all my bras from him," he said with a laugh.

I clinked my coffee cup to his.

"So tell me," he said, "do you want to be my Saturday friend?"

"What would that entail?" I asked.

"We would meet each Saturday morning and do what we will call 'something.'"

"I would like that," I said.

Chapter 29

In April, Walter Knight was in the hospital again. On my way home from the movies with Jon, I stopped at Saint Mordecai, where Candy was keeping vigil. I found her dozing on a fat recliner outside her father's room. I debated waking her, and then gently touched her wrist. "Fox News, anyone?" I said as a greeting.

She sighed with relief. "Thank heaven for you."

I smiled at her exhausted face.

"I am so glad you came. He's on a respirator. This recliner was in the hall. There's another recliner in his room. It's not as wide. We can push it out here if you want to stay awhile. I hope you will stay."

In her father's room, the lights were on although he was sleeping. I looked out the steel-encased window to the dreary street. There was a man with a broken umbrella he was trying to close, heading into the building. The asphalt glistened. An old Volvo splashed by. A red taxi waited.

I walked over to the head of the bed. Walter was motionless, his eyes closed. I could tell that Candy had combed his white hair. She wet a washcloth at the sink and dabbed around his pale forehead and cheeks.

"I keep pressing the morphine button," she said as she did just that. "I don't want him to be in any pain, but I've probably overdosed him by now."

"It's on a meter," I said.

"Really?" she said. "Are you sure?"

"If you're worried, you could stop pressing it. Or talk to the nurse."

"I can't stop. It's the only thing I feel like I can control."

The room was bare, the kingdom of bland in the town of beige.

"I detest this room. At least in the nursing home, he has his life around him. His golf clubs are in his room, leaning against the wall. Isn't that terrific? He would putt them into a plastic ice bucket."

I laughed. "What else is in the room?"

"His tennis racket, a paperweight from his desk, and his lobster trap from Deer Isle."

"Where's Deer Isle?" I asked.

"It's hours north, en route to Acadia National Park. That's where we summered."

"Jon is from Maine. He grew up in Portland. I've never been to Maine."

"You must. Go in the summer or the fall. That's when Maine is an aphrodisiac. My parents met when my mother was visiting her grandparents during July, and Dad, who came every year for the entire summer, stalked her. But I don't think it was called 'stalking' back then. He remembers telling his cousin he wanted to marry her."

"The first time he met her?"

"Very first," she said.

"I have an idea. I can go to the nursing home tomorrow and bring his important things here to the hospital."

"That would be terrific. He'll feel a lot better once his clubs are in the room. His bag belonged to his grandfather. And he has his grandfather's license plate on his car. So much history."

"Do you have any pictures in your wallet?" I asked.

She opened her bag and handed me a wallet-size leather photo album. The first shot was of her mother, about the age we were, with a book in a hammock on a great stretch of lawn. Candy's mother was a patrician with thick white hair. She reminded me of Barbara Bush.

"When he dies, she won't know he's gone," Candy said.

"I'm so sorry." There I was with the "so sorry" again.

"I could say, 'Mom, Dad died today.' Do you know what she would say?"

I shook my head.

"'I requested orange gelatin,'" Candy said sadly.

I placed the pictures around the room, leaning them against the telephone, the ice bucket, a sanitized cup tucked into a white wrapper on the radiator. "I wish I had tape," I said. "I'll get some tomorrow."

There were four pictures of Jumper—skiing, climbing, sailing, and tossing a football. "Did you call your son?" I asked.

"No. He's with his father. And there's nothing he can do."

"He could keep you company. He could see his grandfather."

"It appears *you* are my company."

I knew from her tone it was time for me to shut up.

When she saw that I was wearing heels, she went to her father's cupboard and passed a pair of blue hospital socks to me. I removed my shoes and pulled on the stretchy socks with the rubber bottoms. I dangled my foot. "What do you think?"

"Watching my father die is killing me," Candy said as she pushed the button on the morphine drip.

I moved behind the recliner and turned it so that the seat was facing the door. "Let's push this monster into the hall."

"I don't think it will fit through the door," Candy said.

I pushed forward. "It got in here. It has to be able to go out."

"I don't want him to die today. Don't let him die today," she pleaded with me from the other side of the recliner.

"Today isn't the day," I said.

"Do you promise?" she said as she took her place next to me, pushing and shifting the chair out the door and into the hall.

We positioned the recliner so that it was adjacent to the one she had been dozing on when I arrived. We sat, close to each other, elbows touching, looking forward, chairs erect against the stark putty wall, the visitors gone, the nurses changing their long shifts, the night maintenance man waxing the speckled floor with a machine. Candy rose to administer morphine to her father again.

At eight, I left the hospital to go home and change for my day at work. At nine, Walter was gone.

Alone in a corner at the memorial service for Candy's dad, I was warm in the suit I'd worn at my mother's funeral, the black one Candy had picked out in Westport. But it seemed appropriate to be wearing it.

The conservative attire, the hushed tones, and the lack of the very young and the very old at the funeral gave the service the air of a tidy corporate event, and made me miss my family. I overheard a woman, replete in Burberry—suit, scarf, shoes—discussing how courageous Candy was, listing how much she'd been through. She said Candy's dad was the finest fellow, and it was a shame about her mother and the Alzheimer's and the home.

I wondered whether Harvey would die before me. He was chubby—the size of the overweight guys who are married to short, thin women on situation comedies—a type 2 diabetic with his sugar out of control, a type A personality. On occasion, like the time we had battled over the steak the size of Kansas and he had raged off, I warned him about his weight. But who was I kidding? I was an Olympic-class enabler. *"Here, Harvey, have another twice-baked potato. The romaine is delicious with sugar-coated pralines, honey almonds, plump raisins, and blue cheese crumbles."* There were times I'd turned a bowl of lettuce into a three-thousand-calorie meal. Now I spent a few dark moments every day imagining Harvey losing serious weight the way only a man can—swiftly, and without exercising. I feared his thinness. If he ultimately got into shape, it would prove to everyone how well he was doing—in his new life without me. Unfortunately, the trimmer I imagined Harvey, the more I wanted to eat.

Candy was speaking to her relatives, who were pixieish and perfect, like her. I didn't know a soul in the room, and weary of waiting for the service to start, I escaped to a restroom. When I returned, Candy grasped my hand and pulled me into one of the rooms reserved for the people who were closest to the deceased. We were alone, the sofas and folding chairs pathetically empty.

"Do you want to sit down?" I asked Candy.

She waved my suggestion off. "Brian is here."

At last I would get a live look at the heartbreaker.

"Without my son."

"What do you mean?"

"I was going to send a car to Bosley-Billingsworth for Jumper."

It was hard to believe what I had just heard. She was going to *send a car* to get her son to bring him to his grandfather's funeral? In my family, we had a tendency to pick up our children ourselves on such occasions.

"Then, Brian offered to get him. So I said that was fine."

"So why is Brian here alone? Where's Jumper?" I said, keeping my outrage to a minimum.

"Brian decided school was important and it was better not to disrupt the boy."

Going by her husband's skunk of a record, I figured that Jumper had simply found something better to do. I assumed Candy was thinking that too. But I didn't know how she could think at all since she was now at her father's service without her only child.

"I'm a mess," Candy said, shaking. "But I just turned and walked away from him because I can't start a ruckus."

Demeanor was everything to her. But under the circumstances, I didn't understand how she had maintained it.

"I managed to write a eulogy last night. The problem is, I won't make it through the first paragraph without blubbering. Please, please, read it for me." She reached into her blazer pocket and handed me two lilac pages folded in half. "It's handwritten, but I write very neatly."

"Are you sure you don't want a relative to read it?"

"I want you to read it. I thought about it and thought about it, and I want you to read it." Then, before I could say anything else, she said we had better join the others.

We returned to the chapel. Candy spoke to the funeral director as I took a seat in the first row next to a private nurse, an Ethiopian woman who had taken care of Walter while he lived in the nursing home. I didn't want to unfold the eulogy. I was fearful it would be too painful for me to read. My throat would catch. I wouldn't be able to finish.

Candy joined me. I patted her hand. I watched Brian, who was posing against a pillar. Was he too good to sit down? Or did he want to make sure that everyone saw him—so kind to attend the funeral when Candy and he were kaput?

I had seen Brian in photographs, but I hardly recognized him without his sports equipment, a snow-capped mountain, or a riotous wave in the background. Truth was, he looked even better in person, in a suit and tie. In fact, Brian reminded me of the paternal figure in an advertisement for a gold wristwatch that costs more than a vacation home in Nantucket, a watch passed down for generations.

I had to fight every impulse that I had to keep myself from going right up in his face and asking him how he could hurt Candy and why he didn't bring Jumper. He enraged me, but I knew my fuming was mostly about Elisabeth. *How dare you pummel my daughter? And, by the way, Dr. Bang, you should have brought your son.*

The pastor, a stern, distinguished man, stood at the podium, an exquisite ceramic urn on an adjacent draped table somehow dwarfing him. He recited "The Lord Is My Shepherd" and several prayers I had never heard before. Then he said, "Candy has written a eulogy for her father, and her lifelong friend Marcy Hammer will read it now."

I certainly wasn't her lifelong friend, although it did seem like a lifetime had passed since I'd first bumped into her in the hospital. I felt undeserving and embarrassed by the unexpected honor, but equally moved. I touched Candy's shoulder as I passed to the podium. I cleared my throat and opened the lilac paper. The mahogany banjo clock ticked two o'clock from a corner. A man coughed. I could hear the crinkling of a wrapper. Candy was looking down into her lap, almost studying it.

I read slowly, keeping my eyes on her words.

"Sadly, due to her illness, my mother is unable to be here today."

Someone sneezed in a back row. It threw me off.

"Dad graduated Phi Beta Kappa from Dartmouth and began work at Travelers in Hartford. Twenty years later, he became CEO of our family corporation and facilitated the merger with Aetna. Naturally, I am proud of him as a businessman, but I am even prouder of him as a family man. Dad was not demonstrative, nor free with approving words. His actions told me all that I needed to know. He rose early and went to work early, but each morning, Dad brewed a cup of English breakfast tea for my mother, wrapped it in a cozy, and placed it on her bedside table so she would find it there when she awoke."

I stopped for a moment and caught my breath. I wanted to look at Candy for her approval, but I stared out at the room instead.

"Dad loved Mom eternally. When Mom decided late in life to return to school to finish her doctorate and ultimately teach, she was concerned about the long drive to the university, in Storrs. The campus was a good hour from where we lived and, of course, a more tedious trip in winter snow. Dad insisted that she apply, and her application was successful. Dad

*drove Mom to Storrs many times a week, and he was in the room when she
defended her thesis.*

"*Dad was that way to me as well. On the first day of art school in
Boston, I met a boy I liked immediately, but after a month, he ended our
relationship. One month is a long time for a college girl. I stayed in my
room. I couldn't eat. I couldn't sleep. At eighteen, I was sure my world had
ended. One night, I was surprised to find Dad knocking at my dormitory
door. In his suit with loosened tie, Dad sat down next to me. 'If you miss
one bus, you catch the next,' he said.*

"*Dad then asked me for two glasses. He opened his briefcase and pulled
out a bottle of whiskey. He poured single malt, his drink of choice at the
time—one for him, one for me.*

"*He was and always will be my Walter in the Water.*"

As I concluded the eulogy, choking back tears, all I could think
was *Sixty years. Her parents were married sixty years.* Almost twice the
time Harvey and I had been married. Would anyone honor me, care for
me? I didn't have Alzheimer's. Thank heaven I was healthy. He didn't
as much as have to hand an aspirin to me, and Harvey still took off.
I had read Candy's eulogy. Sadly, there would be no such eulogy for
Harvey or me.

∽

The reception was in a white tent on the rolling lawn of the funeral
home. There were bars, each with one bartender, serving liquor in crystal glasses. There was a long decorative table laden with flowers, cookies,
and cake, along with cloth napkins and fine china plates. In a corner,
there was a table with a small white-and-gold sign: "Dad's Favorite
Dessert." I took a petite whoopie pie filled with pumpkin. I glanced
around, hoping for another look at Brian. Apparently, he had ducked
out at the end of the service.

"Glad to meet you, Candy's best friend," a woman said. She was overdressed for the occasion. For any occasion. I knew immediately she had married mistakenly into the family. She extended her hand. "Pamela. I'm married to Brian's older brother, the good son."

"Marcy Hammer," I said.

"Can you believe Brian didn't bring Jumper?" she said as though we were at an all-girl, all-night pajama party. As she finished her sentence, Candy approached, and I was certain she had heard.

"Candy, I was glad to hear that your mother is better," Pamela said.

"She's as fine as can be expected," Candy said, heading off any further conversation regarding the matter.

Pamela told Candy to keep in touch, then departed.

Candy turned to me. "All day, every day, my mother sits in her wheelchair in the hall, hugging a rag doll in an apron, feeding it with a bottle. And when I come to the nursing home, Mom wants to know whether I brought diapers for her baby. Do you know who she thinks I am? She thinks I'm Hilda. Hilda is the woman who took care of me when I was a child. Hilda wore a hairnet and weighed over three hundred pounds. Marcy, it's all over."

I felt helpless. What was there to say? What could I do?

"Candy, I have an idea. Maybe we could take a ride to Jumper's school." My children always made *me* feel better—even when we were disagreeing.

"Maybe," Candy said.

"Come on. It's a destination. We can take him out for lunch."

"It would be good for me," Candy said.

"We can go on any Saturday," I said.

"I'll call the school to see if we can visit. Jumper has classes and activities on Saturdays."

"Well, we have class, and I'll think of an activity."

Chapter 30

Harvey and I had always been generous to our children, but after the birth of the baby, Harvey became Mr. I'll Pay for That. I knew exactly what was going on: Harvey didn't want our children to think the one-month-old had diminished his love for them, had reduced their rankings and modified their relationships.

As Harvey pandered to our kids with substantial gifts, Ben crowned him the "sultan of Brunei." Amanda informed me about the royal title when she'd returned from a business trip to Paris, and we met in Manhattan at a café with chandeliers, tapestry sofas, and many rugs. When Amanda excused herself, she left her iPad on the seat of her chair.

With nerves on end, I reached over and zipped through her photographs. I saw pictures of merchandise and interiors from different angles, models on a runway, and Amanda with a handsome business-man. As I wondered who he was, I continued searching through the photographs, glancing furtively at the door to the restroom across the café. I held the iPad lower in my lap, almost in my skirt. Then, there it was—a close-up of Harvey Hammer, cradling the month-old baby I had never seen before. Baby Oops—Jorge Pablo Hammer—had copious red hair from Harvey's side of the family, and his mother's—I assumed—dark complexion.

Amanda exited the ladies' room, and I slipped her iPad back onto her chair, hoping she wouldn't recall in exactly what position she had left it.

When Amanda joined me again, she said that she had gotten past her anger at her father. He was a man, a human being. And, even the most revered biblical characters did things that were wrong.

She said that Harvey had told her she'd gotten enough experience working for other companies and had asked her to consider moving back to Connecticut, sooner rather than later, to start at Bountiful. It made sense. Amanda was Harvey's succession plan. She had majored in marketing and then studied part-time until she earned her MBA. She was a hard worker, with Harvey's business sense, and she had left the trainees who began with her in retail wondering which rocket she took off on.

Harvey had always been proud of Amanda, beaming when he thought about her and mentioning her to everyone. When we were out with friends, Harvey would boast about Amanda as though no one else in the universe had a child. These days, he was on the telephone with her constantly, discussing their common interests, such as the division of retail floor space. Their relationship was magnificent, but Amanda wasn't ready to abandon big-city living, a big-city department store, and her nightlife for Harvey's warehouse in the woods. The old Harvey would have known that and respected it. The new Harvey was hopeful she would join his firm once she received her bonus from Bloomingdale's.

∽

Harvey wanted to see me. It said so in an e-mail message. When I opened the message, I was at the office lining up artisans for a charitable exhibition. I replied to Harvey with two words: "Too busy." He pursued me online, responding that he could be at my office in an hour. I didn't like that idea, concerned about any Old West gunslinging between us that other people might see or hear. On the other hand, my curiosity was mounting. I told him to meet me in the rear parking lot.

Harvey wore a new Red Sox baseball cap. Even his beloved Yankees had been traded in. His casual attire was surprising on a weekday morning, but then Harvey was full of surprises.

I would have bet my children's only shoes that he was about to inform me that he had hired a divorce lawyer—as though he had slapped down a retainer yesterday, when I was certain he'd had an attorney in a $3,000 made-to-order suit and $75 paisley socks imported from Italy, before the baby was born. Feldman would have insisted on it. I hadn't heard from any lawyer, but that didn't mean Harvey didn't have one. It didn't matter. I was committed to playing the game of wait and see.

I walked over to Harvey's new car, a black convertible that screamed "No baby seat may be installed in this portion of my midlife crisis." When Harvey emerged, then stood next to me, I moved a few steps toward the trunk.

"The baby must love to ride in this car," I said.

He ignored my remark. "Have you heard from the kids?"

"Of course."

"Did they say anything about me?"

"Sure."

"Did they say what's going on?" he asked.

"Of course." It was tougher than I thought to say almost nothing. No wonder silence was golden.

He kicked a rock at his feet.

I waited.

He placed his hands in his pockets. "The parrot is doing well. Interestingly, he prefers seeds to pellets."

I looked around the parking lot. Jon walked into the office carrying a painting, wrapped in brown paper, for the exhibition. Even though we'd never as much as held hands, I felt connected to him, linked more to him than to Harvey. Jon didn't wave, which meant he didn't see me.

"Who knew?" Harvey said out of nowhere. "You just don't know. How can you ever know what's in another person's head?"

Touché, I thought.

"I'm in the Presidential Suite, and I can't sleep."

"Problem?" I said, proud that I'd used only one word.

"My life is hell," he blurted out.

I wanted to say "Thanks for the good news," but I managed to remain silent. Why was he telling me this? Who unloads on the scorned wife?

"The woman needs a state mental institution—no hall phone, no cigarettes, no visitation; all the mail should be opened, read, and edited before she receives it."

"Who?" I knew precisely whom Harvey was talking about, but I wanted the joy of hearing him say her name aloud.

"My baby mama."

I laughed. It should be unlawful for a man named Harvey to say the words "baby mama."

"That's the terminology today."

"Uh-huh."

"She calls my office incessantly. If an assistant doesn't put her through, she lashes out. If I take the call, she won't ever hang up."

This was fabulous news—what he deserved but not quite enough.

"There's more," he said. "I hired her a live-in nanny, a 32A right-wing Christian from Oklahoma. I'll never understand a girl with a flat chest choosing a soft cup. She needs a padded bra, but she doesn't know that because she's never been to the East Coast before."

Life was tough . . . Then you hired a nanny who'd never been to the East Coast before.

"Madison doesn't touch the baby."

It was unusual to hear her name. She had become the M-word to me. "Maybe it's postpartum depression."

"You never had postpartum depression."

"Yes, I did. You never noticed it."

"When was that?"

"It was after Amanda was born."

"Who could be depressed about having Amanda?"

"Her own mother," I said. "Every afternoon I cried until I couldn't see. I thought of terrible things."

We both remained against the car, looking forward at the driveway instead of at each other. I hated that he still thought motherhood was the giant rainbow lollipop of life. "I lived on a couch in the family room in front of the old big-box TV. I gazed at three hours of soap operas a day. That's fifteen hours a week, for about fifty weeks. That's wasting thirty days of my life. But I didn't care. I spent my days sucking on a Donald Duck pacifier so that I wouldn't binge and gain weight. I still have it in a drawer."

"The weight?"

Okay, so that kind of comment was why I'd married him. "The pacifier," I said.

He looked at me the old way, and I recalled the night we'd met at Cousin Leona's party and our escape to the hallway, where we'd served humor balls back and forth. And I remembered that for a long time, we had a very good time.

"Harvey, what do you want from me?"

"I don't know," he said.

I forced myself to turn toward him. I looked over his shoulder at the full trees on the curving country road beyond.

He stared at me, which was odd, because he hadn't really looked at me in a long time. I thought maybe he could finally see me, the woman who enabled him to lead the life he wanted, often kinder to him than

I was to myself. I was done speaking to him, advising him, making generous excuses for the behavior of his "baby mama."

"Harvey, I have to go."

I walked swiftly back into the office. I collapsed into the seat at my desk. I reached for tissues, spilling my coffee over the call list of volunteer painters, potters, and illustrators for the exhibition, trembling yet relieved I had walked away.

&

"What do you mean, you invited Harvey to Jeremy's wedding?" I asked Dana later that day as she stood in front of my desk at work. I was stunned, as though I had been hit with a Taser.

"I didn't invite him," Dana said. "I had nothing to do with it. Jeremy sent the invitation."

"You're telling me that your son, Jeremy, practically my nephew by dint of how much time I spent with him while he was growing up; your son, whose diaper rash was on fire until I rushed over to your house with the medicated ointment; your son, whose toenails I clipped until he was two because you were such a coward; your son, who called me Mommy 2, didn't know what was happening with Harvey and me?"

"You know how Jeremy feels about Harvey. Jeremy decided on business school because of Harvey. Besides, I didn't know until the invitation had already gone out."

"Well, get the invitation back."

"I can't. I'm in an impossible situation."

"No, I'm the one in the impossible situation," I said.

"Jeremy called Harvey to say he was getting married."

"He did?" Of late, I soured when anyone demonstrated an appreciation of or affection for Harvey, deservedly or not. I knew Harvey meant a lot to Jeremy, but it had never occurred to me that Dana would allow Jeremy to invite him.

"Do you have an ashtray?" Dana asked as she pulled a pack of cigarettes out of her bag.

"You cannot light a cigarette in this office. Besides, I have a lot of work to do. We have a show going up. I don't have time for this."

"So, when Jeremy called Harvey, your generous husband asked if the bride would like a trousseau from Bountiful Bosom. Harvey said Moxie should go to the store on the Upper West Side and see Hannah."

"Hannah? She's still there?" I felt more naive and foolish than ever, realizing that Hannah remained on the payroll, and chances were that One-Eyed Bobby, whom Harvey had also said he was going to fire, was parked on his stool reading the newspaper at the warehouse, dining on blueberry and corn muffins Harvey brought in. I was a smashed 1970 stick shift in a pileup of Harvey's lies. That day at the house, he went on and on about his troubled business, but the man was probably making more money than ever.

"I have no idea who these characters who work for Harvey are," Dana said, "but now the bride loves Harvey too."

I stared at Dana mercilessly and suddenly realized how much I hated her pristine hair. Her waist-length blond locks made her appear younger than anyone our age or anyone ten years younger than us. I detested that she could snack night and day and never gain a pound. I detested her lean, toned body and her sculpted arms. Dana would go sleeveless in an Alaskan blizzard while driving huskies, to display her limbs. At that moment, I disliked everything about Dana Davenport. First, it was Harvey, and now Dana. Was there a soul in this world I could trust?

"I regret that Jeremy insists on inviting Harvey to his wedding," she said. "We had such a row about it—worse than the argument about the color of the ink on that gaudy invitation, which wouldn't have been a problem at all if I had done the copy and design. But, no, they had to go to a commercial printing house. I'm a respected art director and the CEO of an advertising agency, and my son plucks his invitation—with a bow on top—from a horrifying retail catalog in a dreary Boston stationery store. Believe me, the Harvey thing was not the first problem."

Silence. Over the course of my domestic tragedy, I had mastered the art of letting the other person insert foot in mouth by simply remaining quiet myself.

"Believe me, Marcy. I was appalled, out of my mind when I heard that Jeremy had invited Harvey. But Jeremy said it was time we all grew up. Ha. He's thirty, and he's telling us to grow up." Dana sat down on top of a three-drawer file cabinet and crossed her legs. "I understand that this is a disaster, but there is nothing I can do about it. Jeremy's entire wedding is trial by fire. Do you have any idea what it's costing me? And that's with her parents taking out their millionth house mortgage. Just *say* the word 'wedding' in earshot of a caterer or florist or hairstylist, and the prices go up a third."

As far as I was concerned, it wasn't costing her enough. I glared as she put her damn cigarettes back into her bag. Did she actually think she could go now?

"You're turning on your best friend for a free negligee?" I said.

"Stop," Dana said. "I've been divorced. I did it twice to get it right. This is what it's about. He shows up. You show up. Every holiday and occasion sucks. Fortunately for me, Jeremy's father is gone."

"Lovely."

"Well, at least you didn't have what I had with the twins—two different school conferences with the same teacher, year in and year out, hopscotching holidays, alternating birthday parties."

"You're correct. I'm the lucky one," I said as I slumped in my chair. "It's clearly better that I spent my entire life on Harvey."

"Harvey's coming alone, and all of your kids will be there. Do you want to bring someone? You could bring Jon."

"What makes you think Jon would like to be stationed in my minefield?"

"Marcy, did I tell you the wedding cake is made of Oreo cookies?"

Fat chance I gave a hoot what kind of cake was being served at the wedding.

"We'll seat Harvey at another table with the most boring, tedious people in the world, and we'll put his atrocious table in front of the kitchen door. Better yet, I'll place him at a table between two grandmothers who won't stop talking about grandchildren—and they'll have as many pictures as Irving Penn."

I didn't want to hear one more word about the wedding.

"What do you think of Oreo cake?" Dana said.

By the time Dana reached me in my car that evening, I had called the Upper West Side store to find out if Hungry Hannah was, in fact, still employed. She was. I'd berated myself again for my naïveté, but I'd also decided I was not the kind of woman who refused an invitation to her best friend's son's ceremony because her estranged husband would be there. I planned to gather my forces and attend the wedding, without a date but with self-esteem. The wedding would be the first time I'd have to be at a family event with Harvey, but not the last. I had spent more than half of my life with him. I could spend an evening. Besides, he was going alone.

"Dana, I've recouped. I'm fine about the wedding," I said when I answered my cell. I was proud of myself for making this decision. My mother would call it "being the bigger one."

"He's plus one," Dana said rapidly, probably hoping I wouldn't hear.

"You're joking." I was aghast.

"I found out today that Moxie sent the invitation addressed to 'Harvey Hammer and Guest.'"

"What?" I was incredulous.

"I'm sorry."

I had to know. "Dana, is his baby mama his plus one? He claims he's not living with her. He claims she's a maniac. But who knows the truth."

"I guess his plus one is anyone he wants to bring," she said.

"Well, then, count me as his minus one."

"I can't do this without you. I invited only a few other friends so I could get your kids into my count."

"I'm not going to sit by myself watching Harvey and his juvenile delinquent slow-dance to 'For Once in My Life' with their baby between them in a carrier. Or worse, see him enter the room with a new woman."

"Stop worrying about the baby. The wedding is no children, except the flower girl. The baby isn't invited."

"Even for you, this is amazingly insensitive. Go away."

I headed to Food Kingdom, open late, where I could rest my brain in the dairy aisle. I stood staring, valiantly trying to change my delinquent grocery behavior by buying only what I needed for myself. When I had ten items, I pushed my carriage zero miles per hour to the express line. I stood behind a man in work overalls buying an Italian sub and a six-pack of beer. A weary old lady with twisted gray hair and a pail of multiple-cat clumping litter stepped up behind me, and then a single girl, with a tin from the salad bar and a Diet Snapple. As I looked at her, she nodded hello to me. I watched as she sent a text message. I considered the other aisles—the family aisles, the "I want a candy bar, Mom" aisles. I placed my cottage cheese on the checkout counter and answered my phone. It was Dana again.

"Jeremy called Harvey and told him to come alone. He said he didn't want you to feel uncomfortable," she said.

"Really, Dana, what's uncomfortable about my husband dancing with his baby mama while I'm in the ladies' room pinching perfume from the bridal basket so I can spray it in his eyes at the dessert buffet?"

The checkout girl interrupted. "My parents don't get along either," she said.

Chapter 31

It was a May wedding. I arrived alone.

I had never attended a wedding by myself. In college, I'd brought dates. After that, there was Harvey. I thought about all the single women in the world who were alone on special occasions and realized that I had never made an effort to reach out in any way.

I took an aisle seat on the groom's side of the outdoor chapel. The chairs were white with plum ribbons tied to the legs. A justice of the peace—with a mustache and a goatee—was standing at the podium. To his side, two violinists and a cellist were waiting to play. Dana's first cousin, Marlene the Man Eater (that's what Dana always called her), gave me a nod. I returned the greeting.

Dana's friend Wendy waved to me. Coincidentally, Wendy had grown up in Queens with me. When we were kids, Wendy had pushed me over, into a row of hedges in my yard. I dashed into the house to report her to my mom. And what did Mom say? "Marcy, she's your friend. Be the bigger one. Look the other way." With all of my looking the other way, I'm surprised I never sprained my neck.

Dana's sister gave me an air-kiss. She was in a short satin dress with a beige lace overlay and a beret that belonged to Dana.

Elisabeth arrived. I moved one seat down so she could settle next to me on the aisle. The remainder of the row was vacant.

"I like your dress, Mom," Elisabeth said. I had discovered it in my closet with the tags still on.

More importantly, I was wearing a white strapless bra that I had bought online. I knew Harvey would notice immediately, fit maven that he was, that it was not his brand.

"This wedding is so cookie-cutter. The plans must have made Dana irate," Elisabeth whispered, covering her mouth with her hands. Her hair was curled, loose to her shoulders, which were creamy and bare.

Amanda and Ben came from the city. Elisabeth and I moved further into the row. Amanda was too stylish for the occasion—fashion-forward while on a field trip with actuaries.

"Where's Dad?" Ben asked as he adjusted his raspberry tie.

Maybe Harvey didn't know how important he was to Jeremy and Moxie. Perhaps he was delayed at Bountiful, or was talking deductions with Feldman and forgot the wedding. Reminding Harvey about life-cycle events had been my job—and I was now out of work.

Harvey scurried in minutes before the procession began. He tapped Ben's shoulder, and the four of us moved down yet another seat.

A five-year-old flower girl in an eyelet dress skipped down the wedding aisle, dropping snapdragons from a straw basket. She halted midway and looked furtively toward her mother, who waved her on. The guests were smiling, with the exception of Harvey, who, head down, was consulting his phone. I signaled him with my index finger to put the cell in his pocket, but before he saw me, I remembered that I wasn't his caretaker anymore; his rude behavior didn't reflect on me.

Following the flower girl were the bridesmaids, in strapless J.Crew dresses. Harvey glanced up to take in their breasts. *"34B, 36C, 40D,"* I could hear him thinking, proud of the bras compliments of Bountiful Bosom, fitted by Hungry Hannah.

As a violinist played, Jeremy appeared in a tuxedo. We rose as Moxie came into sight. She was chalky and stiff, locked between her parents, who were clutching her as though they were escorts to her execution. Groom approached bride as Harvey responded to an e-mail. Elisabeth saw him with the phone, rolled her eyes, and whispered to me, "What else is new?"

☙

When the ceremony concluded, we remained in our row, chatting as though we were still a family. I was the mom. Harvey was the dad. Elisabeth, Amanda, and Ben played the children. In a hushed tone, Ben sang, "Here comes the cell phone."

Amanda said, "I've never seen anyone answer e-mails at a wedding before. I'm proud you're my dad."

My other kids laughed.

"It couldn't be helped," Harvey said. "There are problems in the warehouse. I own a business. I can't just disappear."

Harvey's phone rang, a tone similar to two deep belches.

He said, "Yes, Feldman," and walked steps away, seeking privacy in a noisy room crowded with wedding guests. We checked the table cards arranged on a sideboard. I was at table 5 with my kids.

"Dad's not sitting with us," Elisabeth said as she opened Harvey's place card.

"That's embarrassing," Ben whispered to her. I pretended I didn't hear.

Harvey returned to us, interrupting the conversation, cutting off Elisabeth midsentence. "That was Feldman. He's tracking a website that's selling merchandise from Bountiful at a discount."

"On Saturday night," I said. It was a statement, not a question. Feldman worked an eight-day week.

"It turns out that a manager is lifting merchandise at the warehouse. Her daughter is selling the filched brassieres online."

I noticed he was studying my chest as he spoke.

"That's not a Bountiful bra," he said.

I hit him with a grenade. "Actually, I went to another place."

"What other place?"

"Let's go to the bar," Ben said to the girls, avoiding the earth tremors he assumed were about to start.

"I thought you were just wearing what you had," he said to me.

"No," I said, savoring the moment.

"You bought a bra?" he said, aghast. "Where? Why?"

Instead of saying I purchased the bra online, which was where I bought it, I said I bought it at Victoria's Secret. He hated Victoria's Secret, but most of all, he wanted to be as big as Victoria's Secret.

"Wow. That really hurts. You bought a brassiere from Victoria's Secret."

"You had an affair and a baby."

"I'm not going tit for tat here."

Suddenly, Dana was next to us, between us.

"Dana, I know you were concerned, but the wedding is wonderful," I said. "And Jeremy looks so incredibly happy."

"Thank you, Marcy. Harvey, may I borrow your cell phone?"

Harvey removed his lifeline from the pocket of his made-to-order suit and gave it to Dana. She grinned a thank-you, strutting off to make what I assumed was a private call. But I couldn't figure out whom Dana would be calling, because anyone she would want to call was at the wedding.

I watched as, from across the room, Dana waved to Harvey, waited until he noticed, grinned from ear to ear, and pointed to his cell phone. Harvey smiled back. I could hear him thinking, *"Glad to help out."*

Then, like a pitcher at a baseball game, Dana wound up wide and hurled Harvey's damn cell phone out the window.

Chapter 32

I was wearing silk pajamas I had ordered from Lord & Taylor, made by a manufacturer Harvey referred to as "those shit heels." I retrieved the Sunday *New York Times* from the driveway, carried my newspaper and coffee up to my room, and lolled in the center of my bed, reading. Ever since the wedding, I had been feeling better. An entire week of feeling better. I called Candy and asked if she wanted to go for a walk.

We met on a path that extended through three states, but Candy and I always traveled the same portion, a two-mile trek that began near the field at Atherton Middle School.

After about half a mile of trying to keep up with Candy's brisk pace, I pretended I needed to retie my sneakers, and Candy had no ethical choice but to stand still while I did.

"How's Elisabeth?"

"She's dating a proctologist. But I won't go there."

"I guess we all have to learn our lessons the difficult way."

"I'm grateful that you forgave me for my deceit, but it amazes me that you actually ask me about Elisabeth."

"There's a reason," she said.

"You have empathy for liars and cheaters?"

She shook her head.

"Spill," I said.

"Firstly, we've been through a lot since the day we ran into each other in the hospital."

"Ha. You call this a lot?"

"And secondly, when *I* met Brian, he was married."

I stopped in my tracks and turned toward her. "You're making that up."

"I wish I was. He had been married twice, each time for about four years, but he had no children. Everyone—my parents, my friends—warned me he was the last man on earth who would be faithful, but I was too young, too infatuated, to believe a word of it. He's a charmer, and he has that effect on women."

A pack of serious runners, with headbands, were approaching us. We moved to the side of the path where the rocks met the trees.

"We were married at the courthouse. Later, we had a proper bash. It was under a white tent. Brian didn't want a fuss. And my parents were content to keep it simple. We served shellfish on blocks of ice, champagne, and a splendid buttercream cake."

We began walking again.

"I made every one of Elisabeth's mistakes. Only I did her one better and married him."

I was breathless again, and this time it wasn't from walking too fast.

"That's my story," Candy said, which meant she was done talking about it forever.

A woman on a bike with a basket honked her rubber horn, as if to say hello. Then a teenager in jeans on a mountain bike passed us quickly on the right.

"No helmet," I said.

"You should try it," Candy said.

"Riding a bike?"

"Not wearing a helmet. Take some chances."

"Breaking news—I already have."

"Are we talking Jon? Is he more entertaining than attending a convention of lingerie manufacturers in Las Vegas?"

"Harvey's association is called LUMP—Ladies' Undergarment Manufacturers and Providers."

"I will never forget that."

"Jon and I get together about once a week, on Saturdays. But there's no romance. He hasn't gotten over his wife yet."

"And you?"

"Yesterday I cleaned out a bathroom cabinet and found a tube of lubricant dated July two years ago. It made me think I wanted to have sex."

"I think you're entitled."

"Do you know what I worry about most?"

"Not a clue."

"My knees."

She looked at my knees, concealed by loose workout pants. "What's wrong with your knees?"

"Promise you won't laugh." I rolled my pants up to my thighs.

She studied my knees, right to left. "Oh, you're right. There are four of them."

"They sag."

"Good grief. We all have body parts we wish we could trade in."

"You don't," I said.

"Then why am I constantly working out and watching what I eat?"

"Okay, what's your body part?"

"My height. Or lack of it."

"Men love small women. But enough talk about me. What about you and a certain Leonardo? Still training?"

"Okay, you're right—we've trained all night."

"And?"

"I plan to keep training."

"He makes you happy."

"I guess he does."

"What's the best part?"

"He tickles my feet," she said.

"Seriously?"

"I'm usually serious."

You never know what goes on in someone else's house, I thought as I picked up a long branch from the ground. I removed the twigs, creating a walking stick, offered the stick to Candy, and she hiked the rest of the trail with it.

As we reached our cars, my phone vibrated. I recognized Feldman's office number; it had been the same from when I married Harvey to when he decided to throw everything away.

"It's Feldman," I whispered to Candy. "He's Harvey's accountant."

"Magnificent Marcy," Feldman said. "How are you?"

"Great," I said.

"How are the kids?"

"Can we get to it, Feldman?"

"What's the hurry?"

"My date just arrived. And he's too young to have patience."

"I see," he said, then paused. "Marcy, we need your signature on a form so I can file your tax return. It's been on extension since April, and Harvey wants it done now. You can stop by the office today, or I can deliver it by messenger—whatever's better for you."

I looked at Candy, who was performing deep knee-bends with the walking stick, and mouthed, "Wants me to sign a form."

"No way," she whispered back.

"Thank you as always," I said to Feldman. "If you drop it at my house, I'll return it as soon as I can."

I waved Candy over next to me.

"Don't be childish," Feldman said sternly. "I want to wrap this up today."

Candy signaled me to hang up.

"I'll call you back," I told Feldman.

"Stop everything," Candy said. "You can't just sign a tax return. You have to find out whether he's filing jointly or separately, and which is most lucrative for you."

"I'm certain that Feldman is looking out for Harvey. I guess I need to consult my own financial person now."

"I want you to call Parker Whitman," she said, slowly reciting the number as I pecked it into my phone. "He's the accountant to the stars."

"Which stars?"

"Every star who lives in Connecticut."

"I'm hiring my own accountant," I said in a singsong. "Crazy, but something about that makes me feel as though I'm in power and grown-up."

"It's your defining moment," she said.

I called Parker Whitman and said I was Candy's best friend. Candy smiled. Whitman said Feldman needed to e-mail our records to him immediately.

I wanted to wait awhile so Feldman and Harvey would get all itchy-scratchy about me signing, but I couldn't help myself. I phoned Feldman from the trail.

"No need to drop the return off," I said pleasantly. "Instead, I'd be very grateful if you forwarded our returns and all of our information to Parker Whitman in Greenwich."

"Parker Whitman? How do you know Parker?" Feldman said, bewildered, as though I had told him to send our returns to the president of the United States.

"How do *you* know Parker?" I asked him, downright gleeful.

"Everyone knows Parker," Feldman said. "Paul Newman swore by him."

"He's my accountant," I said proudly.

"Whitman isn't taking new clients," Feldman said. "And I'm your accountant."

"Not anymore," I said, feeling all kinds of supremacy.

Candy was laughing. I clicked off my phone, made two tight fists, and pummeled the air above me.

Then I said, "Feldman says Whitman isn't taking new clients." I was concerned that I would have to find someone else.

"He's my cousin. He's taking you."

"I wish I could be on the line when Feldman tells Harvey that I hired my own CPA. Harvey's heart will stop. Do you have any idea how great this is?"

"It's a step," she said seriously. "Now you have to think about moving."

"Believe me. That was my move. Harvey doesn't take a breath without Feldman's advice."

"What I mean is that you should move to a new house that befits the new you. There are darling Capes not far from where I live, on Pine Turn. If you are going to live in the country, I say live in the country."

Chapter 33

"Did I get here too early?" I asked on the following Saturday when Candy greeted me in a cobalt robe, collar up, belt tied in the nattiest bow I had ever seen.

"Leonardo just left," she said apologetically. "I'll hop in the shower and be ready in no time."

I couldn't imagine how a perfectionist could hop in the shower to be ready in no time, but I nodded.

I wandered into the kitchen. There was not one magnet or photograph on her refrigerator. She was a blank refrigerator person. I opened the behemoth. She was also an empty fridge person. There were several liters of vodka, a healthy supply of organic yogurt, orange juice, cranberry juice, a coconut, and a pineapple.

I didn't want to feel like I was with the FBI, so I stopped looking around, moseyed back into the living room, and called Dana.

I asked whether there was any news about colleges. Dana had sent the deposit to hold places at Tufts, but she was praying double-time that the girls would be plucked off a wait list at Yale.

"No news from Yale," Dana said drearily before I could ask about fat letters and thin letters in the mailbox.

I had no idea why she thought there were two seniors in the universe who were going to turn down Yale this late in the game, thereby making room for the twins.

"Every day at noon, I drive home from the agency to check the mailbox. I open it slowly, as though it's going to explode. But Yale could still happen," Dana said. "In fact, I bought a Yale sweatshirt for good luck."

"You did? Isn't that putting unnecessary pressure on the twins?"

"Don't be silly. I only wear the sweatshirt when I know the twins won't be around. It's not as though I bought a Yale bumper sticker and slapped it on our car."

"I see the difference," I said, laughing to myself.

☙

In about a half hour, less time than I'd thought it would take, Candy reappeared in a short skirt, a printed blouse, and heels.

I told Candy I needed to punch the boarding school's address into my GPS so we wouldn't get lost—unless, of course, she knew how to get there. We went with the GPS, and after I forgot to make a turn in two-tenths of a mile, the GPS lady became indignant.

"She always thinks she's right," I said to Candy over the lady's voice.

"Who are you talking about?"

"The GPS lady. She's always on her high horse. She thinks she knows something we don't know. She thinks she knows everything."

"Well, she does. She knows how to get there."

"Don't stick up for her," I said.

"Change her language to French."

"That would show her. But I took Spanish in high school."

"I speak fluent French." She rattled off words.

"What does that mean?"

"I'm glad you're going to Jumper's school with me."

I switched to French, and Candy translated. Almost two hours later, we passed a garage for car repairs, a white church, and a fire station, then turned right up a hill surrounded by woods to Bosley-Billingsworth.

The school was centered on a large quad bordered by massive oak and maple trees. We parked in the visitors' lot, near a gray clapboard house, then walked a stone path to the main building, with black shutters and green doors, overlooking the quad, where students were sauntering to class and greeting one another, and a few boys were tossing Frisbees. From the outside, the building gave the appearance of a well-cared-for antique home deserving of a historic plaque, but the shabby interior was another case. Maybe the building was next on the school's list of renovations. As I took inventory, I could feel Candy pick up on my negative thinking.

"Brian went here," she said, as though that explained the dust balls. "And his father went here. And his grandfather went here."

I wondered how far back this was going to go. "Candy, my grandfather dropped out in sixth grade. He made a tennis racket in shop class, and when the teacher criticized the racket, my grandfather hit the teacher over the head with it. Then he walked out of the school, never to return."

"You made that up."

"Right, because I wanted you to think I was from a long line of delinquents."

⌒⌒

Candy opened the door to the main office, where a woman in a tartan blazer with engraved buttons glanced up from her computer and greeted us with an English accent. She clicked her tongue when she finished each sentence. She said Jumper was changing clothes after practice and she would get in touch with the coach. Candy and I sat down on a bench outside the office.

"Here we are, waiting again," she said, listless, tapping her foot.

"No one knows how to wait like we do. If waiting becomes an Olympic sport, we are in."

She turned toward me. Timidly, she put her hand on mine. I was so moved I felt a chill.

"What if we had never met?" she said quietly, seriously.

"I would have missed out on all that Fox News."

"I've never had a girlfriend before."

"How could that be? You went to a girls' school."

"Women don't like me," she said.

"That's ridiculous."

"And I always had a boyfriend—from seventh grade on."

"That's probably why women don't like you."

"I guess I'm saying thank you," she said.

"Well, thank you too," I said.

She smiled a real smile for what I thought was the first time since her father passed away. I wanted to hug her. But I didn't. She wasn't a hugger.

When I felt as though we had waited long enough, a boy appeared in the hall. He was wearing the school uniform—khaki pants and a white shirt—but he had made the outfit all his own, the way popular children always do. His blond hair was in his eyes. He had a wicked smile.

He kissed Candy on the cheek. "Mom, I'm sad about Grandpa."

"I know," Candy said. "I miss him too. Marcy, this is Jumper."

"You'll have to tell me how you got your nickname," I said.

"What do you think?" he said.

"You jumped a subway turnstile in Manhattan?"

Jumper laughed. Candy seemed relieved.

"He loved the children's song about monkeys jumping on the bed," she said. "I would sing it again and again, and he would jump up and down."

"So Dad started calling me 'Jumper.'"

"And it must have been prophecy, because now my son's favorite part of skiing is jumping." She turned her attention back to Jumper. "How are you?"

"We killed Farber-Berkshire in soccer." He pumped his fist in the air.

"That's great," she said.

"We're playing Northville-Hammond tomorrow."

"I brought you something special," Candy said. She reached into her handbag and removed a small box wrapped in foil paper.

Jumper opened the package. It was a pocket watch. He turned it over in his hand several times. Then he said, "Mom, it's nice, but I check the time on my cell phone."

What a sentimentalist, I thought.

"It belonged to your grandfather."

"Oh. Thanks. Can you hold on to it for me? I wouldn't want to lose it or anything."

She placed the watch back in the foil and into her bag, struggling not to reveal her disappointment in his lack of interest. "Would you like to go out for lunch?" she said.

"I don't have time for lunch. I have to go to pottery."

I wanted to say "So you'll make a bowl another time." But he wasn't my child.

"I don't think it would be a problem to miss one class," Candy said. "After all, you didn't go to the memorial service."

It was almost lethally painful that she had to bring out the heavy artillery just to talk her kid into a grilled cheese, especially after we'd traveled for two hours in French.

"I told Dad I wanted to go," he said.

I didn't believe him.

"Whatever," Candy said. "It's done."

I noticed Jumper staring past Candy, down the corridor. There was a girl who at first glance looked to be wearing an oversize navy sweater and nothing else. Less than an inch of pleats stood between her and a *Playboy* photo shoot.

"Come along," Candy said to her son. She opened the door to the main office to sign Jumper out for lunch.

Jumper didn't move from the hallway. "Mom, the closest restaurant is fifteen minutes from here. And I went there with Archer's family. His father owns restaurants in Manhattan. It's kind of a hobby. And he returned his lamb chops—twice."

"Well, it's lunchtime. We won't be ordering lamb chops."

"Archer's mother said the staff was inattentive."

I felt like I was reading TripAdvisor.

"Mom, can't we talk here?"

It seemed the only way Jumper was going to lunch was in handcuffs. Candy surrendered and sat back down on the bench.

I was glad she had some vodka chilling at home.

Elated he had gotten his way, Jumper squeezed close to his mother. I said I was going to make a phone call. I walked to the end of the hall, bearing right as a bell rang and students piled out of the auditorium.

When I returned to the main office, Candy was out front alone. "Boys," she said. As we walked to my car, she asked, "Was your son like this?"

"Well, he's grown up now."

"Your children would have been at the funeral."

"All families are different," I said, to make her feel better.

"In my family, we act as though nothing happened. Then we never discuss what happened, because it never happened."

⁓

The restaurant with the lousy lamb chops and inattentive service was called Ye Ole Tavern. Now we'd had two warnings about the place—one from Jumper and the other from the restaurant's name. It was lunchtime, one o'clock, but there were only a few cars in the parking lot. One was a sedan with the license plate YOTVRN.

"Should we choose another restaurant?" Candy said.

I was hungry. "No, let's go in."

Candy was too worn out by her son to disagree.

At the door, a woman greeted us. She was wearing a colonial dress with a ruffled apron. She asked if we had reservations. When I said no, she said, "Well, let me see what I can do. We have been very busy. The Continental Congress departed a wee moment ago."

Candy and I stared into the oval dining room, where only two tables were occupied.

The greeter said, "I could seat ye in the Pig's Ear, but it's reserved for a large party."

"Any table is fine," Candy said.

"I'll be right back," the greeter said.

"We should go," I said. "This is a mistake."

"I'd like to try this place," Candy said.

Okay, I thought. *What's one more disaster?*

The greeter returned with menus rolled up as though they'd been delivered by Paul Revere. She held a dish with a candle on it, then lit the candle at our table.

A waiter arrived, in a white wig and a uniform that might have belonged to George Washington. "My name is Quincy. Welcome ye. Would ye like to know about our specials this day?"

I nodded.

"Today's special is lamb chops—two thick baby chops, marinated in a barrel for no less than forty-eight hours, grilled while supervised on our own hot coals."

"You marinate your lamb chops in a barrel?" I said.

"Yes," he said.

I couldn't help myself. "Is it a clean barrel?"

Candy looked away so she wouldn't laugh.

"I'll have the house salad," I said. It was tough to ruin iceberg let-tuce—and this was definitely not a fancy-lettuce place.

"I'll have a glass of chardonnay and the lamb chops," Candy said.

"How would ye like ye lamb chops prepared?" the waiter asked as we rolled up our menus.

"However." Candy tied the ribbon around her menu and handed it back to the waiter. My ribbon was somewhere on the floor.

When the waiter left, I said, "I can't believe you're having the lamb chops."

"I am, and they'd better be bad. In fact, this had better be the worst meal of my life."

I smiled.

"He's like his father," she said.

"And very good-looking," I said.

Candy beamed. I was praising her most important piece of work.

"He was asked to model for Abercrombie," she said.

"I can see him on a billboard."

"I didn't let him do it. I don't want him in that world."

"What did Brian think?"

"Go for it, of course."

"Did Jumper want to model?"

"The boy *is* his father's son. But there was no way I would agree to it."

"Every party has a pooper," I said. "That's usually why my children invite me."

The waiter returned with Candy's wine. He brought a woven basket covered with a doily. The muffins were rock-hard. No butter.

"Enough about my life for one day. Any news about Harvey's baby?"

"The baby's on Facebook."

"Do you mean that Harvey's on Facebook?"

"No, but Madison is. She posted a picture of the baby between her two bare breasts."

"Your husband's girlfriend friended you?"

"No, Elisabeth told me. Madison friended my children. And why not? She's their age."

The ridiculous waiter arrived with lunch. My shredded iceberg was in a cracked bowl. I glanced at Candy's plate. "Nice. They put a little lamb chop on your mint jelly."

"It's burned," Candy said. She was smiling. "What a relief this meal is to me."

"You should return it," I suggested.

"I'm not hungry, and if you remember, I don't eat meat."

She pushed the plate to the side, then became adamant. "Elisabeth shouldn't be telling you anything about anyone on Facebook. From this ye old lousy meal on, I suggest that you concentrate on how well *you* are doing. Your children are healthy, accomplished. You worked your way up into a full-time executive position in a stimulating place. And even for a woman a minute older than thirty, you look great."

I could feel myself blush. "Thank you, Your Kindness."

"My absolute pleasure."

"I've been thinking," I said. "Maybe what I need is a man. But I don't know what to do about my body image problems. I can't help thinking that I have the body of a woman passing middle age."

"Is that what's stopping you? With Jon."

"No. Like I've said before, he wants to be friends."

"You could fix that."

"No. I don't think I could."

"Are you a woman or a mouse?"

"Cheese, please."

"Wrong answer, Marcy. Make a list. What do you want next?"

"I'm not a business," I said, brushing her off, although I knew she was determined to make her point.

"You, my friend, are more than a business. You are your *most important* business."

I had never thought of myself in that way. My lifelong business had been my family—what they wanted, what they needed to achieve, their comings and goings, how they felt, how to make them feel better, the orchestrations of our complex lives. But I knew Candy was right. Now was the time to think about me, myself.

"You're moving on. Push off the pier. And don't look back—because the past isn't here anymore."

Chapter 34

When I saw Jon at a meeting to determine the winners of the annual Guild for Good scholarships, he asked if I was interested in going to a poetry reading.

I hadn't been to a poetry reading since college. The only poem I knew by heart was by Robert Frost, about two roads diverging and choosing the one less traveled. I didn't relate to the Frost poem. Maybe when I was young, I had taken less-traveled roads. But from the moment I met Harvey, the road I was on was more crowded, more standstill than an expressway at five thirty p.m. following a multitruck pileup.

As I thought this, I could swear I heard my mother's voice, direct from heaven: *"Marcy, what did you want to do? Live like a hippie?"*

"No, Mom. Not with an advanced degree in marketing from NYU."

But the shake-up in my life had made me realize I'd been stagnant. I had become Harvey's wife, Mrs. Hammer. I had become the mother of Elisabeth, Amanda, and Ben. I had yet to become Marcy.

Jon had said he would meet me at the reading, which was at Price College, the liberal arts school where he taught English in order to support his art. I parked my car in a lot marked "Green Stickers Only." I didn't have a green sticker, but I didn't think the campus police would actually tow my Volvo wagon. It looked way too faculty. I parked next to a Bug with a tattered Dead sticker. Suddenly, I wished I owned the Bug. *Wake up,* I thought. *You are fifty-nine years old. It's too late to be cool.* Then again, I was on campus midweek, meeting a younger man—five years younger and cooler than the subject of a *Rolling Stone* cover—at a poetry reading.

I stopped a young character in a rainbow beanie with braids and asked if he could point me to my destination, Rebecca Horbund Memorial Hall. He kicked the stand on his Columbia ten-speed and pointed across a football field.

"The cement building with the green stripe?" I asked.

He nodded.

I was standing on a magnificent campus with turn-of-the-century buildings, and I was headed for the edifice that looked like a converted Stop & Shop.

Once inside the building, I hunted down the ladies' room so I could check my makeup and hair. The bathroom walls were covered with graffiti. I read the advice someone had written on the stall door: *Mental problems? See Dr. Howard. You would have to be crazy to go to anyone else.*

I found the auditorium. Jon was down front talking to the poet. He spotted me and waved me down to the front, next to a United States flag, a Connecticut flag, and a heavy velvet curtain running across the stage.

Jon greeted me as though the last time he had seen me we were saying good-bye as he rushed the Berlin Wall. He introduced me to the poet, his friend Leanne.

"I've never met a real poet before," I said. "It's an honor."

"Jon's a poet," Leanne said.

I didn't know Jon wrote poetry. I'd always thought of him as a painter with a day job of teaching literature.

Leanne was very pretty—in an ethereal and willowy way. She had wispy, thin hair and feathery bangs. Her gossamer shirt had a Japanese floral motif. I could see her white bra beneath it. I wondered whether it was from Bountiful. I wondered whether she and Jon had ever been more than friends.

Jon and I took our seats. I liked an end seat, but Jon chose fifth row in the middle. We made our way through a passel of students. I sat down. There was a tall, chunky boy with a baseball hat sitting in front of me.

"This won't do," Jon said. "Let's change seats. I know it's only a reading, but I don't want you to have trouble seeing."

Wow, I thought. *This man is so nice.*

Leanne's poetry was about her life in Santa Monica, California. One poem, about the pier there, was dazzling. But the poem I liked best was called "Montana." It was about a shopping avenue in Santa Monica lined with restaurants, fitness palaces, and personal care salons frequented by divorced women with longish hair and yoga clothing, who spend whole weekdays getting work done on their faces and bodies as they're offered champagne. I was so into the idea of it I thought I should hop on a plane right away for a Brazilian butt lift, a pelvic wax, and a blowout. In Leanne's poem, an extraterrestrial descends on Montana Avenue. He returns to his planet reporting that on Earth most women have their pubic hair professionally removed after being served a mimosa.

When the reading was over, I told Jon how much I had enjoyed it. "And what's this I hear about you being a poet?" I said as we stood to leave.

He said Leanne was wrong. He didn't write. He just kept journals.

I thought, *I'd like to see his journals,* but of course I didn't ask to.

I said that I wanted to buy Leanne's new book. He said he had a surprise for me. He reached into his sport coat pocket and handed me the book.

"Thank you so much. That was so kind of you."

Once we were outside the hall, Jon said he was sorry that he couldn't go for a drink; he was Leanne's ride to the airport. I couldn't help myself. I asked.

"Are you seeing Leanne?"

"No," he said.

"Oh."

"But one day, I would like to be seeing you."

Without thought—if I had stopped to think about it, I would never have done it—I reached for his hand. His long fingers closed, wrapped around mine. I heard myself say, "I think our problems will work out."

And I actually believed it.

Marcy Hammer. Sometimes you surprise even yourself.

Chapter 35

Sometime that fall I stopped marking my calendar in black. In fact, I stopped marking it at all. I had grown accustomed to the ten-items-or-less lane of the supermarket. I no longer bought banana cakes and ice cream for visitors I didn't have. When I thought about Harvey, I thought of how miserable he must be. I imagined him in a fine restaurant with the baby. Harvey picks up the baby. The baby belches smelly breast milk and takes a runny yellow shit on Harvey's suit. I had loved the man. And in spite of everything, I still loved him. But I didn't want him back.

～◎～

One September morning, I took a very long walk—seven miles round-trip, my record—on the blissful road near my house. Before starting out, I swallowed a bottomless breath, stretched stiffness from my shoulders, cracked my hands, and rolled my neck from side to side. As I walked, I admired Connecticut as though I had never come upon it before. I revered nature's bounty, the heavenly quiet, the sweet scent of rolling pasture, the classic red barns, and the narrow white farmhouses dating back one hundred years. I saw rambling weathered fences fronting nouveau estates in silent woods. I was appalled by the rise of lifeless double-peaked residences.

I looked up at the sky and searched the clouds for my mother's face. I imagined that she had found my father. She was serving him dinner at a table with a white cloth and silver candlesticks. My mom said, *"I'm so worried about Marcy."* My dad asked if there was any more manna, and the conversation stopped there.

On the way back from my walk, I took in the children chasing each other in circles on a corner, the young mothers with high-end strollers, holding coffee mugs and chatting. I kicked a wayward stone, or two or three, and smiled, delighted by those stones. And, as always, before I took the left turn for home, I looked at the sky, searching the clouds once again for my mother's face.

I felt a surge of energy when I returned home, as though I were a student who had swallowed an upper to stay awake all night. I dashed up the stairs to my bedroom, discarded my denim jacket, and swung open the door to my closet. After a business week in London, Harvey had imported an Old English breakfront, replete with dark leather inlay and drop-leaf lion handles. Small wonder the immense walk-in reminded me of a dressing room in a BBC miniseries. Soon after the breakfront showed up, a crew of construction workers arrived to build a second closet—for Earl Harvey himself.

I stared at the rows of bras, the majority still new and in plastic packages with cardboard. I couldn't reach the uppermost open shelf, so I sprinted to the kitchen and brought back the straw broom. With one swipe of the golden bristles, bras tumbled upon me. Each package featured the Bountiful logo and a sensual shot of a nubile woman reaping the benefits of Harvey's best. I jumped backward to escape the fall of T-shirt bras, racerbacks, halters, push-ups, hook-fronts, and strapless bras. In no way was I athletic, but there were enough Bountiful Bosom sports bras alone to lift the Olympic team of every country since women began participating in sports.

The shoemaker's daughter never has shoes, I thought, *but the brassiere maker's wife has a whole different problem.* I needed a warehouse, because once Harvey had moved his own attire to his new royal closet, he brought home more and more lingerie.

When he came home from Bountiful in the evening, Harvey would often unlatch his briefcase and display his latest bras. Styles I could use and styles I couldn't use. He didn't care. He wanted me to own every one of his products.

Kindly, I would remark about the wondrous bras, leaving lingerie on the kitchen counter while I served him dinner. If, on occasion, I commented that I already had a king's ransom of intimate apparel, too much to ever wear, he took offense, gaping at my ingratitude. Then, concentrating on his meal, he might ask if there was any more Chilean sea bass or Moroccan lamb stew. Well, the man had seen his last Moroccan lamb stew from me.

The number of bras I owned was appalling. I knew I never wanted that much of anything ever again, or anything as big as my house. My new home would be a small older house. It would have a screened-in area with pots of flowers and a pair of wicker rockers I'd refinished myself. That way I could relax on the porch, splitting a very fine bottle of California wine with Candy. Or, just maybe, I would squeeze four narrow chairs in a line, so that when my children all came we could look out at the world together.

The phone rang. I found it hidden under the thongs, bikinis, and hipsters I had pulled out of the breakfront. It was Dana in a rushed voice. She was calling from a noisy street.

"What are you up to?" she asked with a gulp.

"Are you eating something?"

"Diet Coke," she said.

"I'm discarding my remnants of Bountiful Bosom," I said as I cleared the bottom drawer. I sat down on my supply of underwear, in every color ever seen on a woman. Surprisingly, although white bras sold best, Harvey was not fond of all-white bras. Too boring, too expected, too lazy a choice. He often said that if every woman wore white underwear, he would never have followed his family's footsteps. Instead, he would have gone to medical school—not to practice medicine, but rather to become a mogul in pharmaceutical sales.

"You're throwing out everything?"

"Every hook, eye, and underwire," I said with determination.

"If you wait, I could come over. We could burn the bras. I'll come tomorrow night after my board meeting at the agency, and I'll bring an extinguisher."

"This isn't a protest. It's a cleansing. I'm having a fine time on my own."

"But you never really like to be alone."

"I guess I've gotten better at it. What choice did I have?"

"What are you going to do with the bras?"

"I'd like to find a shelter where every woman wears my size."

"What size?" she said.

"36C."

"I'm a D," she said.

"How much of that D is really yours?"

"I can't believe I'm missing the bra burning," she said.

I didn't correct her.

"I'm at college visiting my daughters. The counseling office called me." That couldn't be good.

"I think Jenna is having a meltdown."

"What happened?"

"She hates it here."

"Oh," I said. *Freshman jitters,* I thought.

"She's gained twenty pounds, and she's wearing sweatpants, flip-flops, and a T-shirt that says 'Life Is Shit, Then Your Mother Picks Your College.' She says she's too depressed to go to classes, and she blames me for pushing her into this place. She says that I wouldn't allow her to visit the schools she liked, the ones she really wanted to go to, and that we only saw the schools Monica liked, because Monica and I always like the same things, and that I like Monica better anyway, because Monica is just like me. She says that she had wanted to write her college essay about the original clothing line she had knitted for our dog, but I insisted that she write about the plight of refugees. She wants to transfer to the Fashion Institute of Technology."

"Well, at least she has a plan."

"Now who's the one with the sunny side up?"

"Well, Dana, if she wants to be in fashion, she belongs in a fashion school."

"That's what she said, but I believe in a liberal arts education."

Good luck with that, I thought, thinking of all the times my own mother had advised me to do one thing and I did another. *Sorry, Mom,* I thought. *I miss you, Mom. So much.*

I picked up a flamingo-pink demi bra and twirled it, up high, then low. The label said "Aura of Mystique." I'd thought an aura *was* a mystique. "As long as you called," I said to Dana, "could you tell me Judy's number at work?"

"Judy?" Dana said.

"You know, Judy—your friend, the Realtor."

"You're selling the house?"

"I'm getting a price from Judy."

"You know, you never wanted that house," she said, as though I needed her to remind me.

I remembered when Harvey and I had first seen our home.

It was brand-new. In the living room, my voice echoed when I said, "This house is too big. We don't need a place like this."

"Come here," Harvey cajoled. I joined him as he stood like a peacock looking out on the yard. "Look at the view. Have you ever seen so many trees? We would own every one of these trees. Have you ever thought of owning trees?"

To be honest, it had never occurred to me. City girl.

He pulled me to his chest, speaking sweetly, as though I were a hesitant customer in one of his stores, as though he was determined to make the sale—whatever it took.

"Harvey, we don't need a house like this. It's ridiculous."

"So we won't use what we don't need. *I* would live in this house forever, but if not, it's perfect for resale."

"What resale? We're not buying this house."

The Realtor was in another room, pretending not to listen.

"And what about the kitchen?" Harvey said.

"We don't need two ovens to have dinner. All we need is a phone."

"We'll use the second oven on Thanksgiving to keep your mother's extra stuffing warm. And don't worry about the cost. Feldman said to spend at least this much."

I had never before seen him want anything as much as he wanted this house. I thought carefully about denying him his country wet dream before I said, "I'm not ready to do this—maybe one day, but not now."

Harvey shook his head and asked the Realtor for her card, and we headed back to our apartment in New York, a great and palpable silence in the car.

Months later, on the kind of steamy Saturday in summer when no one who actually lives in Manhattan is *in* Manhattan, I was bathing Elisabeth when Harvey arrived home from Bountiful. He came into the bathroom holding his briefcase. "It's ours!" he shouted.

"What's ours?" I lifted Elisabeth, and Harvey wrapped a thick bath towel around her. He hoisted her in the air, looked into her eyes, and said, "Elisabeth, you have the best daddy in the whole world."

"And why is that?" I asked on behalf of Elisabeth.

"I bought the house," Harvey said with a champagne-popping voice, his eyes still fixed on Elisabeth's face—in other words, not looking at me.

I walked out of the bathroom and didn't speak to him for what seemed like the equivalent of one hundred years on death row. He didn't sleep on the couch, because we didn't have a couch. He slept with me in our queen bed—Elisabeth the buffer zone between us.

At night, listening to him snore, all I could think about was his act of deceit. When I mentioned to my mom on the phone that Harvey and I weren't speaking because he'd bought the house without telling me, I thought she would see it my way. Instead she said, "The man bought a house for his family? That's a crime now?"

Even distance didn't keep her from defending him. "The location is unfortunate, because it's too far from me, but he meant well. He said he'll send a man in a car to pick me up when I want to visit."

I was filling bottles with formula when Harvey entered the kitchen. "I'm sorry I bought the house without consulting you. The Realtor called to tell me that the price was reduced, and my business sense got the best of me."

"So the Realtor called *you*. Why do I think *you* called the Realtor?"

"Feldman called the Realtor. He plays golf with her husband," he said. "Then the Realtor called me."

"It's one lie after another, Harvey."

"Marcy, I'm sorry."

He took my hand. "Please, Marcy, let me do what I know is the right thing for us—for you, for me, for Elisabeth."

"We're married, Harvey," I said as I could feel myself caving. "We don't buy houses without each other."

"I promise that you will be the one to choose the next house. I won't have a word to say about it."

Who knew then that I had been listening to an oracle?

⁓

"Judy is the best," Dana said. "She could sell a house to a fish."

"I know. That's why I want to call her."

"So, what? This means you're good? You're good with the Harvey thing?"

Only Dana could call the failure, demise, and obliteration of my thirty-three-year marriage "the Harvey thing."

"Yes, Dana, I'm good with the Harvey thing. I'm good with the man I spent my most vital years with, the man I have as yet to be legally separated from, the father of my children, who will also be the grandfather of my grandchildren. How are you with your husband thing?"

"Calvin is just fine, thank you," she said. And we laughed.

I stuffed all of the lingerie into clear trash bags, twist-tying the tops. I lugged the bags to my car. I opened the trunk. Slam. Trunk closed, deed done.

I dropped the remains of Harvey in a rusting collection bin at the rear of a dry cleaner with a flashing studded arrow above the low flat roof. I read the blue-on-white signage on the charitable bin. Apparently, the best of Harvey was bound for Africa.

Chapter 36

Amanda came in from California to see me and to speak to Harvey about the bra business. It was December and snowing big, sticking flakes. I left my house and drove to the airport early.

On the way, I thought about my mother. How she would have reprimanded me for traveling in such foul weather. How she was right so many times when I thought she was wrong. How often a mother's love is mistaken for the beliefs of the Stone Age.

I decided I should call my brother.

I thought I heard Mom say, *"I'm gone almost a year. Why didn't you call him already?"*

"Because Max acted like a fool at your funeral?"

"He acted like a fool? Now that's a crime? He's your brother."

"He has a phone."

"You're the bigger one. You're the oldest."

Just maybe, my mother's advice to rise above the deeds of others, to look the other way, to be strong for the people I love, had gotten me through the worst times of my life.

∞

As I approached the sign directing drivers to arrivals, the car slid in the slush from a previous snowstorm and slammed into a snowbank on a sliver of an island. I lost my composure, but felt better, relieved, when I realized that no one was behind me. I caught my breath, removed my tense hands from my gloves, and guided the car back onto the airport road.

Slowly, I pulled in next to the American Airlines arrivals area. No sign of Amanda.

My cell rang. Harvey. For some reason, Harvey had been utilizing Amanda's imminent arrival in town as his excuse to call me relentlessly. Call one: "Do you know which airport?" Call two: "I hope she got a free upgrade to first class. Did she?" Then call three: "I'm positive Amanda is coming to tell me that she's ready to join the business. I'm right, right?"

"What?" I barked as I answered this time, massively annoyed and on the lookout for a police officer who might insist that I move my car immediately. I was idling under a sign that said "No Waiting. Active Loading Only" and couldn't think of anything I wanted to do less than recircle the icy airport. Actually, there was one thing—taking yet another call from Harvey.

"Is she in yet?" he said.

"No. I'm waiting."

"Horrible weather," he said from inside his cozy office, no doubt sitting with a sky-high roast beef sandwich at his desk, swiveling his leather chair to glance at the snow out the window.

"*I* should have gone to get her," he said, and I could hear the rustling of papers.

"She called *me*," I answered.

At the airport, a young policeman approached me.

"No standing," he said firmly.

"I'm waiting for my daughter."

"You'll have to circle until she arrives."

"But it's icy. I almost had an accident."

"You have to circle."

I circled—twice. The cell phone rang.

"What are you doing?" Harvey asked.

"Circling."

"She's not in yet?"

"No, I'm circling with her in the car." *What a dingbat.*

"Call me as soon as you pick her up. I ordered her an amazing desk, and it's being delivered this morning."

"Is it returnable?"

"Marcy, my daughter is joining the business, the business that has been in my family for generations."

"She said that?"

"She doesn't have to say anything. You know that she never flies in."

"Harvey, she said she was coming to talk to you. She didn't say she needed a desk and an office at Bountiful."

"Why else would she fly in?"

Because she misses her mother and father? I couldn't take another second of him. "Oh, I think that's her," I said, even though she was nowhere in sight.

I pulled next to the curb, and within minutes the policeman approached. "Need I repeat myself?" he said, looking straight through me.

⟳

The third time I pulled up, Amanda waved me down, looking all Los Angeles—with dark movie-star sunglasses to block the dizzying gleam of the New England snow, auburn leather boots, which I was sure weren't waterproofed, and two designer duffel bags.

I flipped open the trunk. Amanda quickly deposited her bags in the trunk and herself in the front seat.

"Mom, I thought you would be here when I arrived," she said as a greeting. "You know how I hate to wait. I called your cell and left messages. Why don't you ever check your messages? And who were you talking to?"

"I was talking to Dad."

"That's good."

"Anyway, I was here. I had to circle." Her behind was barely in the seat, and she had already irritated me. "How was your flight?"

"I sat next to the Math-a-Magician."

The Math-a-Magician was a girl who went to high school with Amanda. Amanda never spoke to her unless she needed help with calculus.

"What's she up to?"

"She started a hedge fund. She was named one of the top thirty people under thirty in Los Angeles."

"Top thirty people for what?"

"Top thirty under thirty to watch."

How different my life might have been if I had been born into Amanda's generation.

"Mom, I have to make a call."

Amanda tapped some numbers and started giving bossy orders to someone on the phone. Several calls later there was no sign of her letting up.

I steered nervously in the snow, creeping.

"Amanda, enough with the cell phone. Let's talk."

"Just one more call. I'll text it."

"So why did you decide to fly in?"

"To see you and talk to Dad."

"Amanda, I have to tell you something. Dad set up an office for you. He ordered you a new desk."

"He did not."

"Yes," I said, elongating the word.

"I came in to speak to Dad, daughter to father. I'm not going into the business. I have decided that I am not ready to sit in the woods in a five-story building in Podunk, Connecticut."

"Wow. That's harsh."

"I was offered a big job with Nordstrom. I move to Seattle, for one year. Then who knows?"

"What about Arnold?"

"We're in the process of breaking up. He stood his ground. Said that if I moved to Seattle he was moving on."

"And you're going anyway?"

"Never postpone your life for a man."

Who said that? I wondered. *And why hadn't they said it to me?*

"Mom, I think you should get back with Dad."

"Let me see if I have this right. You're ditching your live-in boyfriend and moving to Seattle, but you think that I should go back to Dad?"

"Give him a chance."

"I gave him a chance," I said.

"After all these years, he deserves another chance."

"I didn't know you were so loyal."

"I'm not. But you are."

I wanted to confirm in no uncertain terms that I wasn't patching up anything with Harvey, but it would have been a waste of breath, and Amanda would have continued the infuriating conversation until I was so exasperated and so distraught that I'd start wondering whether I was making a mistake.

But I wasn't making a mistake. I was moving on. And I was proud of myself for it.

I dropped Amanda at Harvey's office and steered straight for home. My head had never been clearer. I had my friends. I had my work. And, if I drank lots of water, gave up pizza, walked more, and got quality medical care, I had plenty of time to become one of the top eighty women under eighty.

Chapter 37

A few days after Amanda's visit, I received an unexpected phone call.

"Hello," a familiar voice said when I picked up the telephone in my bedroom. "This is Amelia from Sweet Heaven Bakery."

"Hi, Amelia," I said.

"I hope I didn't call at a bad time."

Bad time? I thought. *Let me tell you about bad times.* "No, of course not," I said.

Nervously, she said, "I'm sorry to bother you, but it's that time of year, and I was wondering whether you wanted to order a cake for Mr. Hammer's birthday."

Of course. Do you have any cakes with anthrax frosting? What about "Happy Birthday" inscribed in ground glass?

"I customarily require two days' notice to bake a large cake, but I don't want you to worry about that."

"Thanks for calling, Amelia. But I don't need a cake this year."

"Is Mr. Hammer okay?"

"He's fine." *You have no idea how fine.*

"And you?"

"I'm okay," I said, and I realized that my answer was honest and real, and that I had surmounted the insurmountable. I was the person who deserved to celebrate, to rejoice rising above it all. "Question—do you still bake that incredible chocolate cake with marzipan?

"It's our bestseller. Everyone loves the chocolate and the cherries, and the marzipan."

"I'll come by for one tomorrow."

"We'd be happy to deliver it. What size?"

"Just large enough to look celebratory. Eight to ten people. We're keeping it quite small this year."

"Eight to ten is a minuscule party for you. I remember Mr. Hammer's sixtieth—topsy-turvy butter cake for one hundred, fresh-from-the-farm strawberries and raspberries, whorls of dark-chocolate icing. It barely fit in my SUV."

Harvey had called it "better-than-sex cake." Now I wondered—better than sex with whom?

⟶◦

I was busy and I had made a life, but habits of a lifetime die hard. By the morning of Harvey's birthday, banners that said "Happy Birthday" were running through my head. But I decided that for my own purposes, December 7, Pearl Harbor Day, was no longer Harvey's birthday to me. Seizing a purple marker, I attacked my wall calendar. I purpled out his birth date, the day before, and the one after. I was proud of myself, and I was done.

The cake had already been delivered in a chartreuse box with Sweet Heaven ribbons. I moved my low-fat yogurts, pineapple cottage cheese, a bottle of chardonnay and one of sauvignon blanc, and placed the cake like a grand prize on the center shelf of the refrigerator, keeping the door open and staring at the box. I liked my fridge with a cake in it. A cake in a box meant there had to be people in the house, or coming to the house. That something good was coming up. All the years with Harvey, there were endless cakes. Ice-cream cakes, carrot cakes, banana cakes, cheesecakes, and strawberry shortcakes. A person who had a delicious cake was a person who wouldn't be alone for long.

I meandered around the front of the house, surveying the neighborhood. A metallic sports car I had never seen before headed gradually, tentatively, into my driveway. Harvey shut off the ignition and stepped out. My eyes darted to the top of his head. Harvey had hair—a toupee perched on his skull as though it belonged almost anywhere else. I vowed not to ask what he fed it.

What gave him the right to drop by the house? And what was he up to? I wanted him to turn around and leave, like he was some stranger using my driveway to make a U-turn.

"Marcy," he said, carefully closing the door on yet another midlife crisis.

"Hello, Harvey," I said, forcing a smile.

"No 'Happy birthday'?" he asked.

"Oh, I forgot," I said, delirious with myself for having refrained from the greeting.

"Come on, Marcy. Wish me a happy birthday."

"Happy birthday to you," I said. "You look like a monkey, and you act like one too."

"I wondered whether you'd remember. Can you believe I'm this old? Last night I couldn't sleep just thinking about it, so I ordered a few roast beef sandwiches from room service."

"Seedless rye bread, tomato, heavy on the horseradish, pickle chip on top."

"Do you like it?"

I knew he meant the toupee, but I said, "Roast beef on seedless rye?"

He pointed to his head—as though it needed pointing to.

"You actually care if I like it?"

"Yes, I do. And, in fact, I have something else I want to ask you."

"Ask away, Harvey," I said as though I couldn't care less what was on his mind.

"Would you . . . ? Could you spend my birthday with me?"

Was that the reason he was here? I wasn't even sure I'd heard right. What had happened to Madison? Was this a cruel stunt for a reality show?

"Marcy?

"Yes?"

"It ends at midnight," he said.

I laughed.

"So it's yes." He rubbed his hands together, obviously delighted.

What would be the harm? I could take the high road, the uppermost road in the world. I could choose to be the bigger person, as my mother had always instructed. This one time, I could be the most tremendous person on earth.

"It *is* my birthday," he said.

"I know," I said.

"For I'm a jolly good fellow . . ."

Maybe I could start with his birthday, and then, with hard work, my family might be whole again. But how would I ever forget? The mourning parents on television who claimed they forgave the killer, the killer of a five-year-old child, constantly amazed me. I could never forgive the killer. There was no life sentence long enough for me.

There was a reward in realizing that Harvey needed me. But it was like a prize in a box of Cracker Jack—nothing of value, mislaid in minutes. "I can't," I said, raising my flat hands up as if to halt him.

"Give me a reason."

"There are a million reasons, and I don't owe you a single one of them."

"Maria's moving back to Argentina."

"Maria? I thought her name was Madison."

"Madison is a professional name. Maria's family wants to help with the baby. She has four sisters in Argentina. And you know me, Marcy. You know I took care of her. Right now, I'm providing enough financial assistance for quadruplets. She plans to open a leather outlet, for tourists, in Buenos Aires. She'll sell coats, boots, bags, and wallets. Leather is colossal in Argentina—lots of cattle."

I stared like he was speaking in tongues.

"I asked Feldman to work with her, and he knocked out a business plan." Harvey's voice dripped with pure New England maple syrup, as if his arrangements were beyond what would ever be expected from an established man like him, as though his cash absolved him of all paternal responsibility.

"Harvey Hammer—pleased to provide what every young and single, overwhelmed mother needs—a business plan."

My head was spinning somewhere above me. A Jeep sped by our driveway, teenagers inside, blaring a rap song out the windows. I turned and strutted briskly toward the house.

Harvey shouted, like a lunatic, repeating himself, "She's moving back to Argentina."

I marched into the house, straight as a soldier. I never looked back.

෨

I was lonely. Sorely, I wanted company. I opened the refrigerator door and stared at the chartreuse box with the Sweet Heaven ribbons on top. I had the cake. The cake was for people. I picked up my cell phone. And I called Jon.

"Hi."

"Hi, Marcy."

I swallowed a breath. He had never been to my home, but suddenly I found myself extending an invitation. "Would you like to come over?"

I doubled down by saying I had cake.

"What kind?"

"Chocolate." I knew he loved chocolate.

"Can't get there fast enough."

"Great. That's great."

"Can I bring anything?"

"Just yourself will do."

"No way would I arrive empty-handed. I'll bring a dessert wine."

I didn't need him to bring dessert wine. I had fine ones in the house. But I liked that he thought he should bring something.

I showered, put my hair up in a tortoiseshell clip, my makeup light, and decided on the dress I'd worn that day I went to Harvey's office, the cream-colored wrap from Nordstrom. The truth was, I looked wonderful in that dress, whether it had brought back my husband or not.

I lit the fireplaces in the living and dining rooms. The crackling was romantic. I set the dining table with an embroidered tablecloth, matching napkins, the silverware I reserved for holidays, wineglasses, dainty coffee cups, saucers, and dessert plates from a White House–size collection of china.

Carefully, I placed the cake on an ornate, antique stand that I had thought too fussy when I'd received it as a gift from my mother. Now, it seemed impeccably right.

☙

Jon arrived, in a flannel-lined parka, jeans, a crewneck sweater, and a denim shirt. His nose was a bit red from the cold. He stamped his snow-dusted boots on the sisal rug.

"I had a hard time finding your house," he said, pulling off his heavy boots and placing them neatly next to mine. I liked the way our boots looked together.

"Didn't you use your GPS?"

"I figured I would turn in to a driveway when I smelled chocolate."

He presented a bottle of port. I took his parka, leather gloves peeking out of the pockets, and hung it in the hall closet. I could feel him watching me, and I became concerned that my behind looked wider than I'd thought in the dress. *Plump rumps are in,* I told myself.

When I turned toward Jon, he was looking around the foyer. What was he thinking? That based on this house, my carbon footprint was obliterating the earth?

He pointed to the cap-and-gown pictures in identical frames above the console where Harvey had always dropped his keys.

"Elisabeth, Amanda, Ben," he said. "Elisabeth looks like you."

"She's a doctor," I said.

He posed, with a squint of the eyes, his index finger on his chin. "You might have mentioned that once—or a thousand times."

"Proud mama," I said.

"With reason," he said.

I couldn't decide whether to give him an abbreviated tour of the downstairs of the house or proceed directly into the dining room. I felt needles of anticipation. I wanted to show him around, but I didn't want to appear like I was showing off. Besides, my decor was mostly late Harvey XIV.

"Take me to your cake," Jon said.

I noticed that the fires I had built earlier were dwindling. I considered adding wood.

"Beautiful," he remarked about the dining room. "Did you know that I'm a master fire builder?" He moved the baroque screen, wielded the coordinating poker, and pushed over a reticent log. Flames shot up in the fireplace. "Those are big logs. Did you haul all of them in here?"

"From the yard," I answered, noting that he appreciated what little I had done. "We . . . I . . . ordered a cord for the winter."

At the table, he took in the cake, rubbing his hands together and dramatically licking his lips. "I know this cake. It's from Sweet Heaven Bakery. The chocolate with the marzipan and the cherries."

"Yes."

"I love this cake. This cake is nirvana. If I were going to a desert island and I could take one thing, I would take this cake."

"Sounds delicious, but then what would you do? I mean, after you ate it."

"Easy. I'd call you. To come get me."

He'd call me. If he needed help, he would call me.

My eyes welled. In a way, he'd answered all my questions: Had Harvey done me in? Was I too old to start over? Would I ever be in a relationship again? Did I want to be in a relationship again?

"Mind if I do the honors?" Jon said.

He lifted the knife with the handle that replicated Tiffany stained glass. He danced the utensil about the cake, as if to say "Should I cut here, or should I cut there?"

"Come help me," he said, pulling me close. He stood behind me, wrapping his long arms around me and placing my palms around the knife, his handsome hands enclosing mine.

I could have stood like that forever; I never needed to move again.

I heard a loud knock. More knocks. The side door opened, then banged shut.

"Anyone home?" Dana shouted.

Jon stepped back.

"In the dining room, Dana," I said.

"You're never in the dining room," she said from the kitchen.

"Whose Subaru Outback is in the driveway?" Dana asked as she came in, her Tibetan ski hat and mittens still on. Then she saw Jon. She couldn't have looked more surprised if Harvey had been there feeding cake to his parrot.

"Oh. Hi, Jon," she muttered.

"Good to see you, Dana. How's Calvin?" Jon was friends with Dana's husband.

"Great, great," she said, grinning at me.

"I'm not staying," she said. "Definitely have to go. I dropped by to give Marcy some news, but it can wait."

"You can't do that. You can't say you have news, then not tell it."

"Can I hear it?" Jon asked.

Dana pulled out a chair and sat down at the table, her legs, in jeans, extended. "My son, Jeremy, and his wife, Moxie, are having a baby."

"Grandma Dana!" I shouted, then started clapping. It had been a while since I had heard good news.

Dana turned to Jon. "Tell her to stop with the Grandma Dana. I had Jeremy when I was eleven, and he's having a baby in junior high. If Marcy says Grandma Dana one more time, I'm going back to smoking more than three cigarettes a day."

"Do they know if it's a boy or girl?" I asked.

"It doesn't matter as long as the baby's healthy, doesn't look like Moxie, and doesn't call me Grandma."

"I agree," I said, nodding my head and smiling. "The baby should call you Big Sister."

"It's great, isn't it?" Dana replied, gleaming.

"The best," I said. "I heard a prayer once that I never forgot: 'May you live to see your children's children.'"

"My children are having children!" Dana said.

"How about some cake?" Jon said.

"All right, but just cut me a big piece."

As Grandma Dana teased crumbs with her fork, she told us that Jenna had applied to transfer to the Fashion Institute of Technology in New York.

Jon said he knew the director of admissions.

When Dana excused herself, I accompanied her to the door.

"Do you think he'll make a phone call to FIT?"

"Yes, but after that no more about colleges. Ever."

"This isn't about college. It's about admissions."

"Right."

"Has he ever been here before?"

"No."

"Whoa." She knocked my shoulder. She knocked it again. Three times.

"What's 'whoa'?"

"Don't let him leave his toothbrush. You won't remember which one is his and which is yours."

Now, wouldn't that be nice, I thought.

When Dana drove off, Jon and I leaned back, side by side on the couch in the living room, facing the pleasant fire he had happily coaxed to roaring.

"Coming to your home makes me feel like I know you so much better." He passed a glass of port to me. "For the first time since my wife died, I feel unstuck, unencumbered by the awful memory of it all. It made me think how wonderful it would be to go on a trip with you. Just to Portland. Because that's where I'm from and I think you would like it. I know a terrific five-room inn on the water with a view of the coast from every window. And because I see how much you like fireplaces, I'll ask them to install one just for us."

"Just for us?"

"Just for us."

"One more thing . . ."

I really didn't need to hear one more thing. I was planning on going to Maine with him and considering never coming home again.

"The haddock chowder in the little restaurant in my little inn is easily the best in the world," he said, sipping port. "But . . ."

Please, no ifs or buts. Only ands.

"It's a long drive to Portland," he said.

"That's fine." *More than fine. Double fine. Mighty fine.*

"So we'll go?"

"Just tell me when."

"Next weekend then?" he said, and he kissed me.

"Yes." *Yes to the first kiss of my second life.*

Chapter 38

The leftovers from the cake were still fresh in my fridge when I got a real estate tip from Candy and went to scout a house that she thought I would like.

At 11 Pine Turn, I left the radio on and gazed across the road. There was a yellow house, with white shutters, a gray door, and a walk of blue slate. There was a sign: "For Rent or Sale." I could try it for a year, or buy and make it mine right away.

It was still light, but the house was dark. Sporadically, a snowflake drifted into silence. I lowered my car window. The air smelled delectable, like great logs burning, winter cold in New England. Chimney smoke puffed into the sky from the surrounding homes. The woods were still. I stepped out of my car, in my L.L.Bean boots, and zipped my parka. Quickly, eagerly, excitedly, I crossed the country road. Not a car went by.

I tugged at the screen door that led to the porch, opening and closing it several times, listening to the pleasant squeak of the rusted hinges. There was a lockbox on the weathered front door. I jiggled the lock, hoping, praying that it had been left open accidentally. I thought, *Why isn't anyone incompetent anymore?*

I peered into the windows. I could see two reclining colonial love seats facing each other, an oak-veneer cocktail table between, a braided wool rectangular rug, and an ebony upright piano with sheet music. No personal effects. A Realtor had staged the place—all signs of individuality carted off to Goodwill. But it was as if the sweet yellow house had been readied just for me.

I centered myself on the slat-back cedar porch swing. The sun was almost gone, the moon rising—on my house, the house of Marcy. I was thinking about how much I missed my mother—my mother and her mothering.

How is it that I'm abundantly alive, I thought, *and she's gone forever?*

Then, exactly then, I heard an affirmation from my mother.

"Marcy, you're making the right decision."

"Mom, you thought Harvey was the right decision."

Seconds before, heartbroken, I'd mourned her absence, so why when hearing advice from my mother was I always a snarly fourteen?

"What did I know? And what did he know? He knew brassieres. Move into the house and invite your friends. I'll bring my cinnamon-apple stuffing and a nice roasted turkey."

"I'd like that. More than anything."

I looked up, up into the sky.

"Please don't worry. Don't worry, Mom. I'm okay."

Acknowledgments

I am indebted to my brilliant agent, Joelle Delbourgo. She brought my novel to Kelli Martin, executive editor of fiction at Amazon Publishing. Kelli is insightful, delightful, dedicated, and responsive. Every communication is a great education.

It was a privilege to work with Tiffany Yates Martin, developmental editor extraordinaire. I owe a lot to the careful eye of copyeditor Elizabeth Johnson. Also, Phyllis DeBlanche for proofreading. I thank the Amazon and Lake Union production and marketing teams, as well as Janet Perr for the cover.

I gratefully acknowledge Jennifer Belle, bestselling author of four wonderful novels, including *High Maintenance* and *The Seven Year Bitch*. As a longtime member of Jennifer's writing workshop in Greenwich Village, I have been the fortunate recipient of her unparalleled encouragement and guidance—both of which were integral to the writing of this book.

I thank my fellow writers in Jennifer's workshop, most especially Desiree Rhine, Julie Flakstad, Lisa Liman, Katie Sammis, Raina Wallens, Aaron Zimmerman, Renee Pettit, and Erin Hussein.

Special mention goes to Lanie Robertson, author of many great plays, including *Lady Day at Emerson's Bar & Grill.* I thank my cherished friend for copious detailed notes resulting in a better book—and most important—for his wise and witty counsel regarding literature and life.

I am grateful to Anne Greene, director of the Wesleyan Writers Conference. And I appreciate the early enthusiasm of novelist Anne Bernays.

For many reasons, I thank Julie Edmonds (my first reader), Jeff Lesh, Jay Johnson, Nolan Robinson, Kenneth Klein, Nancy Shapanka, Gwen Dreilinger, Rachel Dreilinger, and Dr. Henry Jacobs. Also, the Writers Room, Avon Free Public Library, and NYU.

Colleen Lorenz—you always turn up when I need you. And this time I needed you to read.

It's good to have sisters. And there are none better than mine. I thank Sandra Simon Klein (devoted reading teacher for thirty-five years) and Debra Simon (editor and publisher of *Carolina Woman* magazine) for assisting me with *Lift and Separate*—and for a lifetime of loud holidays and support.

About my daughters: My attorney Marisa Rothstein is a constant source of inspiration. What's more, she always comes to my rescue, and always cheers me on. Sharyn Rothstein is a playwright and television writer. She is the person I turn to, often at midnight, for top-notch professional advice. See or read Sharyn's award-winning plays *By the Water* and *All the Days*. I am inspired by, and aspire to, her artistry.

Most of all, I thank my husband, Alan. I thank him for looking for my novel in Brentano's on Eighth Street and University Place and all the incredible fantastic things that have happened—because of him—since then.

Frieda and Leo Simon. We hear you.

Lucien. Frankie. Sydney. Your names are in a book.

About the Author

For more than twenty-five years, Marilyn Simon Rothstein owned an advertising agency in Connecticut. She grew up in New York City, earned a degree in journalism from New York University, began her writing career at *Seventeen* magazine, and married a man she met in an elevator.

Marilyn received a master of arts in liberal studies from Wesleyan University and a master of arts in Judaic studies from the University of Connecticut.